Eliza Southgate Bowne

Letters of Eliza Southgate

Eliza Southgate Bowne

Letters of Eliza Southgate

ISBN/EAN: 9783337392246

Printed in Europe, USA, Canada, Australia, Japan

Cover: Foto ©Andreas Hilbeck / pixelio.de

More available books at **www.hansebooks.com**

Letters of

Eliza Southgate,

Mrs. Walter Bowne.

Born, September 24, 1783.
Married, Spring of 1803.
Died, February 19, 1809.

Aged 25 years.

Bowne Family Record.

Thomas Bowne, Born in Matlock, Derbyshire, England, 1595; died 1677.

X John, Son of Thomas, born in Matlock, 1627; married Hannah Field, of Flushing, L. I., 1656; died 1695.

Samuel, Son of John, son of Thomas, born 1667; married Mary Becket, 1691; died 1745.

Samuel, Son of Samuel, son of John, son of Thomas, born 1692; married Sarah Franklin, 1724; died 1767.

James, Son of Samuel 2d, son of Samuel, son of John, son of Thomas; married Caroline Rodman.

Walter, Son of James, son of Samuel, son of Samuel, son of John, son of Thomas, born 1770; married Eliza Southgate, of Scarborough, Me., 1803; died 1846.

Children of Walter Bowne.

Walter, Born 1806; married Eliza Rapalje, 1826; died 1877.

Mary King, Born 1808; married John W. Lawrence, 1826; died 1874.

X "Built in 1661 the "Old Bowne House" Flushing L. I. still occupied by his descendents.
1887

Southgate Family Record.

John Southgate, born in Combs, Suffolk County, England; married Elizabeth ——, of Combs.

Richard, Son of John, born in Combs, March, 1671; married, October 17, 1700, Elizabeth Steward; died in Leicester, Mass., April, 1758.

Steward, Son of Richard, son of John, born in Combs, September 18, 1703; married, March 28, 1735, Elizabeth Scott of Palmer, Mass.; died December, 1764.

Robert, Son of Steward, son of Richard, son of John, born October 26, 1741; married, June 23, 1773, Mary King, daughter of Richard King of Scarborough, Me., and sister of Hon. Rufus King; died November 2, 1833.

Children of Robert Southgate mentioned in these letters:

Isabella,	Married	Joseph C. Boyd,	Died	1821.
Horatio,	"	Abigail McClelland,	"	1864.
Eliza,	"	Walter Bowne,	"	1809.
Octavia,	"	William Brown,	"	1815.
Miranda,	"	—— Tillottson,	"	1816.
Arixene,	"	Henry Smith,	"	1820.
Mary,	"	Grenville Mellen,	"	1829.

Letters of Eliza Southgate while at School.

Medford, January 23, 1797

My Mamma:

I went to Boston last Saturday, and there I received your letter. I have nothing new to communicate to you, only my wishes to tarry in Boston a quarter if <u>convenient</u>.

In my last letter to <u>Father</u>, I did not say anything respecting it, because I did not wish Mr. Wyman to know that I had an inclination to leave his school, but only because I thought you would wish me to come home when my quarter was out. I had a great desire to see my family, but I have a still greater desire to finish my education. Still, I have to beg you to remind my <u>friends</u> and acquaintance that I remain the same Eliza, and that I bear the same love I ever did to them, whether they have forgotten me or not.

Tell my little brothers and sisters I want to see them very much indeed. Write me an answer as soon as you can conveniently. I shall send you some of my work which you have never yet seen,— it is my arithmetic. Permit me, my honored mother, to claim the title of

Your affectionate daughter,

ELIZA SOUTHGATE

MRS. MARY K. SOUTHGATE.

2

Medford, May 12, 1797.

Honored Parents:

With pleasure I sit down to write to the best of parents, to inform them of my situation, as doubtless they are anxious to hear. Permit me to tell something of my foolish heart. When I first came here, I gave myself up to reflection, but not pleasing reflection.

When Mr. Boyd left me I burst into tears, and instead of trying to calm my feelings, I tried to feel worse. I begin to feel happier, and will now gather up my philosophy and think of the duty that now attends me, to think that here I may freely drink of the fountain of knowledge. But I will not dwell any longer on this subject. I am doing nothing but writing, reading, and ciphering: there is a French master coming next Monday, and he will teach French and dancing. William Boyd and Mr. Wyman advise me to learn French, and Mr. E. L. Boyd says it is not best to learn French yet, if I do at all.

I wish you to write me very soon what you think best, for the school begins on Monday. Mr. Wyman says it will take up but very little of my time, for it is but two or three days in the week, and the lessons only two hours long. Mr. Wyman says I must learn geometry before geography, and that I had better not begin either till I have finished ciphering. We get up early in the morning, and make our beds and sweep the chamber. It is about as large as our kitchen chamber, and a little better finished. There are four beds in the chamber and two persons in each bed. We have chocolate for breakfast and supper.

Your affectionate daughter,

ELIZA SOUTHGATE.

Medford, May 25, 1797.

My Dear Parents:

I hope I am in some measure sensible of the great obligation I am under to you, for the inexpressible kindness and attention which I have received of you, from the cradle to my present situation in school. Many have been your anxious cares for the welfare of me, your child, at every stage and period of my inexperienced life to the present moment. In my infancy you nursed and reared me up, my inclinations you have indulged, and checked my follies,— have liberally fed me with the bounty of your table, and from your instructive lips I have been admonished to virtue, morality, and religion. The debt of gratitude I owe you is great, yet I hope to repay you, by duly attending to your counsels and to my improvement in useful knowledge.

My thankful heart with grateful feelings beat,
With filial duty I my parents greet:
Your fostering care hath reared me from my birth,
And been my guardians since I've been on earth:
With love unequaled taught the surest way,
And checked my passions when they went astray.
I wish and trust to glad declining years,
Make each heart gay, each eye refrain from tears.
When days are finished, and when time shall cease,
May you be wafted to eternal peace,

Is the sincere wish of your dutiful daughter,

ELIZA SOUTHGATE.

Medford, June 9, 1797.

Dear Mother:

I am sensible of my being deficient in my duty, in not complying with your request sooner, but perhaps I am not so negligent as you may imagine. It was so rainy when I was in Boston that I could not go out, and Mrs. Boyd advised me not to get them until the spring ships came in. Your bonnet cost 9s., and the veil 1s. 6d., and the ribbon 2s. 6d. I should have gotten satin ribbon, but I could not get any that was so handsome; but if you don't like it, I will get some satin. The children's were 6s. apiece. I did not trim your bonnet, for I was afraid it would get tumbled. They trim them with a large rose bow before, and a great many ends to the ribbon, and a bow and streamers behind, and not let the ribbon go round the crown; and trim the children's in the same manner; or nothing but a ribbon round the crown. You may trim them with any color you please, but I think pink will look best for Arexine. You must line them with the same color you trim them with, if you please: bonnets like yours are worn very much by old and young. I got me one; it is shaped very much like yours; it is blue satin and straw. Sarah's ear-rings cost me 13s. 6d. Be so kind as to write me very often, and I shall feel much more contented in perusing your letters, and in following your advice. Please to send those things that you have got ready as soon as you can conveniently; I want them very much. I have concluded not to learn French; I am very sorry I began. I hope I have not displeased you. I go to dancing, for I thought I had better go the first quarter with the others.

I am your affectionate daughter,

ELIZA SOUTHGATE.

MRS. MARY K. SOUTHGATE.

Medford, June 13, 1797.

Dear Mother:

With what pleasure did I receive your letter, and hear the praises of an approving mother. It shall be my study to make you happy. You said you hoped I was not disappointed in not learning French. I hope you think I have too much <u>love</u> and <u>rever-</u> ence for my parents, to do anything amiss that <u>they</u> thought most proper for me. I was very happy to hear that you had received the bonnets, and I hope they will suit you.

I have never received a letter from Horatio since I have been here. I expect to begin geography as soon as I have done ciphering which I hope will soon be, for I have got as far as Practice. Tell Isabella and Mama King that some letters from them would give me great pleasure, and that I hope to experience it soon. I should have written to Mama King, but I had not time; yet I intend to the first opportunity. I have found the nubs, and sent them to Portland. I received your letter by my brother Boyd, and was very much surprised to hear that Octavia was going to have the small-pox. Please give my love to Harriet Emerson and Mary Rice, and tell them that I intend to write them very soon, and shall expect some letters from them. Give my love to all my friends, and tell them that I often think of them, and I hope they will not forget

Your affectionate daughter,

ELIZA SOUTHGATE.

3

Medford, 25th   *1797.*

Dearest Mother :

I received your packet of things the 20th inst., and was very glad of them. If you will be so kind as to send me word whether the ear-rings were in the basket, I will be much obliged to you : I have forgotten whether I did or not. Write me word if you like your bonnet and the children's. I hope you do. Give my love to Sarah and all the children, and kiss Arexine and Robert for me. Never did I know the worth of <u>good parents</u> half so much as now I am from them. I never missed so much, and above all things our cheese and butter, which we have but very little of, but I am very contented. I wish you could send me up my patterns, all of them, for I want them very much indeed, for I expect to work me a gown.

I am, with <u>all due</u> respect, your dutiful daughter,

ELIZA SOUTHGATE.

Medford, August 11, 1797.

Dear Parents:

It is a long time since I received a letter from you, and I have neglected my duty in not writing home oftener. I shall send you with this some of my pieces, and you will see if you think I have improved any. The Epitaph on the Hon. Thomas Russell was the first one that I wrote.

My brother Boyd never came to see me when he was up; only called and delivered me the letter. I have never heard anything since from Boston, nor seen any of my acquaintance from there. I have not been to Boston since election. I expected to have gone to Commencement, but I did not. I fear the time alloted to my stay here will be too short for me to go as far as I wish, for I shall have to go much farther in arithmetic than I had any idea of, then go over it again in a large book of my own writing; for my instructor does not wish to give me a superficial knowledge only. He says, if I am very diligent, he thinks that nine months from the time I came will do if I cannot stay longer. I should feel happy, and very grateful, if you thought it proper to let me tarry that time. I have ciphered now farther than Isabella did. I have been through Practice, the Rule of Three, and Interest, and two or three rules that I never did before.

I would thank you to write me word if you are willing for me to stay so long. With wishing you health, and all the happiness which you are capable of enjoying, permit me to subscribe myself,

Your affectionate and most dutiful daughter,

ELIZA SOUTHGATE.

Medford, August 14, 1797.

My Dear Mother:

I am very sorry for your trouble, and sympathize with you in it. I now regret being from home more than ever, for I think I might be of service to you, now the children are sick. I hope they will be as much favored in their sickness <u>now</u> as they were when they had the <u>measles</u>. I am very sorry that Jane has broken her arm, for it generally causes a long confinement, and I fear she has not got patience enough to bear it, without a great deal of trouble.

I suppose Isabella will be very much worried about her baby. I would thank you to write me very often now, for I shall be very anxious to hear from the children. I believe I have got some news to tell you, that is, I have found one of your acquaintance and relation,— it is Mrs. Sawyer. Before she was married her name was <u>Polly King</u>, and she says that you kept at their house when you were in Boston. I believe I have nothing more to request, only for you to give my love to all the children, and <u>kiss</u> each of them for <u>me</u>, and tell them to be as patient as they can. Give my respects to my father, and tell him I want to receive a letter from him very much.

I am your ever affectionate and dutiful daughter,

ELIZA SOUTHGATE.

MRS. MARY K. SOUTHGATE.

Medford, September 30, 1797.

Dear Mother:

You mentioned in yours of the 16th inst., that it was a long time since you had received a letter from me, but it was owing to my studies, which took up the greater part of my time : for I have been busy in my arithmetic, but I finished it yesterday, and expect now to begin my large manuscript arithmetic. You say that you "shall regret so long an absence"; not more certainly than I shall ; but having a strong desire to possess more useful knowledge than I at present do, I can dispense with the pleasure a little longer of beholding my friends, and I hope I shall be better prepared to meet my good parents, toward whom my heart overflows with gratitude. You mentioned in your letter about my winter clothes, of which I will make out a memorandum. I shall want a coat, and you may send it up for me to make, or you may make it yourself, but I want it made loose with a belt. I wish you to send me enough of all my slips to make long sleeves that you can, and I wish you could pattern my dark slip to make long sleeves. I want a flannel waist and a petticoat, for my white one dirts so quick that I had rather have a colored one. I have nothing more to write, only give my love to all who ask after me. I have just received a letter from Horatio ; he is very well.

Your ever affectionate daughter,

ELIZA SOUTHGATE.

MRS. MARY K. SOUTHGATE.

Medford, November 10, 1797.

You mentioned in your letter, my dear mother, that Cousin Mary informed you that I expected to go to the ball. I did think that I should go, but I altered my mind; I had two or three invitations, but I would not accept of anything.

My cloak, likewise, you mentioned something about, which I shall attend to when I go to Boston at Thanksgiving; for then is a vacation of a week. I had a letter from Horatio yesterday; he was well. Isabella wrote me word that my father had got the rheumatism very bad, which I am sorry to hear; if the wishes and prayers of Eliza would heal the wound, it would not long remain unhealed. My love to all the children; tell them I don't dare to tell them how much I want to see them, nor even think. My love to all that ask after me.

May all the happiness that is possible for you to enjoy be experienced, is the sincere wish of

Your affectionate daughter,

ELIZA SOUTHGATE.

MRS. MARY K. SOUTHGATE.

Medford, December 16, 1797.

My Dear Father:

I received yours with pleasure, and was happy to hear that you were better. I hope you will continue growing better until the complaint is entirely removed. I came from Boston yesterday, after spending vacation there. I went to _the theater_ the night before for the first time, and Mr. Turner came into the box where I was. I did not know him at first, neither did he me, but he soon found me out. With this I shall send some prices. My respects are justly due my good mother, and my love to all who ask after me, the children in particular.

I hope to improve to your satisfaction, which will amply reward me for all my pains. I must conclude with wishing you health and happiness.

Your ever affectionate daughter,

ELIZA SOUTHGATE.

ROBERT SOUTHGATE.

Medford, January 9, 1798.

My Good Father:

The contents of your letter surprised me at first. It may sometime be of service to me, for while I have such a monitor, I never can act contrary to such advice. No, my father; I hope by the help of Heaven never to cause shame or misery to attend the gray hairs of my parents or myself, but, on the contrary, to <u>glad</u> your declining years with happiness, and that you may never have cause to rue the day that gave me existence.

My heart feels no attachment except to my family. I <u>respect</u> many of my friends, but <u>love</u> none but my parents. Your letter shall be my guide from home, and when I again behold our own peaceful mansion, then will I again be guided by my parents' happiness. Their happiness shall be my pursuit. My heart overflows with gratitude toward you and my good mother. I am sensible of the innumerable obligations I am under to you.

You mention in your letter about my pieces, which you say you imagine are purloined. I am very sorry if they are, for I set more by them than any of my pieces. One was The Mariner's Compass, and the other was a geometrical piece. I spent Thanksgiving at Mrs. Little's and Christmas here. I have finished my large manuscript arithmetic and want to get it bound, and then I shall send it to you. I have done a small geometry book, and shall begin a large one to-morrow—such a one as <u>you</u> saw at Mr. Wyman's, if you remember. It is the beginning of a new year. Allow me, then, to pay you the compliments of the season. I pray that this year to you may prove

A year of health, prosperity, and love.

My quarter will be out the eighth day of next month. It will be in about four weeks. I wish you would write me soon how I am to come home, for I wish to know. I should be very glad if <u>you</u> could make it convenient to come for me, for I wish <u>you</u> to come. Give my love to Irene, and tell her I believe she owes me a letter. If you please you may tell the part of my letter which concerns my school affairs. My love is due to all who will take the trouble to inquire after me. Tell Mama I have begun her turban and will send it as soon as I finish it. When I see her I will tell her why I did not do it before. Accept my sincere wish that my parents may enjoy all the happiness that ever mortals know. Still I hope I am your dutiful daughter.

ELIZA SOUTHGATE.

ROBERT SOUTHGATE, ESQ.

5

Boston, January 30, 1798.

My Honored Father:

By Captain Bradbury I was informed that you wished me to come home with him, which I should have complied with had not I seen my Uncle William to-day, and he informed me that you had concluded to let me spend some time in Boston, which I was very glad to hear. I shall now wait until I hear certain, which I wish you to send me word by the next boat. I shall inclose in this a card of Mrs. Rawson's terms, which you may peruse. Until then, I remain, with the same affection,

Your dutiful daughter,

ELIZA S——.

ROBERT SOUTHGATE, ESQ.

Boston, February 13, 1798.

Honored Father:

I am again placed at school, under the tuition of an amiable lady, so mild, so good, no one can help loving her; she treats all her scholars with such a tenderness, as could win the attention of the most savage heart, though scarcely able to receive an impression of the kind. I learn embroidery and geography at present, and wish your permission to learn music. You may justly say, my best of fathers, that every letter of mine is one which is asking for something more,—never contented. I only ask; if you refuse me, I know you do what you think best, and I am sure I ought not to complain, for you have not yet refused me anything that I have asked. My best of parents, how shall I repay you? You answer, By your good behavior. Heaven grant it may be such as shall repay you.

A year will have rolled over my head before I shall see my parents. I have left them at an early age to be so long absent, but I hope I have learnt a good lesson by it; a lesson of experience, which is the best lesson I could learn. I have described one of the blessings of . . . in Mrs. Rawson, and now I will describe Mrs. Wyman, as the nurse. She is the worst woman I ever knew; nobody knows what I suffered from the treatment of that woman.

I had the misfortune to be a favorite with Miss Haskell, and Mrs. Wyman treated me as her own evil heart dictated; but whatever is, is right,—I learnt a good lesson by it. I wish you, my father, to write me an answer soon, and let me know whether I may learn music. Give my best respects to my mother, and may it please the <u>Disposer of all Good</u> to restore me safe home to the bosom of my family. I never was happier in my life. My heart overflows with gratitude to my heavenly Father for it, and may it please him to continue in you "his favor which is life, and his lovingkindness which is better than life," is the sincere wish of

Your daughter,

ELIZA SOUTHGATE.

Boston, May 12, 1798.

My Dear Parents:

Now, at the end of the week, when my hopes are almost exhausted of seeing my brother, I attempt to address you: a task which was once delightful, but now painful, since my mother's last letter. I see my errors, and if I can hope they will no longer be remembered by my parents, I shall again be happy. My mother's letter greatly surprised me, after having received so different a one from my father,— indeed, my parents, did you think I would any longer cherish a passion _you_ disapproved, after expressing your disapprobation? It was enough; your wishes _are_, and always _shall be_, my _commands_.

I have spent a week of painful anxiety; no letter, no brother, no father has come, and I am now in painful expectation to receive a letter to-night, but I dare not hope it will be so. Do, my father, as soon as you receive this, send for me as soon as possible; for my quarter at Mrs. Rawson's was out last Saturday, and as circumstances are, I thought proper not to go to Mr. Boyd's. I beg of you to send for me home directly, for I only board at Mrs. Rawson's now; for I am in expectation of seeing or hearing every day, and, therefore, I have not begun any more work. My time is spending without gain. I am at Mrs. Frazier's, and have been here ever since Thursday. I shall go back to Rawson's to-night, and there wait for further orders. Time hangs more heavy than it ever did before.

I am, with the most sincere respect and affection, your daughter,

ELIZA S———.

Boston, February 7, 1800.

After the toil, the bustle, and fatigue of the week, I turn toward home to relate the manner in which I have spent my time. I have been continually engaged in parties, plays, balls, etc., etc. Since the first week I came here, I have attended all the balls and assemblies,—one one week and one the next. They have regular balls once a fortnight and regular assemblies once a fortnight, so that I have been every Thursday to one or the other.

They are very brilliant, and I have formed a number of pleasing acquaintances there. Last night, which was ball night, I drew No. 52. Drew a Mr. Snow—bad partner; danced with Mr. Oliver, Mr. McAndrews, Mr. McPherson until one o'clock. They have charming suppers—table laid out entirely with china.

I had a charming partner always. To-day I intend going to Mrs. Codman's. Engaged to a week ago, but wrote a billet saying I was indisposed; but the truth of the matter was, I wanted to go to the play to see Bunker Hill, and Uncle wished I should; therefore, I shall go. I have engagements for the greater part of next week. To-morrow we all go to hear Fisher Ames' Eulogy; and in the morning going to look at some instruments, we have one picked out that I imagine we shall like—$150—a charming toned one, and not made in this country. I am still at Mrs. Frazier's. She treats me with the greatest attention. Nancy is indeed a charming girl. I have the promise of her company the ensuing summer. I have bought me a very handsome white satin skirt. Richard Cutes went shopping with me yesterday morning; engaged to go to the play next week with him. For mourning for Washington, the ladies dress as much as if for a relation—some entirely in black; but now many wear only a ribbon with an urn painted on it. I have not yet been out to see Mrs. Rawson and Miss Haskell, but intend to next week. Uncle Williams has been very attentive to me indeed—carried me to all the plays three or four times, and to all the balls and parties excepting the last, to which I went with Mr. Andrews.

Give my best respects to Papa and Mamma, and tell them I shall soon be tired of this dissipated life, and almost want to go home already. I have a line to write to Mary Porter. I must conclude with saying how much I think of you, and accept the sincere affection of

Yours,

ELIZA SOUTHGATE.

Boston, June 12, 1800.

To Octavia, at Mrs. Frazier's:

In the hospital! Bless your heart, I am not there. Who told you I was? Mr. Davis, I know. If you see him, tell him I shall scold him for it. Martha has heard the same. True, I had some idea of going in, but gave it up as soon as I heard Dr. Coffin did not attend. Horatio did likewise. Your last to Mamma is dated from Mrs. Frazier's. How, Octavia, shall we discharge the debt of gratitude which we owe her? It had exceeded my hopes of payment before you went; surely it is now doubled. You mention nothing of any letters from me. I have written several, and in one told you particularly that Mamma wished you by all means to take lessons in music. You don't tell us what you have done since you have been in Medford. Martha writes me that you are to spend part of vacation at Mrs. Trumen's. What has become of Ann and Harriet? I am out of patience waiting for them. Why don't they write? It is an age since I have had one line. Col. Boyd, I hope, will bring some letters from all of you. I have heard that Eleanor Coffin received attentions from Sam Davis when in Boston. Did you hear of it? Martha writes me, too, that Mr. Andrews is paying attention to a young lady in Boston, but does not mention her name,— <u>Miss Parkman</u>, I guess; he was said to be her swain last winter. Mary Porter went home last week. I went with her. She has now gone to Topsham, to tarry until Uncle returns. I anxiously expect a letter from Ann or Harriet, to know the reason that they don't hasten their visit. I am learning my twelfth tune, Octavia. I almost worship my instrument. It reciprocates my sorrows and joys and is my bosom's companion. How I long to have you return! I have hardly attempted to sing since you went away. I am sure I shall not dare to when you return. I must enjoy my triumph while you are absent. My musical talents will be dimmed when compared with the luster of yours. Pooh! Eliza, you are not serious. No, I will excel in something else, if not in music. Oh, nonsense! this spirit of emulation in families is destructive of concord and harmony. At least, I will endeavor to excel you in <u>sisterly affection</u>. If you outshine me in accomplishments, will it not be all in the family? Certainly. How I wish I had a <u>balloon!</u> I would see you and all my friends in Boston in a trice. I have not got one. Do tell me is Ann the same dear, good

friend and as much my sister _romp_ as ever? Tell her I am so affronted with her that I won't speak to her. Sister Boyd is over,—won't go home this week. About your work, I will go downstairs and ask Mamma. A _mourning piece_ with a figure in it, and two other pictures,—mates. Figures of females I think handsomer than landscapes. Mrs. Rawson knows what is best,—thus says Mamma; she don't wish any scenes. Mr. Little, the bearer of this, another beau I send you; and here is poor _I_, not a bit of a one. _Dr. Bacon_, and even him Cousin Mary,—selfish creature!—has lugged off his _heart_ and left the remainder here; so we might as well have a stump. Poor soul! his face looks like a _peony_—one continual blush; I suppose, for fear of hearing his name mentioned; and she—unreasonable creature!—thinks he is not all perfection. Unaccountable taste! he is very delightsome, surely. How long shall I rant at this rate! I long to go to Portland, and there I shall see some being that looks like a beau,—or a monkey,—or anything you please. To supply the loss, I often look out of the window, till my imagination forms one out of a tree, or anything that I see. We can imagine anything, you know.

Bless my soul! Mr. L. is waiting. Give my love, respects, everything to all.

ELIZA.

OCTAVIA SOUTHGATE, a Sister.

Topsham, July 1, 1800.

I must again trouble my dear mother, by requesting her to send on my spotted muslin. A week from next Saturday, I set out for Wiscassett, in company with Uncle William and Aunt Porter. Uncle will fetch Ann to meet us there, and as she has some acquaintance there, we shall stay some time, and Aunt will leave us there, and return to Topsham. So long a visit in Wiscassett will oblige me to muster all my muslins, for, I am informed, they are so monstrous smart as to take no notice of any lady that can condescend to wear a calico gown; therefore, dear mother, to insure me a favorable reception, pray send my spotted muslin by the next mail after you receive this, or I shall be on my journey to Wiscassett. I shall go on horseback. How I want my habit! I wish it had not been so warm when I left home, and I should have worn it. I am in hopes you will find an opportunity to send it by a private conveyance before I go; but my muslin you must certainly send by the mail. Aunt Porter's little Rufus is very sick; he, poor child, was born under an evil star, and I believe Pandora opened her box upon him when he first came into existence. The mumps, I believe, now afflict him; night before last we were alarmed for fear of his having the quinsy; but I believe he is in no danger of that at present. I wish to hear from home very much.

ELIZA. •

I shall anxiously wait the arrival of the next mail after you receive this.

Topsham, July 3, 1800.

I believe, my dear mother, that you meant to give me a very close lesson in economy, when you cut out the shirts for me to make. You had measured off the bodies of two, and cut them part way in, and also the sleeves were marked; after I had cut these off, there was about a quarter of a yard left.

I now wanted the collars and all the trimmings. I made out, after a great deal of planning, to get out the shoulder-pieces, wrist-bands, one pair of neck gussets, and one of sleeves. Do send the collars. One pair of neck gussets and one sleeve are still wanting. I shall send this on by Mrs. Smith, and if you can find out when she returns, I wish you would send me some linen and some more shirts to make, as I shall soon finish these, and can as well finish making up the piece here as at home. I was very sorry I did not wear my habit down, as I shall want it when I go to Wiscassett,— if you can possibly find an opportunity, I wish you would send it to me. Aunt Porter's child is one of the most troublesome ones I ever saw; he cries continually, and she is at present destitute of any help, except a little girl about twelve years old. I wish, my dear mother, that you would forward all letters that come to Scarborough for me immediately. I hope you will enjoy yourself in Portland this week. I was almost tempted to wish to stay a week there; there were so many parties, and so gay everybody appeared, that I longed to stay and take part. I forgot all about it before I got to Topsham. Much as I enjoy society, I am never unhappy without it. I cannot but feel happy that I was brought up in retirement, since from habit, at least, I contracted a love for solitude. I never feel alone when I have my pen or books. I feel that I ought to be very happy in the company of such a woman as Aunt Porter, for I really don't know of any one whose mind is more improved, and which makes her both a useful and instructing companion. Her sentiments and opinions are more like those I have formed than any person I know of. I think my disposition is like hers, and I feel myself drawn toward her by an irresistible impulse. Not an hour but she reminds me of you, and I sincerely think her more like you than your own sister.

I shall write you when I go farther east. I don't know what I shall do about writing to Octavia, as Mrs. Rawson told her that I wrote on an improper subject when I asked her in my letter if Mr. Davis was paying attention to Eleanor Coffin, and she would

not let her answer the question.   This is <u>refining too much</u>, and if I can't write as I
feel, I can't write at all.   Now I ask you, Mamma, if it is not quite a natural question,
when we hear that any of our friends are paid attentions to by any gentleman, to ask a
confirmation of the report from those we think most likely to know the particulars?
Never did I write a line to Octavia but I should have been perfectly willing for you or
my father to have seen.   You have always treated me more like a companion than a
daughter, and, therefore, would make allowances for the volatile expressions I often make
use of.

I never felt the least restraint in company with my parents which would induce me
to stifle my gayety, and you have kindly permitted me to rant over all my nonsense. And
I strictly believe it has never injured me.

I must bid you good-night.

ELIZA.

Pray don't forget to send some more shirts.   I wish my father or you would write
me while I am from home.

MRS. MARY K. SOUTHGATE.

Bath, Sunday, September 13, 1800.

Mr. Moses Porter:

There are some kinds of indisposition that, instead of weakening the faculties of the mind, serve only to render them more vigorous and sprightly, and, in proportion as the body is debilitated, the mind is strengthened. I have every reason to believe that the imagination never soars to such lofty heights as it does in sickness. But, where am I, and what about? Well may you ask the question. Believe me, cousin; I have attempted to finish this letter four times this day. I cannot account for my inability to write; it used to be the joy of my life. Nothing delighted me so much as to steal into the chamber by myself and scribble an hour; but since I received your last, I have often attempted to answer it, but in vain. I have a stubborn brain. It must be coaxed, not driven. I find there is nothing so tedious as to write when we are not in the mood for it: you may easily see I am not in one at present. Now, for heavens! see what I have written, and find the chain that connects. When I began, I meant to say I had been quite unwell ever since I left Portland; that some disorders only served to give vigor to the mind, and —but I meant also to say mine was altogether of a different nature; but, as I left that out, so I had better done the other. O Lord! 'tis too bad. I'll not write another word till I think I can understand it after it is written. I am low-spirited, stupid, and everything else.

Wednesday.

Now I shall really think I have no soul, if I find myself as destitute of ideas as I was on Sunday. I have just been viewing the most delightful prospect I have seen this long time, and yet it has left no greater impression on my mind than objects passing before a mirror. I shall think myself devoid of every faculty that constitutes us rational beings. I think Nature has done everything to render Bath pleasant. The window at which I now sit commands a most delightful water prospect. The river is about a mile in breadth at this place. The opposite banks are—sublime or beautiful. What if I for a moment should take a poet's license, and, by the force of imagination, project steep and ragged rocks, bid them stoop with awful majesty to reflect their

gloomy horrors in the wave! See you not that enormous precipice whose awful summit was ne'er profaned by human footstep? Does not your blood freeze as it creeps along your veins? Behold again that barren waste! The ax or the plow has never clothed it with a borrowed charm nor robbed it of those Nature bestowed on it. It still boasts its independence of the labor of man. But, to leave fiction for reality, the surface of the water is a perfect mirror. I never saw it so perfectly smooth. At this moment there is a boat passing rowed by two men. The reflection in the water is so distinct, so very clear, it looks like two boats. I admire to see a boat _rowed_. It seems to look like arms or wings moving with graceful majesty, while the boat cuts the liquid bosom of the water, leaving as it recedes a widening track. There is always to me something very charming in the rowing of a boat. There is music in the motion; and what can be more graceful and majestic than the motion of a ship under sail? Yesterday there was a big vessel here. 'Twas within hearing,—very near. I never was more forcibly struck than at the moment. I longed to prostrate myself in humble admiration as she approached with a slow, commanding, celestial air. At the moment I am sure it gave me a better idea of the awful grandeur of a deity than anything I had ever seen. I saw Juno! dignified gracefulness; such as I had read of, but could not conceive. I have often in reading been disagreeably struck by the epithets used for the motion of the gods. Sometimes they make them glide through the air, sometimes approach with a solemn _step_, and many other words I do not recollect. Nor do I at present think of any words that would answer better. Yet to glide seems stealing along.—to move rapidly and imperceptibly. A bird glides through the air; yet there is nothing celestial in the flight of a bird. It seems to be properly applied to _fairies_. Something light and airy should glide. That a fairy should glide along seems right,—just as I have an idea of them; and then for a god to _step_! that seems too groveling,—too like us mortals! Yet that, in my opinion, is better than the other. The place on which this house stands seems to project a small degree toward the water. I believe there is not a room in the house that does not command a view of the water. In front there is a kind of a cove; the water makes in several rods. The river is broad and straight. The land rises gradually from it a half mile, but I think it is to be regretted that the inhabitants have built under the hill, or rather, that they did not prefer climbing a little higher. However, I think it must have a fine appearance from the water. Last year I recollect sailing along in front of the settlement, and remarked how much more compact it looked than it really is, the houses rising one above the other in such a manner that every one was seen distinctly. I think nothing can be more beautiful than a town built on a sloping ground ascending from so fine a river as this part of the Kennebec. All the navigation belonging to the different ports on this river above Bath pass directly by here, and several times I have

seen twelve or fourteen at a time. To me, who have been brought up amidst salt marshes and flats, this fine river affords much novelty and amusement. I cannot but confess the sensations I feel in viewing it are more pleasing than those produced by the stagnant water in a Scarborough salt pond. I have almost filled my sheet without saying a word about your letter. Indeed, I have forgotten what was in it. At the time you gave it to me, I know I received it with much pleasure, as it robbed me of some painful moments. After Horatio's recovery, I sat down one evening to write you, but I had only written the day of the month when a most violent clap of thunder (the same that struck Mr. Hooper's house) shook the pen from my hand and the desk from my lap. I do not imagine even by this omen that I offend the strictest laws of virtue and propriety by continuing to write you; therefore, should something equally powerful wrest the pen from my hand, depend upon it, I will seize it with renewed vigor and dare assure you of my esteem, etc.

ELIZA.

I shall go to Wiscassett on Monday. Expect to hear from me after I return to Bath. While there, I shall have no time. I expect to have important communications to forward from a certain pair of sparkling eyes which are far more eloquent than her tongue. Now, I have half a mind to be affronted. I know at this time as soon as you have read this you are tumbling it into your pocket as waste paper, to ponder on the brilliancy of the said eyes. Well, I shall see them soon, and shall be tempted to ask some atonement for the damages I may suffer. Write me often while I am here. It is your _duty_.

Scarborough, September 14, 1800.

I suppose I ought to commence my letter with a humble apology, begging forgiveness for past offenses, and promising to do better in future, but no, I will only tell you that I have been so much engaged since I got home from Topsham, that I could not write you. Martha tells us you were in Boston last Sunday. <u>Mamma</u> thinks, Octavia, you are there too much,—we do not know how often, but we hear of you there, very often indeed. I think, my dear sister, you ought to improve every moment of your time, which is short, very short, to complete your education.

In November terminates the period of your instruction,—the last, perhaps, you will receive ever, only what you may gain by observation. You will never cease to learn, I hope; the world is a volume of instruction, which will afford you continual employment,—peruse it with attention and candor, and you will never think the time thus employed misspent. I think, Octavia, I would not leave school again until you finally leave it. You may—you will think this is harsh; you will not always think so—remember those that wish it <u>must</u> know better what is proper better than you possibly can. Horatio will come on for you as soon as your quarter is out: we anticipate the time with pleasure. Employ your time in such a manner as to make your improvements conspicuous. A boarding school, I know, my dear sister, is not like home: but reflect a moment: is it not necessary, absolutely necessary, to be more strict in the government of twenty or thirty young ladies, nearly of an age and different dispositions, than a private family? Your good sense will tell you it is. No task can be greater than the care of so many girls. It is impossible not to be partial, but we may conceal our partiality. I should have a poor opinion of any person that did not feel a love for merit superior to what they care for the world in general. I say this, not because I think you are discontented,—far from it: your letters tell us quite the reverse, and I believe it. Surely, Octavia, you must allow that no woman was ever better calculated to govern a school than Mrs. Rawson; she governs by the love with which she always inspires her scholars. You have been indulged, Octavia; so we have all. I was discontented when I first went from home. I dare say you have had some disagreeable sensations, yet your reason will convince you you ought not to have had. You had no idea when you left home of any difference in your manner of living. I knew you would easily be reconciled to it, and,

therefore, said but little to you about it.   Yesterday Miss Haskell's letter, which I so much wished for and so highly prized, was sent me.   Tell her to trust no more letters to the politeness of Mr. Jewett, for he will forget to deliver them.   He has been studying in the same office with Horatio ever since he returned, and never told him he had a letter for me till I told Horatio to ask him.   I've got it at last, and will answer it as soon as I have an opportunity, which I expect soon : my letters are of too little consequence to send by post.   Tell Miss Haskell how highly I am obliged to her for every letter, and how much it gratifies me to have her write thus.

My love and esteem ever await our good Mrs. Rawson, and I hope she does not intend my last letter shall go unanswered.   Susan Wyman is still remembered as the companion of my amusements in Medford.

Irene joins me in love to her.   Betsey Browne, my love to her likewise.   Family are all well, Octavia.   Sister Boyd is here,— has been with us several days.   Let us hear from you when you have an opportunity.   I should like to know how many tunes you play, but you have never answered any of my inquiries of this kind : therefore, I suppose I ought not to make them.

Your

ELIZA.

OCTAVIA.

To Moses Porter, a favorite Cousin.

September, 1800.

My most charming cousin, most kind and condescending friend, teach me how I may express the grateful sense I have of the obligations I owe you. Your many and long letters have chased away the spleen; they have rendered me cheerful and happy, and I almost forgot I was so far away from home. Oh, shame on you! Moses, you know I hate this formality among friends : you know how gladly I would throw all these fashionable forms from our correspondence, but you still oppose me ; you adhere to them with as much scrupulosity as to the Ten Commandments ; and, for aught I know, you believe them equally essential to the salvation of your soul. But, Eliza, you have not answered my last letter! True : and if I had not answered it, would you never have written me again? I confess that I believe you would not ; yet I am mortified and displeased that you value my letters so little ; that the exertion to continue the correspondence must all come from me ; that if I relax my zeal in the smallest degree, it may drop to the ground without your helping hand to raise it. I do think you are a charming fellow!—would not write because I am in debt. Well, be it so, my ceremonious friend. I submit ; and, though I transgress by sending a half sheet more than you ever did, yet, I assure you, 'twas to convince you of the violence of my anger, which could induce me to forget the rules of politeness. I am at Wiscassett. I have seen Rebecca every day. She is as handsome as ever, and we both of us were in constant expectation of seeing you for two or three days. You did not come, and we were disappointed. I leave here for Bath next week. I have had a ranting time, and if I did not feel so offended, I would tell you more about it.

ELIZA.

As I look around me, I am surprised at the happiness which is so generally enjoyed in families, and that marriages which have not love for a foundation on more than one side at most should produce so much apparent harmony. I may be censured for declaring it as my opinion that not one woman in a hundred marries for love. A woman of taste and sentiment will surely see but a very few whom she could love, and it is altogether uncertain whether either of them will particularly distinguish her. If they should, surely she is fortunate, but it would be one of Fortune's random favors, and such as we have no right to expect. The female mind, I believe, is of a very pliable texture; if it were not, we should be wretched indeed. Admitting as a known truth that few women marry those whom they would prefer to all the world if they could be viewed by them with equal affection, or rather that there are often others whom they could have preferred if they had felt that affection for them which would have induced them to offer themselves,—admitting this as a truth not to be disputed, is it not a subject of astonishment that happiness is not almost banished from this connection? Gratitude is undoubtedly the foundation of the esteem we commonly feel for a husband. One that has preferred us to all the world, one that has thought us possessed of every quality to render him happy, surely merits our <u>gratitude</u>. If his character is good,—if he is not displeasing in his person or manners, what objection can we make that will not be thought frivolous by the greater part of the world! Yet I think there are many other things necessary for happiness, and the world should never compel me to marry a man because I could not give satisfactory reasons for not liking him. I do not esteem marriage absolutely essential to happiness; and that it does not always bring happiness, we must every day witness in our acquaintance. A single life is considered too generally as a reproach. But, let me ask you, which is most despicable,—she who marries a man she scarcely thinks <u>well</u> of to avoid the reputation of an old maid, or she who, with more delicacy than to marry one she could not highly esteem, prefers to live single all her life, and has wisdom enough to despise so mean a sacrifice to the opinion of the rabble as the woman who marries a man she has not much love for must make? I wish not to alter

9

the laws of nature; neither will I quarrel with the rules which custom has established and rendered indispensably necessary to the harmony of society. But every being who has contemplated human nature on a large scale will certainly justify me when I declare that the inequality of privilege between the sexes is very sensibly felt by us females, and in no instance is it greater than in the liberty of choosing a partner in marriage. True, we have the liberty of refusing those we don't like, but not of selecting those we do. This is undoubtedly as it should be. But let me ask you, my dear girl, what must be that love which is altogether voluntary, which we can withhold or give, which sleeps in dullness and apathy, till it is requested to brighten into life? Is it not a cold, lifeless dictate of the head? Do we not weigh all the conveniences and inconveniences which will attend it? And after a long calculation in which the heart never was consulted, we determine whether it is most prudent to love or not.

How I should despise a soul so sordid, so mean. How I abhor the heart which is regulated by mechanical rules, which can say "thus far will I go and no farther," whose feelings can keep pace with their convenience, and be awakened at stated periods,—a mere piece of clockwork which always moves right. How far less valuable than that being who has a soul to govern her actions, and though she may not always be coldly prudent, yet she will sometimes be generous and noble, and that the other never can be. After all, I must own that a woman of delicacy never will suffer her esteem to ripen into love unless she is convinced of a return. Though our first approaches to love may be involuntary, yet I should be sorry if we had no power of controlling, nay, of conquering, them if occasion required.

There is a happy conformity or pliability in the female mind which seems to have been a gift of nature to enable them to be happy with so few privileges; and another thing,—they have more gratitude in their dispositions than men, and there is a something particularly gratifying to the heart in being beloved, if the object is worthy; it produces a something like pity, and "pity melts the heart to love." Added to these there is a self-love which does more than all the rest. Our vanity ('tis an ugly word, but I can't find a better) is gratified by the distinguished preference given us. There must be an essential difference in the dispositions of men and women. I am astonished when I think of it, yet— But I have written myself into sunshine; 'tis always my way, when anything oppresses me, when any chain of thoughts particularly occupies my mind and I feel dissatisfied at anything which I have not the power to alter, to sit down and unburden them on paper. It never fails to alleviate me, and I generally give full scope to the feeling of the moment; and as I write, all disagreeable thoughts evaporate, and I end content that things shall remain as they are. When I began this, it absolutely appeared to me that no woman, or rather not one in a hundred, married the man she should prefer to all the

world,—not that I ever could suppose that at the time she married him she did not prefer him to all others, but that she would have preferred another if he had professed to love her as well as the one she married. Indeed, I believe no woman of delicacy suffers herself to think she could love any one before he had discovered an affection for her. For my part, I should never ask the question of myself, Do I love such a one, if I had no reason to think he loved me; and I believe there are many who love that never confessed it to themselves. My pride, my delicacy, would all be hurt if I discovered such <u>unasked-for</u> love, even in my own bosom. I would strain every nerve and rouse every faculty to quell the first appearance of it. There is no danger, however. I could never love without being beloved, and I am confident in my own mind that no person whom I could love would ever think me sufficiently worthy to love me. But I congratulate myself that I am at liberty to refuse those I don't like, and that I have firmness enough to brave the sneers of the world and live an old maid, if I never find one I can love.

To Moses Porter, a Cousin and great Favorite.

October, 1800.

I want to write, yet I don't want to write to you, my <u>ceremonious</u> cousin, but at the same time I can think of nobody else, and am compelled to address you. My last was dated from Bath, so is this. Since then I have made a visit to Wiscassett,—oh, I believe, yes, I did write a few lines from there by Uncle Thatcher. I had forgotten that I wrote any more than the letter I finished before I left Bath. I wish I could give you an account of my spending my fortnight at Wiscassett, which would amuse you as much as the reality did me; but that is impossible. I have seen so many new faces,—I was going to say new <u>characters</u>, but they were generally such as we see every day,—so many handsome ladies, so many fine men; indeed, I have seen a little of everything. Mr. Wild and Mr. Davis (of Portland) kept at Mrs. Lee's. Mr. Wild is a most charming man, sensible, animated, genteel, and apparently has one of the mildest and most amiable dispositions in the world. Mr. Davis you know. There was a Miss Paine, daughter of Judge Paine, spent two or three days at Mrs. Lee's. She was — was — Lord, I can't tell you what — you may have heard of her — celebrated for her wit; lost her lover by expressing it rather too severely, poor soul; it was a sad affair. She has at length become sensible of the impropriety of her conduct, and now hopes to atone for it by flattering every gentleman she sees. Time will show whether this plan will succeed. She talks incessantly, laughs always at what she says herself. At table, where the judges, lawyers, and a dozen gentlemen and ladies were seated, Miss Paine engrossed all the conversation. I defy any person to be in the room with her and not be compelled to converse with her; not by the irresistible force of her charms,— they are rather on the wane. If you look at her, she asks what you were going to say. "I know you was going to speak by your looks." Of course my gentleman walks up; how can he help it.' In this manner she draws a whole swarm around her. The poor souls rattle out their outrageous <u>complaints</u>, trembling with fear; for, the moment their ardor to please appears to abate, she rouses them to a sense of their duty by a lash of her tongue.

Sunday.

Now, I can't bear to be hurried, and I must submit to be, or not send this by Mama King. Last night when I began this, I felt quite disposed to throw away an hour—for my letters to you are <u>thrown away</u>, as you won't take the trouble to answer them — without consulting anything but my feelings. I began, and soon found to my mortification that

I ought to have consulted my candle; for, as if piqued at my neglect, it took "French leave to doze," and broke off my description of Miss Paine in the most striking part. I do not resume the subject; 'twould be a profanation of this day to scandalize a frail sister. My mind is full of charity and Christian love. I hope I shall not stumble against some unlucky thought that may derange its present peaceful state. Now, cousin, don't you think it unpardonable, don't you think it a violation of all the laws of politeness, that you should neglect writing me merely because I owed a letter? I should not be surprised if you counted the words in your and my letters, and settled the account by some rule in arithmetic. But let me entreat you not to estimate mine by the weight, but the _number;_ in that case, I am equal to anybody. But if, unhappily for me, you should weigh them with critical exactness, 'twill take many of them to repay you for one of yours. I feel assured you must have adopted this method, and sincerely ask your pardon for doubting a moment that this was the true cause.

What prevented your coming to Wiscassett? I thought you had determined upon it. Rebecca and I used to expect you every day. Believe me, I was asked a dozen times if you were not absolutely engaged to Miss Rice. How such things will get about. I told everybody that asked me that I was your confidante, and, of course, must keep your attachment a secret, for which I am prepared to receive your _thanks._ Mr. Kensman has been down to Wiscassett. He attended the courts, as he says, to acquire a better knowledge of the _law;_ but I should imagine he mistook the _ladies_ for the law, as he makes them his constant study; but I leave so dangerous a subject, or my feelings should deprive me of the power to finish this sheet. I shall probably return home the beginning of next month. If I have a letter due from you, according to your new arrangements, I beg you to forward it as soon as possible. However, I have not the vanity to suppose there is more than a dozen lines as yet; perhaps when I have written a dozen more letters, I may be richly rewarded with _one from_ you. Where is Mary? How does she do? Rebecca wrote her while I was in Wiscassett, and told me undoubtedly she is expected to spend the winter there. I must finish. Uncle calls ——

ELIZA.

I believe it is about the 10th day of October Ellen Coffin is going to be married to a widower and three children,— think of that, sir! I had a letter from her last week. She is not coming home till she leaves Portland as Mrs. Derby.

Octavia:

After a fortnight very pleasantly spent in Wiscassett I return to Bath. In my last I mentioned that Judge Lowell's family were expected in Wiscassett. They came immediately after. Eliza, the youngest, brought letters from Ellen Coffin: thus I very readily got acquainted with them. Judge Lowell appears to be one of the mildest, most amiable of men. Mrs. Lowell is a fine, lady-like woman, yet her manners are such as would have been admired fifty years ago: there is too much appearance of whalebone and buckram to please the depraved taste of the present age. Nancy L., the oldest daughter, is making rapid strides to old age,—the finger of time begins to furrow her cheek, and has stolen the blush of youth from her countenance; yet her eyes sparkle with intelligence, she is animated, sensible, enthusiastic, and very easy and pleasing in her conversation and manners. You would be delighted with her conversation,—'tis elegant and refined; she has no airs. Eliza is a little, charming, sweet creature; she is about seventeen or eighteen, short, fat, and a blooming complexion, handsome blue eyes, light hair, beautiful dimples, artless and unaffected in her manners. Indeed, I was delighted with her, she is so perfectly amiable in her appearance. I was much pleased at an acquaintance with them. At Wiscassett I was invited to accompany them to Bath: as they were going in a boat, I accepted with pleasure. In the morning, which was Thursday, they called for me, and I went with them as far as Turkham's, where they kept. At last, after a long debate, it was thought too hazardous to go by water while the wind blew so violently: 'twas determined to go by land. Mr. Lee took the two Miss Lowells and myself in his <u>carriage,</u> which holds four very charmingly: Judge Lowell and wife in a chaise, with a boy to carry it back; Judge Bourne in a chaise with a boy; and Mr. Merrill on horseback. About five miles on our way, Mr. Lee took Mr. Merrill's horse, and he got in with us. He sang us a number of songs; we had a charming time. At the ferry Mr. Lee, Mr. Merrill, and the boys left us with the chaise; we then all got into a boat and landed at Uncle's wharf.—'tis about three miles, a most charming sail. Indeed, we had a very pleasant time. They went directly to Page's, and in the evening I went up to see them; left them at eight, and with real regret. I had passed some very pleasant hours in their society. They set out in the morning for Portland. Only

think of Eleanor going to be married! 'Tis no more than I expected, and believed it the moment I heard it. Poor Mrs. Summers! what an affecting loss she has met with. My heart bleeds while I think how _very_ fond she was of the little creature.—she was a _lovely_ child. How do all do at home? I long to get home. I never wanted to see home more in my life, yet I am very happy here. I wish Mamma would send me my habit or great-coat to ride home in; send it by Uncle. Pray get the instrument tuned. If you see _Moses_ soon, tell him I think it impossible to find words to express my obligations to him for his many and long letters; yet I shall endeavor to convince him I have a due sense of them. I shall make all the return in my power. I was going up to Topsham this week; I wish to very much. But, Mama King and Uncle both going, Nancy would be quite alone. I must stay to comfort her. As to Aunt Porter, I believe she will think I am never coming to Topsham.—I begin to think so myself; what can I do? However, I must; I shall go as soon as Uncle returns, and stay till I return home. I want to see Aunt Porter very much. Write me soon and tell me all the news. Has Papa gone to Salem?

ELIZA.

Scarborough, December 16.

I am sorry to have given Aunt Porter such an opportunity of charging me with neglect in executing her commission. But I can easily convince her I did not deserve censure; for until last Friday I never received yours of November 22d, and I shall execute that part of Aunt's request which I can in Scarborough, but the patterns of satin I cannot get in Saco nor in Scarborough. The gown patterns I shall inclose. The one with a fan back is meant just to meet before, and pin the bobbins in string, belt, or anything. The other pattern is a plain waist, with strips of the same stitched on, and for white lace between with bobbin or cord.

I have a muslin done so, with black silk cord, which looks very handsome, and I have altered my brown silk into one like the other pattern. I was over at Saco yesterday, and saw one Mary had made in Boston. It was a separate waist, or, rather, the breadths did not go quite up. The waist was plain, with one stripe of cording set in behind, and the rest of the waist perfectly plain. The skirt part was plaited in box plaits, three of a side; which reaches to the shoulder-strap, and only enough left to meet straight before, as is one of the patterns I have sent. You ask so many questions that I hardly know how to answer them.

Isabella is almost recovered; her family well. The baby, I believe, will be named Charles Orlando. The assemblies begin on Thursday, as also do <u>Saco</u> assemblies. Probably I shall go to next Portland assembly. You ask how Mrs. Little and Lama do. A strange question. Lama is well, or was last Thursday, and Mrs. Little is soon to be married to Mr. Bowman, of Exeter.

Papa has been confined to the house a week yesterday, by a wound on his leg which he made with an ax. He wounded the tendon which leads from the great toe up. He cut it a little above the ankle. It has been very painful. Give my love to Aunt. Tell her I shall not be able to come down this winter, for my next route will be to Boston. Write me the next opportunity, respecting the sables and the trimmings, and how Uncle goes to Boston, that I may be in readiness. Family all well.

ELIZA.

Portland, March 10, 1801.

To Moses:

Thank you for your being so particular in your description of your Eastern tour. I told you that Wiscassett would delight you,—ease and sociability, you know, always pleased you. By the bye, Jewett thought <u>Saw</u> was the land of milk and honey; such fine, buxom girls, so easy and familiar. Dorcas Stores charmed him most,—her haughty, forbidding manners corresponded with the dignity of her sentiments, so he says; something congenial in their disposition, I think. But he has made his selection. Miss Weeks is handsome, censorious, animated, violent in her prejudices, genteel, impatient of contradiction, speaks her sentiments freely, has many admirers and many enemies; on the whole, a pleasant companion among friends. How think they will do together? Jewett you know. Last evening I was out at Broad's. We had only seven in our party, a very pleasant one.—Jewett, Horatio, William Weeks, and Charles Little were our beaux; Miss Weeks, Miss Boardman (from Exeter), and myself the ladies. Mr. Little is engaged to Miss Boardman. He is an open, honest, unaffected, plain, clever fellow. She has a pleasant face, an open, guileless heart, plain, unaffected manners, a clumsy shape, easy in company, but it is rather the ease which a calm, even temper produces than that which is acquired in polite circles. I think they are as much alike as possible; 'twill be a pleasant couple. We played cards, talked and wrote crambo after we had scrubbed the backs of two packs of cards, cut half of them up and ate our supper. We set out for home about one o'clock. You say in your last that if reports are true, I am on the highway to matrimony. You know what I have always said with regard to those things. If they are true, well and good; if they are not, let them take their course: they will be short-lived. I despise the conduct of those girls who think every man that pays them any attention is seriously in love with them, and begin to bridle up, look conscious, fearful lest every word the poor fellow utters should be a declaration of love. I have no idea

that every gentleman that has a particular partiality for a lady thinks seriously of being connected with her, and I think any lady puts herself in a most awkward situation to appear in constant fear or expectation that the gentleman is going to make love to her. I despise coquetry. Every lady says the same, you will say; but if I know myself at all, my heart readily assents to its truth. I think no lady has a right to encourage hopes that she means never to gratify, but I think she is much to blame if she considers these little attentions as a proof of love; they often mean nothing, and should be treated as such. The gentleman in question, I own, pays me more attention than many other gentlemen, yet I say sincerely I don't think he means anything more than to please his fancy for the present. I pride myself upon my sincerity, and if I ever am engaged, I trust it will be to one whom I shall not be ashamed to acknowledge. Our intimacy has been of long standing. He and Enoch Jones were Martha's most intimate acquaintances. They were there almost every evening. "There comes Enoch and William," we used to say as soon as we heard the knocker in the evening. I was always at the doctor's a great part of the time I spent at Portland. I could not be intimate with them. I liked them both,— they were pleasant companions, and I was always glad to see them come in. Since that time Enoch has been gone most of the time, and William has been left alone. True, he has this winter been more attentive to me than usual. He lent me books, drawing, and music; he used often to be my gallant home from parties if I walked, and if I rode he helped me to the sleigh; yet, every gentlemen does the same,—all have a favorite, some for a month and some a little longer. It seems like making you a confidant to talk thus, but I say many things which would appear ridiculous if communicated to a third person, and I know you would have too much delicacy to communicate anything which would hurt my feelings. I have heard all these stories before, yet I must act and judge for myself. I know better than any other person how far they are true, and I candidly confess that he never said a word to me which I could possibly construe into the most faint or distant declaration of love. Then think for a moment how ridiculous it would be for me to alter my conduct toward him. No! while he treats me as a friend, I shall treat him as such; and let the world say what they will, I will endeavor to act in a manner that my conscience will justify,—to steer between the rocks of prudery and coquetry and take my own sense of propriety as a pilot; that will conduct me safe. I would not have been thus particular, but I felt unwilling that you should be led into an error that I could easily remove from your mind. It would seem like giving a silent assent. As I profess to write as I think to you, and to speak openly on all occasions, I felt that I ought to say more to you on this affair than I ever have to any other. Let the world still have it as they will. I confess it would be more pleasing to me if my name was not so much talked about; yet, what Johnson says of an author may apply to a person who is

11

much known in the world, that " his name, like a shuttlecock, must be beat backward and forward or it falls to the ground." I recollect in a former letter you asked why I did not say more of particular characters, and among my acquaintance select some and give you a few characteristic sketches. The truth is, I felt afraid to. I did not know but you might mention many things which would make me enemies. I am always willing to speak my opinion without reserve on any character, because I should take care that I spoke it before those who would not abuse the frankness. But letters may be miscarried, may fall into hands we wot not of. But I never think of these, or, I am sure, I should burn this in a moment. Another thing: it requires a quick discernment, a correct judgment, and a thorough knowledge of the world, of human nature, to form a just character of any one that we are not intimately acquainted with. However, we all of us form our opinion of every person we see: and whatever I shall say, or have said, you must recollect is only the opinion of one who is oftener wrong than right, and you can form no correct idea of any character from what I say.

ELIZA.

Scarborough, Sunday, March, 1801.

Congratulate me ; I am at last at home. Come and see us. We expect Miss Tappan to-morrow, and Pauline, and Miranda. I wish much to see Miss T. I think I shall like her, but tell her she does not know what she lost last week. A young gentleman came several miles out of his way only to see her, and she was not here, and he returned to Portland with a heavy heart. Jewett says she is rather shy. I meant to have written more about Wiscassett, about Miss R., but I must leave that for another letter. I have a great deal to say on that head. Exercise the same coolness and judgment as in choosing a horse. I heard a gentleman make exactly the same observation, and yet that very gentleman is raving distractedly in love. He is a little calm now, but he was a madman. He, like you, is always upon extremes ; extravagant beyond all bounds.

More hereafter.

A man of your gallantry might make a small exertion to confer an obligation on two of the fair. Octavia and myself are very anxious that Miss Tappan should make us a visit. My father will bring Miranda home, but our chaise is broken so much that 'tis impossible to use it in its present state ; none to be hired or borrowed. Why can't you take a chaise, and bring over Pemhire and Miss Tappan ? and besides gratifying me with their presence, I shall be very glad to see you. No coaxing, Eliza. But I am in earnest. Come, and you may see some of Martha's letters from London and Bath. I will tell you everything I can think of, and perhaps invent something, if all these won't do. Lord, bless me ! I should not have to urge every one so hard to come and see me. I am, I should be, discouraged. But, seriously, I wish you to come very much. But if you think it impossible, or, rather, very bad, don't mind what I say. However, come ; I shall expect you.

ELIZA.

Scarborough, Tuesday Night, 1801.

Dear Mother:

We have got Miranda all fixed : only her clothes to be washed, or, rather, ironed. You have undoubtedly got all things ready for her, or you would not send for her immediately. I suppose we shall send her over in the stage, as the riding is as yet too bad to go in the chaise. She wants some handkerchiefs, and a pair of cotton gloves to wear to school ; she had three pair of white mitts, and I have given her another pair. I think she must have another dimity skirt. Her jaconet muslin we could not fix, for it wants a new waist, sleeves, and a hem put on the bottom, and we could get no muslin to pattern it. You can buy a piece, and it can be sent on any time : she will not want it immediately. Charles says you told him I must send to you for anything I wanted.

I want nothing so much as some new linen and some English stockings. Excepting the two fine pair, I have nothing but home-spun ones. I should like half-a-dozen pair ; four at least. If you see anything that would be light and handsome for summer gowns, I should like you to get them.

Why can't you go and see McLellan's ? Perhaps he may let you have one reasonably. I think there are some for twelve shillings a yard. They would not come to more than eight or ten dollars. You can look at them at least. I should like one very much. Sally Weeks has taken one of them.

We do very well here, and all goes on charmingly. Arexine loses her thimble, her needle, and anything to avoid work. Sally Selaid has been here ever since Miranda returned, and you know when they are together there must be romping. However, Frederic has gone to carry her home to-day. Miranda must have my little trunk. Octavia and I both want little trunks. My old one is a good size. How is sister ? Give my love to her. Kiss the children. I really miss them, and our own don't seem more natural than they did. The little Isabella (so they say) is Aunt Eliza's favorite. I love that little thing dearly ; I never loved an infant more in my life. Isabella says 'tis because it has blue eyes. She <u>will</u> make me selfish. I had a letter from Martha

yesterday, the _third_ since you left. She mentions Uncle Rufus's family in all of them. In her last but one, she says Aunt King is confined. She had dined there the Sunday before, and they requested her to bring yours and my father's profiles, which I gave her some time before you went away.

She carried them, and Uncle thought them good likenesses. She admires Uncle Rufus. She says when he first called on her he staid two hours, but she could have talked with him _two days._ In her last she says she was to have been introduced at court, but the confinement of Aunt King prevented. As soon as she gets out, she is to be introduced. She shall write again, she says, by the " Minerva," and send me the fashions. Mr. Smith, the Russian, was here last week; brought me some letters from P——. I am now writing to Martha, to send by William Weeks. 'Twill be a fine opportunity, and I shall write as much as I can. Mrs. Coffin will be delighted with this opportunity. Don't come home, Mamma, till you have staid as long as you wish, for I do not know anything at present that requires your presence.

I think I make a very good manager, and tell Sister Boyd I am astonished to find how much I have improved in my _house-wife_ talents this last winter. The children will allow me absolute rule among them, but I have the worst of it. They do very well, considering what a young gay mistress they have. I sometimes get up to dance, and all of them flash up to help me, and when I am tired I find it difficult to stop them: as I set the example, I am obliged to put up with it. I have not been out of the yard since I came home, till this afternoon. I rode a mile or two on horseback, just to breathe the fresh air. I never was so contented in my life, though I have not seen any one but Mr. Smith these three weeks almost. I have not had an hour hang heavily upon me. 'Tis charming to get home after being absent so long. I believe you will think I am never going to leave off.

Your affectionate daughter,

ELIZA S——.

Scarborough, Me., Thursday, April 8, 1801.

I have been thinking on that part of your letter which interests me most,— respecting the propriety of conduct, opinion of the world. I don't exactly recollect what I wrote in my last, but I am positive you have mistaken my meaning, or, at least, have taken what I said on too large a scale. As a general rule of conduct, in so extensive a sense as you talk about, such doctrine would, indeed, be pernicious; but whatever I said I meant to apply to this particular case, and perhaps did not express myself so clearly as I ought to have done. You have described principles which I have ever condemned as those I now act upon. Perhaps I shall find it impossible fully to explain my sentiments on this subject. It is of a delicate nature, and many things I shall say will probably bear a misconstruction. However, I trust your candor to judge with lenity, and to your knowledge of my heart to believe I would not intentionally deviate from the laws of female delicacy and propriety. Reputation undoubtedly is of great importance to all, but to a _female_ 'tis everything. Once lost, 'tis _forever_ lost. Whatever I may have said, my heart too sensibly tells me I have none of that boasted independence of mind which can stand collected in its own worth, and let the censure and malice of the world pass by, as "the idle wind which we regard not." I have ever thought that to be conscious of doing right was insufficient, but that it must appear so to the world. How I could have blundered upon a sentiment which I despise, or how I could have written anything to bear such a construction as you have put upon a part of my letter, I know not. When I said that I should let these reports pass off without notice, or pretending to vindicate myself, 'twas not because I despised the opinion of the world, but as the most effectual method to preserve it. _You_ say, as well as myself, that whatever we say in vindication of ourselves only makes the matter worse. When I said that, I meant not to alter my

conduct while my conscience did not accuse me. I had no idea that you would suppose my conduct toward him had ever been of a kind that required an alteration, or anything more pointed than to any other gentleman. I supposed you would infer from what I said that it was such as propriety and a regard for my reputation would sanction. I know not what you think it has been, but if I can judge of my own actions,— their motives I know I can, but I mean the outward appearance,—I have never treated him with any more distinction than any other gentleman, nor have appeared more pleased with his attentions than with another's. Believe me, I have kept constantly in view the opinion of the world, and if you knew every circumstance of my life, you would be convinced my feelings were "tremblingly alive" to all its slanders. But "something too much of this." You who know my disposition may easily conceive how often I subject myself to the envenomed shafts of censure and malice. By that gayety and high flow of spirits, which I sometimes think my greatest misfortune to possess, sometimes I err in judgment,— don't always see the right path. Sometimes I see it, yet the warmth and ardor of my feelings force me out of it. Yet in this affair I feel confident I have acted from right principles. There are a thousand trifling things that at times influenced my conduct which you cannot know, and you may be surprised when I say that his attentions were of a kind that politeness obliged me to receive. Nor should I ever have suspected they meant anything more than gallantry and politeness, had not the babbles of the world put it into my head. You have been misinformed in many respects, I am convinced. You mentioned his constant visits at Sister Boyd's. I declare to you he never was there a half dozen times the three months I was in Portland, excepting the morning after the assemblies, when the gentlemen all go to see their partners. Neither was I his constant partner at assemblies. I never danced but two dances in an evening with him all winter, excepting once, and then there was a mistake. This surely was nothing remarkable, for I always danced two with Mr. Smith at every assembly we were at. I danced with one as with the other. True he was my partner at two parties at Broad's. I at the time asked Horatio, when he mentioned the party, why he would not carry me. He said, if I was asked by any other, to say I was going with my brother would be considered as a tacit declaration that I had an aversion to going with him; therefore, 'twould have been folly. You cannot judge, unless you know a thousand customs which they have in Portland. But I declare to you, cousin, I am much gratified that you told me what you thought. Had you locked it in your bosom, I should never have had an opportunity to vindicate myself. I beg of you always to write with freedom. Always write with the same openness you did last; 'tis one of the greatest advantages I expect to derive from our correspondence. I enjoin it upon you, as you value my happiness. I told you I would show you some of Martha's letters. I had one from her since I wrote you, in which she says I must

on no condition whatever show her letters.   However, I will read you some passages in some of them.   You shall see some parts.   I will make my peace with — indeed, I know she would not object.   I love to show you her letters, because you feel something as I do in reading them.   You admire her as you should, the friend of

ELIZA.

P. S. I wrote this letter last night, intending to keep it by me to send whenever I please; all the family were absent,— left me reading. I read your letter; the house was silent, and I was entirely alone. I knew I should not have another opportunity as convenient for giving you my sentiments,— no fear of intrusion; I therefore take my pen and scribble what I send you.   But I believe I must adopt your plan, and send it immediately to the office: but I repent, and burn it. I find in reading it that I have said not half I meant to: but I will send it away immediately.   I am almost ashamed to answer you so soon,—'tis so unlike the example you set me, that I suppose you will say 'tis a tacit disapprobation of your conduct.

MR. MOSES PORTER,
        BIDDEFORD.

Scarborough, Sunday, May, 1801.

When one commences an action with a full conviction they shall not acquit themselves with honor, they are sure not to succeed. Impressed with this idea, I write you. I positively declare I have felt a great reluctance ever since we concluded on the plan. I am aware of the construction you may put on this; but, call it affectation or what you will, I assure you it proceeds from different motives. When I first proposed this correspondence, I thought only of the amusement and instruction it would afford me. I almost forgot that I should have any part to perform. Since, however, I have reflected on the scheme as it was about to be carried into execution, I have felt a degree of diffidence which has almost induced me to hope you would forget the engagement. Fully convinced of my inability to afford pleasure or instruction to an enlarged mind, I rely wholly on your candor and generosity to pardon the errors which will cloud my best efforts. When I reflect on the severity of your criticisms in general, I shrink at the idea of exposing to you what will never stand the test. Yet, did I not imagine you would throw aside the critic and assume the friend, I should never dare, with all my vanity (and I am not deficient), give you so fine an opportunity to exercise your favorite propensity. I know you will laugh at all this, and I must confess it appears rather a folly, first to request your correspondence and then with so much diffidence and false delicacy, apparently to extort a compliment, talk about my inability and the like. You will not think I intend a compliment, when I say I have ever felt a disagreeable restraint when conversing before you,—often, when with all the confidence I possess I have brought forward an opinion, said all my imagination could suggest in support of it and viewed with pleasure the little fabric, which I imagined to be founded on truth and justice, with one word you would crush to the ground that which had cost me so many to erect. These things I think in time will humble my vanity. I wish sincerely that they may.

Yet I believe I possess decent talents, and should have been quite another being had they been properly cultivated. But as it is, I can never get over some little prejudices which I have imbibed long since, and which warp all the faculties of my mind. I was pushed on to the stage of action without one principle to guide my actions; the impulse of the moment was the only incitement. I have never committed any grossly imprudent action, yet I have been Folly's darling child. I trust they were rather errors of the head

13

than the heart, for we all have a kind of inherent power to distinguish between right and wrong, and if before the heart becomes contaminated by the maxims of society, it is left to act from impulse, though it have no fixed principle, yet it will not materially err. Possessing a gay, lively disposition, I pursued pleasure with ardor. I wished for admiration, and took the means which would be most likely to obtain it. I found the mind of a female, if such a thing existed, was thought not worth cultivating. I disliked the trouble of thinking for myself, and therefore adopted the sentiments of others, fully convinced to adorn my person and acquire a few little accomplishments was sufficient to secure me the admiration of the society I frequented. I cared but little about the mind. I learned to flutter about with a thoughtless gayety,—a mere feather, which every breath had power to move. I left school with a head full of something, tumbled in without order or connection. I returned home with a determination to put it in more order: I set about the great work of culling the best part to make a few sentiments out of, to serve as a little ready change in my commerce with the world. But I soon lost all patience (a virtue I do not possess in an eminent degree), for the greater part of my ideas I was obliged to throw away, without knowing where I got them or what I should do with them. What remained I pieced as ingeniously as I could into a few patchwork opinions. They are now almost worn threadbare, and as I am about quilting a few more, I beg you will send me any spare ideas you may chance to have that will answer my turn. By this time I suppose you have found out what you have a right to expect from this correspondence, and probably at this moment lay down the letter with a long, sage-like face to ponder on my egotism. 'Tis a delightful employment; I will leave you to enjoy it while I eat my dinner. And what is the result, cousin? I suppose a few exclamations on the girl's vanity to think no subject could interest me but where herself was concerned, or the barrenness of her head that could write on no other subject. But she is a _female_, say you with a _manly contempt_. O you lords of the world, what are you that your unhallowed lips should dare profane the fairest part of creation! But, honestly, I wish to say something by way of apology, but don't seem to know what. It is true I have a kind of natural affection for myself: I find no one more ready to pardon my faults or find excuses for my failings,—it is natural to love our friends.

I have positively not said one single thing which I intended when I sat down. My motive was to answer your letter, and I have not mentioned my having received it! Your opinion of Story's Poems I think very unjust. As to the _man_, I cannot say, for I know nothing of him, but I think you are too severe upon him. A man who had not a "fiber of refinement in his composition" could never have written some passages in that poem. What is refinement? I thought it was a delicacy of taste which might be acquired, if not anything in our nature. True, there are some so organized that they are

incapable of receiving a delicate impression; but we won't say anything of such things. I
just begin to feel in a mood for answering your letter. What you say of Miss Rice,—I
hardly know how to refuse the challenge; she possesses no quality above mediocrity, and
yet is just what a female ought to be. Now what I would give for a little _logic_, or for
a little skill to support an argument! But I give it up, for though you might not convince
me, you would _confound_ me with so many _learned_ observations, that my vanity would
oblige me to say I was convinced, to prevent the mortification of saying I did not understand you. How did you like Mr. Coffin? Write soon and tell me. We expect you
to go to the fishing party with us on Tuesday. Mr. Coffin told us you would all come.
You must be here by nine o'clock (not before) in the morning. My love to the girls, and
tell them—no. I'll tell them myself.

ELIZA.

TO MR. MOSES PORTER,
      BIDDEFORD.

Scarborough, June 1, 1801.

As to the qualities of mind peculiar to each sex, I agree with you that sprightliness is in favor of females, and profundity of males. Their educations, their pursuits, would create such a quality, even though nature had not implanted it. The business and pursuits of men require deep thinking, judgment, and moderation; while, on the other hand, females are under no necessity of dipping deep, but "merely skim the surface"; and we too commonly spare ourselves the exertion which researches require, unless they are absolutely necessary to our pursuits in life. We rarely find one giving one's self up to profound investigation for amusement only. Necessity is the muse of all the great qualities of the mind; it empties all the hidden treasures, and by its stimulating power they are "polished into brightness." Women, who have no such incentives to action, suffer all the strong, energetic qualities to sleep in obscurity. Sometimes a gleam of genius gleams through the thick clouds with which it is enveloped, and irradiates for a moment the darkness of mental night. Yet, like a comet that shoots wildly from its sphere, it excites our wonder, and we place it among the phenomena of nature, without searching for a natural cause. Thus it is the qualities with which nature has endowed us, as a support amid the misfortunes of life and a shield from the allurements of vice, are left to molder in vain. In this dormant state they become enervated and impaired, and at last die for the want of exercise. The little airy qualities which produce sprightliness are left to flutter about like feathers in the wind, the sport of every breeze. Women have more fancy, more lively imagination, than men. That is easily accounted for. A person of correct judgment and accurate discernment will never have that flow of ideas which one of a different character might; every object has not the power to introduce into his mind such a variety of ideas; he rejects all but those doubly connected with it. On the other hand, a person of small discernment will receive every idea that arises in the mind, making no distinction between those nearly related and those more distant. They are all equally welcome, and consequently such a mind abounds with fanciful, out-of-the-way ideas. Women have more imagination, more sprightliness, because they have less discernment. I never was of opinion that the pursuits of the senses ought to be the ——; on the contrary, I believe it would be the destruction to happiness. There would be a degree of rivalry exist incompatible with the harmony we wish to establish. I have ever thought it necessary that each should have separate sphere of action. In such a case there will be

no clashing, unless one or the other should leap their respective bounds; yet, to cultivate the qualities with which we are endowed can never be called infringing the prerogative of man. Why, my dear cousin, were we furnished with such powers, unless the improvement of them would conduce to the happiness of society? Do you suppose the mind of women the only work of God that "was made in vain"? The cultivation of the powers we possess I have ever thought a privilege (or I may say duty) that belonged to the woman species, and not man's exclusive prerogative. Far from destroying the harmony that ought to subsist, it would fix it on a foundation that would not titter at every jar. Women would be under the same degree of subordination that they are now; enlighten and expand their minds, and they would perceive the necessity of such a reputation to preserve the order of happiness of society. Yet you require that their conduct should always be guided by that reason which you refuse them the power of exercising. I know that it is generally thought that in such a case women would assume the right of commanding; but I see no foundation for such a supposition. Shall I repeat that they would perceive the necessity of such a submission?—not a blind submission to the will of another, which neither honor nor reason dictates. It would be criminal in such a case to submit, for we are under a prior engagement to conduct in all things according to the dictates of reason. I had rather be the meanest reptile that creeps the earth, or cast upon the wide world, to suffer all the ills "that flesh is heir to," than live a slave to the despotic will of another. I am aware of the censure that will ever await the female that attempts the vindication of her sex; yet I dare to brave that censure that I know to be undeserved. It does not follow (Oh, what a pen!) that every female who vindicates the capacity of the sex is a disciple of Mary Wollstonecraft. Though I allow her to have said many things which I cannot but approve, yet the very foundation on which she builds her work will be apt to prejudice us so against her that we will not allow her the merit she really deserves. Yet, prejudice set aside, I confess I admire many of her sentiments; yet, notwithstanding, I believe, should any one adopt her principles, they would conduct in the same manner; and upon the whole, her life is the best comment on her writings. Her style is nervous and commanding; her sentiments appear to carry conviction along with them, but they will not bear analyzing. I wish to say something on your natural refinement, but I shall only have room to touch upon it if I begin; therefore, I'll leave it until another time. Last evening Mr. Samuel Thatcher spent with us, we had a fine "dish of conversation" served up with great taste, fine sentiments dressed with elegant language, and seasoned with wit. He is really excellent company,—a little enthusiastic or so, but that is no matter. In compassion, I entreat you to come over here soon, and make me some pens. I have got one that I have been whittling this hour, and have at last got it to make a stroke. It liked to have given me the tic.) I believe I must give up all

14

pretension to _profundity_, for I am much more at home in my female character, though no argumentative style is conformed to my taste. I never could do anything by rote. When I get a subject I am incapable of reasoning upon, I play with it as with a rattle, for what else should I do with it? But I have kept along quite in a direct line. I caught myself "upon the wing" two or three times, but I had power to check my nonsense. I send you my sentiments on this subject as they really exist with me. I believe they are not the mere impulse of the moment, but founded on what I think truth. I could not help laughing at that part of your letter where you said the seal of my letter deprived you of some of the most interesting part of it. I declare positively I left a blank place on purpose for it, that you might not lose one precious word; and now you have the impudence to tell me that the most interesting part was the blank papers. It has provoked my ire to such a degree that I positively declare I never will send you any more blank papers I can possibly avoid, "to spite you."

ELIZA.

Portland, July 17, 1801.

I almost at this moment wish myself in your situation,—meeting old acquaintance, shaking hands with old friends, and telling over with renewed pleasure your college frolics. I can almost see you convulsed with laughter, hear you recount the adventures of the last year, while imagination brings every boyish frolic to your view, unimpaired by time. What a world of humor! what flashes of wit! what animated descriptions! Oh, these social meetings! How they animate and inspire one! How they lighten the cares and multiply the joys of life! I wish you would write about Commencement. I heard yesterday that Sam Fay, of Concord, delivered an oration the 4th of July. I should admire to see it; I know it must be fine. In my opinion he is a man of excellent talents, capable of writing on the occasion an oration that would reflect great honor on himself. The sentiments must be noble and generous. He possesses so much feeling, there must be many glowing passages in it. If it is printed, I beg you will get me a copy, and I will confess myself greatly obliged. Last time I attended the <u>theater</u> Speed the Plough was performed, and I assure you very <u>decently</u>. The characters in general were well supported. Billius, in Farmer Ashfield, really outdid himself; he threw off the monkey and became a good, honest clown, and did not, as he usually does, outstrip the bounds of nature and all other bounds. Mrs. Powell, a Miss Blandford, delighted us all. How I admire that woman! She is perfectly at home on the stage, and yet there is no levity in her appearance; she has great energy, acts with spirit, with feeling, yet never rants. Her private character we all know is exceptionable. Mr. Downie, as a young <u>buck</u>, is very pleasing; he has a most melodious voice in speaking, and has a very easy, <u>stylish</u> air; good figure, though small. As for Mrs. Harper, she is my aversion; for, as Shakspere says, she will "tear a passion to tatters, to very rags," and she is too indecent ever to appear on the stage. Harper is a fine fellow; he appears amidst the common herd of players, and has as much judgment in supporting his part as any one I ever saw; and even in comic characters I think he excels Billius: he has much greater resources within himself. Billius gains approbation by distorting his face and playing the monkey, while Harper adheres more strictly to nature. In Billius we cannot help seeing the player

through the thin disguise, and Billius, not the character he presents, is continually in our minds. S. Powell is contemptible as a player (and I believe as a man); he puffs and blows so incessantly that it is enough to put one into a fever to see him. He does not know in the least how to preserve a medium, but takes a certain pitch and there remains: he cannot gradually bring his passion to the height, but thunders it out, without any preparation, and the unvarying monotony of his voice is disgusting. I am sure by his strutting and bellowing, Hamlet would think he was made by one of "Nature's journey-men." But it is time to have done with players, for you will think my head turned indeed if I rant about them any longer; but it has served to fill up a part of my letter, and I assure you that alone is a sufficient reason why I should give them a place. Society, bustle, and noise frustrate all my ideas. I cannot write anywhere but at home. I am ashamed that things of so little consequence should turn my head, but 'tis a melancholy truth. Oh, you malicious fellow! don't talk to me about my favorite topic, "female edu-cation"; don't tell me of your philosophical indifference. O Moses, you can't leave the subject; every word that could any way dart at it is marked. I believe you do itch to commence the attack. Well, rail on; you shall not say it is in compassion to me that you desist. God forbid that your greatest enemy should ever inflict so severe a punish-ment as to prohibit you from speaking on your "favorite topic." I fancy you have for-gotten that it is not, Mr. Indifference; your ironical letter has had a wonderful effect, but perhaps not the desired one. I blush not to confess myself most contemptibly infe-rior to my antagonist. You ought to blush, but from a different cause. But I had for-gotten myself and was taking things too seriously. I am not slow at taking the hint; perhaps my presumption merited the reproof. I receive it, and will endeavor to profit by it. And pray, cousin, how does Mr. Symmes's coat suit you. His "haughty humil-ity," his "condescending pride." You have assumed the habit, and I hope will ever clothe yourself with it when you meet your inferior antagonist. You have a fine imag-ination, and have pictured a chain of delightful events which will probably exist there alone. Yet I should have no objection to your being a true prophet. We all can plan delightful schemes, but they rarely ever become realities; but no matter, we enjoy them in imagination. I expect from you a particular account of yourself when you return; you will have many amusing anecdotes to tell me, if you will take the trouble. I have just read your last, and perceive something in it that at first I did not pay much attention to. You say all you have said on the subject of female education was merely the thought of the moment, written not to be received, but laughed at. What shall I think —that you think me too contemptible to know your real sentiment? I should be very unwilling to admit such a suspicion; yet, what can you mean? With the greatest apparent serious-ness you speak of the sincerity with which you conduct this correspondence: was that

likewise meant to be laughed at? I had flattered myself, when I commenced this correspondence, to reap both instruction and amusement from an undisguised communication
of sentiments. I had likewise hoped you would not think it too great a condescension to
speak to me with that openness you would to a female friend. However, I shall begin to
think it is contrary to the nature of things that a gentleman should speak his real sentiments to a lady. Yet, in our correspondence I wished and expected to step aside from the
world and speak to each other in the plain language of sincerity. I have much to say on
this subject, but unfortunately my ideas never begin to flow until I have filled my paper.
Do not imagine from what I have said that the most disagreeable truths will offend me.
I promise not to feel hurt at anything you write, if 'tis your real sentiments. But,
cousin, don't trifle with me; do not make me think so contemptibly of myself as you will
by not allowing me your confidence. Promise to speak as you think, and I will never
scold you again.

ELIZA.

Cousin, I wish you would write a list of your mother's children, names and ages,
those that have <u>died</u>, together with the others. We are going to send them out to Uncle
Rufus, as he requested it some time since. By Martha it will be a fine opportunity. As
soon as convenient, send them over.

TO MR. MOSES PORTER,
       BIDDEFORD.

Portland, July, 1801.

To Octavia:

Tired, stupid, and sleepy, I feel that I can write nothing instructive or amusing. Oh! these summer balls are not the thing, but it was much more comfortable than I expected. My ears were continually assailed with lamentations that you were not present. Mr. Kensman would certainly have gone out for you (so he said), had he ever been at our house; he really asked one or two gentlemen to go. He's a frothy fellow,—he rattles without a spark of fancy, and stuns you with his volubility, as anything empty or hollow always makes the most noise. I told him I received a letter from you yesterday. He gave a pious ejaculation to heaven, turned gracefully on his heel, and entreated in the most humble manner that I would grant him a sight of one line. I refused, as I thought him too insignificant an admirer to be so much honored.

Col. Boyd arrived last night. I found him in the parlor when I went down to breakfast; he inquired for you. Mr. Derby and Mr. Coffin will leave town to-day or to-morrow for Boston. They undoubtedly will call and see you; 'twill be a good opportunity to send me the money, if Mamma pleases. Harriet will sail to-morrow; she sends an abundance of love.

ELIZA.

Topsham, October 29, 1801.

Moses Porter:

Why, you unaccountable wretch! you obstinate fellow! you malicious, you vain, you —
I am run out. I will e'en call in the assistance of Sir John Falstaff to help me exclaim
against you. Provoking creature! with one scrawl of your pen to banish such delightful
thoughts. I was applauding myself for my condescension in writing so often without
answers. I exulted in the thought of your shame and confusion as the proofs of my
superiority, so much above the little forms that narrowed your own heart. How did I
see you hanging your head with penitence and sorrow, while your face glowed with conscious shame! Oh, 'twas delicious! Every day I reflected on it with renewed pleasure.
I felt assured that nothing prevented your writing but an aversion to acknowledging how
humble, how little, you felt. Yet the letter at length arrived. My hand trembled with
delight, a glow of triumph flushed my face; I saw the humiliation so grateful to my
vanity. I was at the Lieu table. I hurried the letter into my pocket. I had no wish
to read it. I knew — I thought I did — what it must contain. I could scarcely breathe, —
vanity, exultation, revenge (sweet sensation), gave me unusual spirits. I stood and
called five. I was sure of a palm flush! 'Twas impossible anything could go wrong.
'Twas a frail hope: I got nothing. — was lieued. Never mind it, thought I, the letter is
enough. I played wrong, discarded the wrong card, knocked over the candlestick, spill
my wine. Positively, if it had been a love-letter, a first declaration, it would not put me
in a worse flustration. But ah! 'twas so different; I did not blush, look down, tremble,
fear to raise my eyes: my heart did not dissolve away in melting tenderness. Heyday!
I had no notion of telling you what I did not do, but what I did. Well, then, I sat
so upright, I was a foot taller. I looked at everybody for applause. I wondered I did
not hear them exclaim, O generous, exalted girl! I demanded it with my eyes; 'twas all
in vain. I heard nothing but " Eliza, you must follow suit. Why do you play that card?
You will certainly be lieued." I was vexed, I thought of the letter; all was sunshine
again. I am called. — dinner. O Lord! this eating seems to clog all my faculties. I
never write with half so much ease as when I am half-starved. I believe it is true that
poets ought not to live well. But, begging your pardon for leaving you so in the lurch,
I had forgotten that the letter was as yet unopened in my pocket. Well, then, we did not
break up till late. After I retired to bed, out came the letter. I was sleepy, and had a
great mind not to open it till morning. However, I thought I would, to have the satisfaction of the confirmation of my hopes, not once thinking of the stroke that should
annihilate them. It came; how shall I tell you my consternation! " Description falters
at the threshold." Yet I did not rave. I did not tear my hair in a frenzy of passion.
I did not stand in mute despair. No, I collected all my dignity and stood fixed and
immovable. I was convinced it was obstinacy alone; 'twas envy, 'twas a something that
prevented you giving me what you knew I deserved. I am called again.

Portland, Nov. 10, 1801.

I had almost determined to light the fire with this scrawl, but upon second thoughts I withdrew my hand from the devouring flames, and saved it from the fate it so justly merits. Yet, we have such a partiality for our own offspring, we rarely ever treat them with the severity they deserve. I ought to tell you where I am, but this letter has nothing like method in it,—but never mind. I began it immediately after I received your last. I wrote while the first impressions it made were on me. Unluckily, I was called from the pleasing task while in the midst of it, and as I never feel the same two hours together, I was unable to continue as I began,—'twould have been cold and studied,—so I left it. I threw it into my trunk, determining not to have anything more to do with it. I had grown amazingly wise. I wondered how I could suffer myself to write such nonsense. To-day I have received an invitation to the <u>second</u> wedding of Capt. Stephenson: I shall go. I thought I would write you a line to let you know I was still in existence, and on my way home. I could not find any paper, and was compelled to tumble over my trunk to find this. I have a world of news to tell you, but I don't know that you would care a farthing about any of it. Mary has been at Boston: Capt. Stephenson told me all about it. Tell her I hear she has got a heap of fine things, at which, together with her ladyship, I hope to have a peep. I have something of vast importance to say to <u>her</u> likewise: a thing on which depends the life and happiness of a fellow-creature. O Mary! who would have thought cruelty one of the failings of your heart! But I shall out with this secret to you before I am aware of it. Now, I have a great mind to turn this into a letter to Mary: I have as much again at this moment to say to her as I have to you, but she would not know what to make of some of it. I expect to be at home on Saturday next. Bring Mary over Sunday,—mind, and don't disobey. Horatio will be with me. I am in a monstrous hurry. I must send more blank paper than I ever did before, for which you will thank me, as I think you once told me that the blank paper in my letters always afforded you the most pleasure,—not exactly so, but something like it.

Adieu.

ELIZA.

To the Same.

Scarborough, December 4, 1801.

"I give you thanks," as Parson Fletcher says, for your dissertation upon apologies and old sayings. You have stored up enough to fill a volume, if I should take your last as a specimen of quantity. However, they are things I trouble myself but little about, and I should rather be inclined to join in railing against them than in enumerating their good effects. I perceive that you were much more inclined to be their advocate after supper than you were before you had just laid down your pen. After venting all your spleen and ill-nature (occasioned by your impatience for roast beef) upon these poor, harmless sayings, you return with an entire new set of sentiments on the subject; you commence to advocate them with more vehemence than is usual with you, and conclude by making them the foundation of every virtue. Now, I have endeavored to find some natural cause for this sudden change, but cannot. Was it that you heard one trickle from the lips of some favorite fair with eloquence too powerful to be resisted? Or, was it a bumper of wine which proved so warm a friend to them? Or, was it the good-natured effect of the roast beef which, exhilarating your spirits, made you look with an eye of pity and compassion on these poor, neglected things, and endeavor, by rubbing off the rust and polishing them anew, to compensate for your malicious endeavors to lessen their—— But, after all, I must confess I am a great enemy to them, in conversation particularly. I never knew a person who made a frequent use of them but I pitied them for the scanty portion of ideas which must have drawn them to such a paltry theft; and, moreover, if I must steal the idea, I would clothe it myself, lest its garment should betray me. I dislike them because they are in everybody's mouth; the greatest fool on earth has sense enough to use them with as much propriety as any other; and you will find every old beggar has his wallet stuffed full of them, ready to launch out on every occasion. I don't know, however, but that you are perfectly right in what you say in their defense. I am inclined to believe what you say is just; but I have so often seen instances of their meaning being perverted to answer some vicious purpose, that I am compelled to believe that the balance is against them. "So much for old sayings." But now as to apologies, I must, with due reverence, beg leave to differ from you in my opinion of them. I am by no means inclined to think they are never used; but when we know ourselves in fault, and that we ought always to suspect the sincerity of any one who made them, you certainly must have known instances where they were essentially necessary, and not to have made them would have proved an obstinacy of disposition quite as disagreeable as insincerity. I hate this parade and nonsense about independence which every gentleman often puts on; it always proves that the

reality is small when such a fuss is made for the appearance. I know some gentlemen who boast of never having made an apology, yet at the same time would say and do a thousand things much more derogatory to their independence than fifty apologies, such as any man of sense might make. I should like to see our fine gentlemen more careful in avoiding anything that would require an apology, and not, like cowards, skulk behind their flimsy shield of independence for defense or security. I have as great an aversion to cringing apologies made on every occasion as you possibly can have, and should always suspect the sincerity of them. If this class are the greater part of them, still I can conceive, nay, I have known instances when an apology has heightened my opinion of a person instead of lessening it. If we are in fault, ought we not to confess it? If we are not in fault, ought we not to exculpate ourselves? I should like a person who valued my approbation very little if he knew I had every reason to censure him, and yet would not, by a single word, convince me I had been deceived. However, I did not mean to dip so far into this weighty subject; 'twould have been better to have touched the edges, and away. Now, really, Moses, I write in pain. If I am not good-natured, you must attribute it all to the cold, which makes my fingers tingle. I can't write below, there is such a gabbing. 'Tis a cold, comfortless night; the rain patters against the windows, and the wind whistles round the house: it sounds like December. Oh, that was an unlucky word; I feel gloomy at the sight of it. The storm has driven all my thoughts back to myself for shelter. I am at this moment so selfish and cross that I would not walk ten steps to do good to any one. Our old windows here clatter so that I can hear nothing else. I shall begin to think the candle burns blue, and that I hear the groans of — between the blasts of wind, which sound hollow and dreary. Even now the shadow of my pen on the wall looked like a man's arm, and, as true as I live, here is a winding-sheet in the candle. Oh, these hobgoblin stories! We never get rid of them. I sometimes, when sitting alone after all are asleep in the house, get my imagination so raised that I look in fearful expectation that the tall, martial ghost of Hamlet will stalk before my eyes, or that some less dignified one will step through the key-hole or pop down chimney. Ghosts,—what a howling wind that is! Nonsense; what was I going to say,—something about ghosts, and all not warming my fingers. I declare, this shall be the last letter I will write from the fire! December, and writing in the chamber without fire; oh, monstrous! But here I am at the end without saying one of the things I meant to. I never, when I sit down to, write anything I wish or intended to when I began. You found my letter, you say; 'twas not worth the finding, as it was too late to answer the purpose I wish. Write me often. I have been entertained with Johnson's Life. We are alone, write often.

L. S.

Portland, January 24, 1802.

Now, at this moment, imagine your friend Eliza half double with the cold, two children teasing and playing around the table, sister and nurse talking all the time, and you will then be prepared to receive a letter abounding with sound reasoning, profound argument, elegant language, and a profusion of sublime ideas. But do not stare if I intersperse, by way of relieving your mind, a few little Jacky Horner stories, which I am obliged to gabble out by wholesale to stop the children's mouths. If I had not had a most retentive memory, I should have forgotten we were corresponding. I can put up with such a tardy, indifferent, reluctant correspondent, when I myself set the example; but we ladies are so accustomed to attention from gentlemen, that I can hardly bring myself to put up with your neglect. I have a thousand times determined to wait just as long before I answer your letter as you do before mine are noticed, and you have nothing to prevent but—pshaw! I am only spending time to give you something to laugh at. I must honestly acknowledge, however, that your last letter was very acceptable, though I was piqued at your neglecting me so long. I wish I felt adequate to giving an opinion on your perfect character, but, as I have told you before, I cannot think when all is noise and confusion around me. But I have endeavored in vain to find fault with it. I am really sorry that your sentiments so perfectly coincide with my own, for you have said all I think on the subject, and much more than I could have expressed; therefore, I am compelled to assent to all you have said. I am very glad we do not agree on every subject, for our letters (mine, I mean) would be very uninteresting: indeed, they have no merit to part with. I do not mean to send your perfect character away without a more intimate acquaintance: when I feel in a proper mood for it, I will take it up and examine every quality separately. I have the outlines impressed on my mind, but I cannot refer to your letter, for it is up in my trunk, and I feel no disposition to leave the fire. With your permission, I will lie by till another time. In the mean time, let us descend from these important discussions to the trifling occurrences of the day. With great satisfaction we again behold the ground covered with snow, for we are almost freezing here; it has been almost impossible to obtain wood to keep us warm, and I declare I have thought a log-house a clay chimney—the bell rings—I must stop ——.

Portland, Monday, February 1, 1802.

The sudden ringing of the bell last Monday stopped me in the midst of a very homely catalogue of blessings; 'tis not worth finishing, and if it was, I could not take up a broken sentence and finish it a week after it was begun. I have in vain attempted to finish this sheet, but I find I am entirely unfit to write. I hold my pen firm in my hand, look this side and that side, yet still cannot think. Scarborough—desolate, dreary Scarborough!—is the only place from whence I can write with ease. Nothing present engages my attentions, and I then have leisure to turn over the rubbish which I have collected from home, ponder on things past, and anticipate those to come. 'Tis something like dreaming,—we are insensible to everything around us. The imagination is unchecked by the operation of our senses, and soars beyond the boundaries of reality. Pray read over this last half page and see if you cannot tell how I feel, look, and act at this moment,—if your penetration does not discover a something unlike my letters in general, cold and studied. I will not, I cannot write. Another post must pass and no letter: yet, 'tis labor, 'tis pain to write thus.

Sunday, February 8, 1802.

To see the dates of this sheet, one would immediately conclude that my ideas flowed periodically, and that I had stated periods to "unpack the heart"; but 'tis because I cannot take my pen and write at the moment I feel an inclination,—not to defer it till a more convenient time, when I most probably should feel indifferent about it. Now, I am aware what you are about to infer from such a dull, studied letter as this is. The "seven days twice run" has put something into your head that ought not to be there, and you are laughing in your sleeve at the discovery. Now, I am not, after the manner of our sex, going to protest it is false; that there is no foundation for such a report, and counterfeit anger that I don't feel.—for these things always are viewed as a modest confirmation of the truth, and frequently are considered the greatest proof that can be brought. It is folly to give importance to such stories by appearing to feel interested, and the only way to destroy them is to hear and let them pass with perfect indifference. Time will certainly show what is true and what is not, and the only method is to let them take their course; they will sink to oblivion if not fed by our own folly. I own 'tis unpleasant to hear such things, but every girl must prepare herself for such vexations. It has one good effect.—that of making us more circumspect in our conduct. I do not say I am not in love, if your penetration has not discovered that I am: neither will what I say convince you. How such a report came to you, I do not know. I had hoped it would wither and die in the hot-bed of a scandal from which it sprang. If you lived here, you would not be surprised at anything of the kind. I declare to you I don't know the girl in town of whom the same is not said. The prevailing propensity th.s winter is match-making, and at the assemblies there is no other conversation. Such and such a one will make a match because they dance together. Another one is positively engaged because she does not dance with him. If a lady does not attend the assembly constantly, 'tis because her favorite swain is not a member. If she does, 'tis to meet him there. If she is silent, she is certainly in love. If she is gay and talks much, there must be a lover in the way. If a gentleman looks at you at meeting, you are suspected. If he dances with you at the assembly, it must be true, and if he rides with you, 'tis "confirmation strong as proof of holy writ." I am vexed to have spent so much time on this subject, but I care nothing about it. 'Tis well I have found something to fill my sheet, and had it not been for that lucky seven days twice over, I should not have finished it this month, and the finishing now has been a week's work.

Adieu.

ELIZA.

17

Sunday, February 14.

Only think, Moses, I was from home when you passed through town! I did not expect you as soon, although you said you should return on Friday. I thought <u>something</u> might detain you in Wiscassett or Portland longer than you expected, but you are one of those odd fellows which nothing can turn aside,— no, not even the most sparkling pair of black eyes in the world could detain you a moment longer than you first intended. What a philosopher in this age of gallantry to remain steadfast! It will come at last, Sir Moses. Bellamy says there is as much time for love as for death, and every one as surely, one time or the other, will feel it. I expected to see you throw off the philosopher and assume the man: one more trial, and I will pronounce you invulnerable. For Miss T. this one is reserved. I long to see how you will look when (to use a vulgar phrase) you are struck down. Pray write me as soon as you receive this, and tell me about your journey. Don't wait as long as you commonly do.

Adieu.

ELIZA.

Portland, March 1, 1802.

*Such a frolic! Such a chain of adventures I never before met with: nay, the page of romance never presented its equal. 'Tis now Monday,— but a little more method, that I may be understood. I have just ended my assembly's adventure,— never got home till this morning. Thursday, it snowed violently: indeed, for two days before, it had been storming so much that the snow-drifts were very large. However, as it was the last assembly, I could not resist the temptation of going, as I knew all the world would be there. About seven I went downstairs, and found Charles Coffin, the minister, in the parlor. After the usual inquiries were over, he stared awhile at my feathers and flowers: asked if I was going out. I told him I was going to the assembly. "Think, Miss Southgate," said he, after a long pause, "think you would go out to **meeting** in such a storm as this?" Then assuming a tone of reproof, he entreated me to examine well my feelings on such an occasion. I heard in silence, unwilling to begin an argument that I was unable to support. The stopping of the carriage roused me. I immediately slipped on my socks and coat, and met Horatio and Mr. Motley in the entry. The snow was deep, but Mr. Motley took me up in his arms and sat me in the carriage without difficulty. I found a full assembly, many married ladies, and every one disposed to end the winter in good spirits. At one we left dancing, and went to the card-room to wait for coach. It stormed dreadfully. The hacks were all employed as soon as they returned, and we could not get one till three o'clock: for about two they left the house, determined not to return again for the night. It was the most violent storm I ever knew. There were now twenty in waiting: the gentlemen scolding and fretting, the ladies murmuring and complaining. One hack returned: all flocked to the stairs to engage a seat. So many crowded down that 'twas impossible to get past. Luckily, I was one of the first. I stepped in, found a young lady, almost a stranger in town, who keeps at Mrs. Jordan's, sitting in the back seat. She immediately caught hold of me, and begged if I possibly could accommodate her, to take her home with me, as she had attempted to go to Mrs. Jordan's, but the drifts were so high the horses could not get through,— that they were*

compelled to return to the hall, where she had not a single acquaintance with whom she could go home. I was distressed, for I could not ask her home with me; for sister had so much company that I was obliged to go home with Sally Weeks, and give my chamber to Parson Coffin. I told her this, and likewise that she should be provided for, if my endeavors could be of any service. None but ladies were permitted to get into the carriage. It presently was stowed so full that the horses could not move. The door was burst open, for such a clamor as the closing of it occasioned I never before heard. The universal cry was, "A gentleman in the coach! let him come out." We all protested there was none, as it was too dark to distinguish; but the little man soon raised his voice, and bid the coachman proceed. A dozen voices gave contrary orders. 'Twas a proper riot. I was really alarmed. My gentleman, with a vast deal of fashionable independence, swore that no power on earth should make him quit his seat; but a gentleman at the door jumped into the carriage, caught hold of him, and would have dragged him out, if we had not all entreated him to desist. He squeezed again into his seat, inwardly exulting to think he should get safe home from such rough creatures as the men; should pass for a lady; be secure under their protection, for none would insult him before them,—mean creature! The carriage at length started, full of ladies, and not one gentleman to protect us, except our lady-man who had crept to us for shelter. When we found ourselves in the street, the first thing was to find out who was in the carriage, and where we were all going; who first must be left. Luckily, two gentlemen had followed by the side of the carriage, and, when it stopped, took out the ladies as they got to their houses. Our sweet, little, trembling, delicate, unprotected fellow sat immovable whilst the two gentlemen that were obliged to walk through all the snow and storm carried all the ladies from the carriage. What could be the motive of the little wretch for creeping in with us I know not. I should have thought 'twas his great wish to serve the ladies, if he had moved from the seat; but 'twas the most singular thing I ever heard of. We at length arrived at the place of our destination. Miss Weeks asked Miss Coffin (for that was the unlucky girl's name) to go home with her, which she readily did. The gentlemen then proceeded to take us out. My beau, unused to carrying such a weight of sin and folly, sank under its pressure, and I was obliged to carry my mighty self through the snow, which almost buried me. Such a time! I never shall forget it. My great grandmother never told any of her youthful adventures to equal it. The storm continued till Monday, and I was obliged to stay; but Monday I insisted, if there was any possibility of getting to sister's, to set out. The horse and sleigh were soon at the door, and again I sallied forth to brave the tempestuous weather (for it still snowed) and surmount the many obstacles I had to meet with. We rode on a few rods, when, coming directly upon a large drift, we stuck fast. We could neither

get forward nor turn round. After waiting till I was most frozen, we got out, and with the help of a truckman the sleigh was lifted up and turned toward a cross-street that led to Federal street. We again went on. At the corner we found it impossible to turn up in turn, but must go down and begin where we first started, and take a new course: but suddenly turning the corner, we came full upon a pair of trucks heavily laden. The drift on one side was so large that it left a very narrow passage between that and the corner house: indeed, we were obliged to go so near that the post grazed my bonnet. What was to be done? Our horses' heads touched before we saw them. I jumped out: the sleigh was unfastened and lifted round, and we again measured back our old steps. At length we arrived at Sister Boyd's door, and the drift before it was the greatest we had met with. The horse was so exhausted that he sank down, and we really thought him dead. 'Twas some distance from the gate, and no path. The gentleman took me up in his arms, and carried me till my weight pressed him so far into the snow that he had no power to move his feet. I rolled out of his arms, and wallowed till I reached the gate; then, rising to shake off the snow, I turned and beheld my beau fixed, an immovable. He could not get his feet out to take another step. At length, making a great exertion to spring his whole length forward, he made out to reach the poor horse, who lay in a worse condition than his master. By this time all the family had gathered to the window; indeed, they saw the whole frolic, but 'twas not yet ended: for, unluckily, in pulling off Miss Weeks's bonnet to send to the sleigh, to be carried back, I pulled off my wig, and left my head bare. I was perfectly convulsed with laughter. Think what a ludicrous figure I must have been, still standing at the gate, my bonnet half-way to the sleigh, and my wig in my hand! However, I hurried it on, for they were all laughing at the window, and made the best of my way into the house. The horse was unhitched, and again set out, and left me to ponder on the incidents of the morning. I have since heard of several events that took place that assembly night much more amusing than mine. Nay, Don Quixote's most ludicrous adventures, compared with some of them, will appear like the common events of the day.

E. S.

March 12, 1802.

William Weeks is going to Philipsburg, and thinks of returning by the way of Scarborough; if so, will leave this at our house, otherwise can return it to me. I have not yet seen Miss Jewett, but I hear she has returned. Did your Saco party come, as you expected? Give my love to Miss Tappan, and tell her nothing but the fame of her beauty would carry this young man so many miles out of the way. I found he was very desirous of calling at our house, therefore wrote by him. Tell her she must answer for the mischief done by leading young men astray from their path. I will estimate the loss it will be to William: he will ride six or eight miles further than necessary, fatigue his horse, wear out his sleigh-runners, and certainly be detained three hours. Now, as we know a gentleman's time is much more valuable than a lady's, it must be a real loss to him: three dollars a day for posting books any common accountant would have, and allowing him but just so much, his loss would certainly amount to four or six shillings on that score. I speak merely of the loss on the score of interest: how deeply it may affect him otherwise may be better imagined from the ravages she has committed in Mr. Orr's heart than from anything I can say. This short visit may derange all his reasoning faculties, and give a different hue to all his future prospects; it may give him a disrelish for all amusements, and make him sigh for the calm serenity of domestic life: — to sum up all together, it may make him in love. But I shall have no time to say anything else if I run on with this any further. To-morrow I expect to go to Gorham, return the same evening, or Sunday morning. I am still at Mrs. Coffin's, but shall return to sister when I come from Gorham. We have had a number of pleasant parties this week: Tuesday Mrs. Robert Boyd had a charming one; Wednesday had a large one here, and to-day all going to Capt. Robinson's, where we expect to dance. To-morrow I go to Gorham. I wrote to Mamma requesting money to buy a lace shade. I called to look at them again, and the shopkeeper told me he was mistaken in the price, for it was twenty-one shillings per yard, instead of the whole pattern, which makes a vast difference. I, of course, think no more of lace shades, but I still think of some money. I have

but four cents in the world, not enough to pay the postage of a letter; pray send me a little immediately. I shall send you a description of the assembly, which I believe you may read to my mother if you wish; 'twill amuse her, I know. I wish you would look in the old desk among my papers, and get a little drawing-book,—directions for drawing printed in a pamphlet,—and give to William to bring over. I hope the snow will last till Mamma comes over and I return home; 'tis delightful weather. How do the daisies and gillyflowers? Mrs. Parker is going to give me some flower seeds. I hear frequent inquiries for you,—when are you coming in town? Tell Miss Tappan I had the honor of dancing a voluntary dance with Mr. Orr at the last assembly. " The floor was very unyielding," etc., etc. I did not tell you any one's adventures but my own on that eventful night. Poor Mr. Orr, impatient to get home, plunged into the snow without waiting for a carriage, and, unfortunately, turning up street instead of down, got most to Mr. Vaughn's before he discovered his mistake, and was obliged to turn round and worry his way back again. He was half dead when he got to his lodgings. Eunice Deering was tumbled over, and when Mr. Little took her from the carriage——

To Moses Porter.

Portland, May 23, 1802.

I received your apology, and am satisfied. 'Tis not the manner of making apologies I think most of, but that long dissertation on the subject continually obtrudes itself on your mind whenever you feel conscious an apology is necessary. But while I am convinced nothing but the fear of appearing inconsistent prevents your making those said apologies, I will not complain; let them come "edgeways" or any other way, so long as I am convinced you feel their necessity. But I have been pondering on your new plan of life, yet I confess it does not appear to me so delightful as to you. It sounds well, "tickles the fancy," cuts a pretty figure on paper, and would form a delightful chapter in a novel. Our novelists have worn the pleasures of a rural life threadbare. Every love-sick swain imagines that with the mistress of his heart he could leave the noisy, tumultuous scenes of life, and in the shade of rural retirement feel all the delightful security and peace ascribed to the golden age: the philosopher and the poet fly to this imaginary heaven with as much enthusiasm as the lover. Then, say they, we can contemplate the beauty and sublimity of nature free from interruption; then the reflecting mind can find endless subjects for contemplation! Here all is peace and love! No discord can find place among these inno-cent and happy beings; they live but to promote the happiness of each other, and their every action teems with benevolence and love. Yet, let us judge for ourselves. We all have seen what the pleasures of rural life are; and whatever poets may have ascribed to it, we must know there is much depravity, and consequently as much discontent in the inhabitants of a country village as in the most populous city. They are generally ignorant, illiterate, without knowledge to discover the real blessings they enjoy by comparing them with others, continually looking to those above them with envy and discontent, and imagine their share of happiness is proportionate to their rank and power. I am convinced that a country life is better calculated to produce that serenity and happiness we are all in pursuit of than any other, but those who have ever been accustomed to it have no relish for its pleasures; and those who quit the busy scenes of life disgusted by the duplicity or ingratitude of the world, or oppressed by the weight of accumulated misfortune, carry with them feelings

and sentiments which cannot be reciprocated. Solitary happiness I have no idea of; 'tis only in the delightful sympathies of friendship and similarity of sentiments that genuine happiness can be enjoyed. Your mind is cultivated and enlarged, your sentiments delicate and refined; you could not expect to find many with whom you could converse on a perfect equality, or, rather, many whose sentiments could assimilate with yours. Were I a man, I should think it cowardly to busy myself in solitude; nay, I should be unwilling to confess I felt myself unable to preserve my virtue where there were temptations to destroy it. There is no merit in being virtuous when there is no struggle to preserve that virtue; 'tis in the midst of temptations and allurements that the active and generous virtues must be excited in their full force. One virtuous action, their temptations and delusions to surmount, would give more delight to my own heart, more real satisfaction, than a whole life spent in mere negative goodness. He must be base indeed who can voluntarily act wrong when no allurement draws him from the path of virtue. You say you never dipped much in the pleasures of <u>high life</u>, and therefore I should have but little to regret on that score. In the choice of life, one ought to consult their own dispositions and inclinations, their own power and talents. We all have a preference for some particular mode of life, and we surely ought to endeavor to arrive at that which will most probably insure us most happiness. I have often thought what profession I should choose were I a man. I might then think very differently from what I do now, yet I have always thought, if I were conscious of possessing brilliant talents, the <u>law</u> would be my choice; then I might hope to arrive at an eminence which would be gratifying to my feelings. I should then hope to be a public character, respected and admired; but, unless I was convinced I possessed the talents which would distinguish me as a <u>speaker</u>, I would be anything rather than a lawyer. For the dry sameness of such employment as the business of an office all my feelings would revolt, but to be an eloquent speaker would be the delight of my heart. I thank heaven I was born a woman. I have only now to wait patiently till some dear fellow shall take a fancy to me and place me in a situation I am determined to make the best of, let it be what it will. We ladies, you know, possess that "sweet pliability of temper" that disposes not to enjoy any situation, and we must have no choice in these things till we find what is to be our destiny; then we must consider it the best in the world. But, seriously, I desire to be thankful I am not a man. I should be content with moderate abilities,—nay, I should not be content with mediocrity in anything; but, as a woman, I am equal to the generality of my sex, and I do not feel that great desire of fame I think I should if I were a man. Should you ever become an inhabitant of Boxford, I make no doubt you will be very happy, because you will reap all the advantages and disadvantages. Yet, I do not think you qualified for the laborious life farmers generally lead, and it requires a little fortune to live an independent farmer, without labor.

Rebecca would do charmingly. I knew you were imagining her the partner of all your joys and cares, of all your harmony and content, when you charmed yourself with your descriptions of rural happiness; with her you imagine you could quit the world, and almost live happy in a desert. So may it be. I know none but a lover could paint the sweets of retirement with such enthusiasm. Yes, my turn now to rail a little; the world has also linked _you_ to a certain person as firmly,—nay, _more_ so than it ever did me; but, however, I will not press too closely on this subject. I shall not expect that candid confession I made you, as your feelings and mine are so different on the two subjects. I want to ask you a question, which you may possibly think improper; but if so, do not answer it. Is Mary really engaged to Mr. Coffin? I hear so from so many persons, and in so decided a manner, I cannot doubt. I would ask her, but in these things there is so much deception in finding out; however, I think I should never deny such a thing when I once became so. However, enough of this. I am now in Portland; shall return to-morrow to Scarborough, where I shall be very happy to see you and Mary; so I depend upon your bringing her over very soon. Adieu! Dinner is ready, and I have nothing to say worth losing it for. Write me often. I shall be at home alone these two months to come. Remember, you have it in your power to amuse and gratify

ELIZA.

To the Same.

Portland, May 28, 1802.

I hardly know what to say to you, cousin. You have attacked my system with a kind of fury that has entirely obscured your judgment, and instead of being convinced of its impracticability, you appear to fear its justness. You tell me of some excellent effects of my system, but pardon me for thinking they see distaste by prejudice rather than reason. I feel fully convinced in my own mind that no such effects would be pardoned. You ask if this plan of education will render me a more dutiful child, a more affectionate wife, etc. Surely it will. Those virtues which now are merely practiced from the momentary impulse of the heart will then be adduced to from principle; a sense of duty, and a mind sufficiently strengthened not to yield implicitly to every impulse, will give a degree of uniformity, of stability, to the female character which it evidently at present does not possess. From having no guide for our conduct, we have acquired a reputation for caprice, which we justly deserve. I can hardly believe you serious when you say that the enlargement of the mind will inevitably produce superciliousness and a desire of ascendency. I should much sooner expect it from an ignorant, uncultivated mind. We cannot enlarge and improve our minds without perceiving our weakness, and wisdom is always modest, unassuming. On the contrary, a mind that has never been exerted knows not its deficiencies, and presumes much more on its powers than it otherwise would. You beg me to drop this crazy scheme, and say no more about enlarging the mind. As it is disagreeable, and you are too much prejudiced even to listen with composure to me when I write on the subject, I quit it forever. Nor will I again shock your ear with a plan which you think has nothing for its foundation either just or durable, which against imagination gave birth to a presumptuous folly cherished. I fear I have rather injured the cause than otherwise, and what I have said may have more firmly established these sentiments in you which I wish to destroy. Be it as it may, I believe it is a cause that has been more injured by its friends than its enemies. I am sorry that I have said so much, yet I said no more than I really thought, and still think, just and true. I beg you to say no more to me on the subject, as I shall know it will be only a favor of politeness which I will dispense with. You undoubtedly think I am acting quite out of my sphere in attempting to discuss this subject, and my presumption probably gave rise to that idea, which you express in your last, that however unqualified a woman might be, she was always equipped for the discussion of any subject, and overwhelms her hearers with

her "clack." On what subject shall I write you? I shall either fatigue and disgust you with female trifles, or shock you by stepping beyond the limits you have prescribed, as I cannot preserve a medium. I fear I shall be obliged to relinquish the hope of pleasing,—of course, of writing. Good-night: I am sleepy and stupid.

Monday.

Oh, how I hate this warm weather! It deprives me of the power of using any exertion; it clogs my ideas. I ask no greater felicity than the pleasure of doing nothing. I intended to amuse you with some of the trifles of the day, but I shall scarcely do them justice this morning. Friday night we had a ball; the hall was decorated with much taste,—'twas fitted up for the "Masons." At the head of the room there was a most <u>romantic little house</u>: four large pillars, formed of green and interspersed with flowers, supported a kind of canopy, which was arched in front, with this inscription, "Here peace and silence reign."—filled with a parcel of girls <u>whining</u> sentiment and silly fellows spouting love. It produces a most laughable scene. The deities to whom it was dedicated withdrew from the sacred retreat which was so profaned, and noise and folly reigned supreme. So sweet a place, so fine an opportunity for making speeches,—'twas irresistible: even you would have caught a spark of inspiration from the surrounding glories, and felt a degree of emulation at the flashes of genius that blazed from every quarter. Invention was on the rack; the stores of memory were exhausted, and folly blushed to be so outdone. Mr. Symmes sat down to overwhelm me with a torrent of eloquence, yet his compassionate heart often prompted him to <u>hesitate</u>, that I might recover myself. Such stores of learning did he display, such mines of wisdom did he open to my view, that I gazed with astonishment and awe, and scarce believed " that one small head could carry all he knew." Mr. Hirsman, with a countenance that beamed with benevolence and compassion, gazed on all around. While a benign smile played round his mouth, and dimpled his polished cheek, the laughing loves peeped from his eyes, and aimed their never-failing darts. Rush girl! too, too near hast thou approached this divinity: the poisoned dart still rankles in thy heart. " The lingering pains of hopeless love unpitied I endure, and feel a wound within my heart which death alone can cure."

Monday Night.

You will easily perceive that I am obliged to write where and when I can. I have not quite so much leisure as when at Scarborough, and though in the very place to hear news, I have no faculty of relating what I hear in a manner that could interest you.

Last evening I spent in talking scandal (for which God forgive me), but 'twas too tempting an occasion to be resisted. I wish you were acquainted with some of the Portland ladies; I would then tell you many things that might amuse. But I dare not introduce you to them, lest I should entirely mistake their character, and that when personally acquainted with them you would be confirmed in your opinion of my wanting penetration in studying character. Yesterday I spent the day with Martha. I wish you were acquainted with her; she is truly an _original_. I never saw one that bore any resemblance to her. She despises flattery, and is even above praise; beautiful without vanity, possessing a refined understanding without pedantry, the most exquisite sensibility connected with all the great and noble qualities of the mind. She knows that no woman in America was ever more admired; she has received every attention which could be paid, and yet is exactly as before she left Portland,—the same condescension, the same elegance and unaffected simplicity of manners, and the same independent and noble sentiments. Perhaps I am blinded to her faults, yet I think she deserves all I say of her; nay, more, for she "outstrips all praise, and makes it halt behind her." They have determined to go to England; in two months, at farthest, they will leave America, not to return for two years. Two years! how many events will have taken place! Perhaps ere that I shall rest in the tomb of my fathers, forgotten and unknown! Perhaps, oppressed with care and borne down with misfortune, I shall have lost all relish for life; all hopes of pleasure may have ceased to exist, and the grave of time closed over them forever. I grow gloomy. I wish I could write anything, but I have never felt a relish for writing since I have been in Portland; at home it supplies the place of society, but here I need no such attention. Write by the post, if you have no other opportunity. The players will commence acting next Wednesday.

ELIZA.

1802.

Now, Mamma, what do you think I am going to ask for? — a wig! Eleanor has got a new one just like my hair, and only five dollars; Mrs. Mayo, one just like it. I must either cut my hair or have one. I cannot dress it at all <u>stylish</u>. Mrs. Coffin bought Eleanor's, and says that she will write to Mrs. Samson to get me one just like it. How much time it will save in one year! We could save it in pins and paper, besides the <u>trouble</u> at the assembly of my head, for nobody had long hair. If you will consent to my having one, do send me over a five-dollar bill by the post immediately after you receive this, for I am in hopes to have it for the next assembly. Do send one word immediately, if you can let me have one. Tell Octavia she must write soon, and that there are many inquiries after her.

ELIZA.

Arrived in Salem, met Mrs. Derby at the door, who received us joyfully. At tea-time saw the children,—fine boys, very fond of Ellen, and are managed by their father with great judgment. How few understand the true art of managing children, and how often is the important task of forming young minds left to the discretion of servants, who caress or reprove as the impulse of the moment compels them. Here are we convinced of the great necessity that mothers, or all ladies, should have cultivated minds, as the first rudiments of education are always received from them; and at that early period of life, when the mind is open to every new impression, and ready to receive the seeds which must form the future principles of the character,—at that time, how important is it to be judicious in your conduct toward them. In the evening Mr. Hasket Derby came in on his return from New-York. He is a fine, majestic-looking man, though he strikes you rather heavy and unwieldy on his first appearance; he says little, yet does not appear absent; has traveled much, and in his manners has an easy, unassuming politeness that is not the acquirement of a day. Wednesday morning had an agreeable tête-à-tête with Ellen, talked over all our affairs; in the afternoon rode out to Hasket Derby's farm, about three miles from Salem, a most delightful place; the gardens superior to any I have ever seen of the kind, — cherries in perfection. We really feasted. There are three divisions in the gardens, and you pass from the lower one to the upper, through several arches rising one above the other. From the lower gate you have a fine perspective view of the whole range, rising gradually until the sight is terminated by a hermitage. The summer-house in the center has an arch through it with three doors on each side, which open into little apartments, and one of them opens to a staircase, by which you ascend into a square room, the whole size of the building. It has a fine, airy appearance, and commands a view of the whole garden. Two large chestnut-trees on each side almost shade it from the view when seen from the sides. The air from the windows is always pure and cool, and the eye

wanders with delight and admiration over the extensive landscape below, so beautifully variegated with the charms of nature; imagination luxuriates with delight, and as it plays o'er the beauties of an opening flower, imperceptibly wanders to the first principles of nature, its wonderful and surprising operation, its harmony and beauty. The room is ornamented with some Chinese figures, and seems calculated for serenity and peace. 'Tis like the pavilion of Caroline, and I almost looked around me for the music of the guitar and books; but I heard not the tramplings of Lindorf's horse, nor did I seem to hear the echo of his voice. "Listen to love, and thou shalt know indifference, or to bless the foe." Certain it is, however, I thought of Caroline the moment I entered. We descended, and, passing through the arch, proceeded to the hermitage, which terminated the garden. It was scarcely perceptible at a distance; a large weeping-willow swept the roof with its branches and bespoke the melancholy inhabitant. We caught a view of the little hut as we advanced through the opening of the trees. It was covered with bark; a small, low door, slightly latched, immediately opened at our touch; a venerable old man was seated in the center with a prayer-book in one hand, while the other supported his cheek, and rested on an old table which, like the hermit, seemed molding to decay; a broken pitcher, a plate, and tea-pot sat before him, and his tea-kettle sat by the chimney; a tattered coverlet was spread over a bed of straw which, though hard, might be softened by resignation and content. I left him, impressed with veneration and fear, which the mystery of his situation seemed to create. We returned to the house, which was neat and handsome, and from thence visited the greenhouse, where we saw oranges and lemons in perfection. On one orange-tree there were green ones, ripe ones, and blossoms. Every plant and shrub which was beautiful and rare was collected here, and I looked around with astonishment and delight. At the upper end of the garden there was a beautiful arbor, formed of a mound of turf, which we ascended by several steps, formed likewise of turf, and 'twas surrounded by a thick row of poplar-trees, which branched out quite to the bottom, and so close together that you could not see through. 'Twas a most charming place, and I know not how long we should have remained to admire if they had not summoned us to tea. We returned home, and Mr. Hasket Derby asked if we should not like to walk over to his house and see the garden. We readily consented, as I had heard much of the house. The evening was calm and delightful, the moon shone in its greatest splendor. We entered the house, and the door opened into a spacious entry; on each side were large, white marble images. We passed on, by doors on each side opening into the drawing-room, dining-room, parlor, etc., etc., and at the farther part of the entry a door opened into a large, magnificent oval room, and another door opposite the one we entered was thrown open and gave us a full view of the garden below. The moon shone with uncommon splendor; the large marble vases, the images, the mirrors to correspond

with the windows, gave it so uniform and finished an appearance that I could not think
it possible I viewed objects that were real. Everything appeared like enchantment. The
stillness of the hour, the imperfect light of the moon, the novelty of the scene, filled my
mind with sensations I never felt before. I could not realize everything, and expected
every moment that the wand of the fairy would sweep all from before my eyes, and leave
me to stare and wonder what it meant. You can scarcely conceive anything more superb.
We descended into the garden, which is laid out with exquisite taste; an airy irregular-
ity seems to characterize the whole. At the foot of the garden there was a summer-house
and a row of tall poplar-trees, which hid everything beyond from the sight, and formed
a kind of walk. I arrived there, and to my astonishment found through the opening of
the trees that there was a beautiful terrace, the whole width of the garden. 'Twas twenty
feet from the street and graveled on the top, with a white balustrade round; 'twas almost
level, and the poplar-trees so close that we could only occasionally catch a glimpse of the
house. The moon shone full upon it, and I really think this side is the most beautiful,
though 'tis the back one. A large dome swells quite to the chamber windows, and is
railed round on top, and forms a delightful walk; the magnificent pillars which support
it fill the mind with pleasure. We returned into the house, and on passing the mirrors
I involuntarily started back at seeing so much company in the other room. We entered
the drawing-room, which is superb, furnished with blue and wood color. There was the
grand piano, the most charming instrument I ever heard. Mr. and Mrs. Derby, Mr.
Hasket D., Frank Coffin, and myself were the party. I was requested to play, and took
my seat at the instrument and had just begun playing, when a slight noise in the entry
made me turn my head. A gentleman entered, and was introduced as Mr. Gray,—made
a most graceful bow and took his seat, and I resumed my playing. We rose to depart,
and Mr. G. accompanied us home. I was delighted with his conversation, which was
sensible, unassuming, and agreeable. I scarcely saw his face, as there was no light.
Thursday, at home all day. In the evening walked in the garden. The evening was
uncommonly fine. The moon shines brighter in Salem than anywhere else. Here, too,
is an elegant garden, full of fruit-trees, the walks kept as nice as possible, and shaded on
each side by plum-trees; very handsome summer-house, where we sat an hour or two,
rambled in the garden all the evening, which was the finest I ever saw,—so very light
that, as Shakspere says, "'twas but the daylight sick, only a little paler." There is
something in a fine moonlight evening exquisitely soothing to the soul. I have felt as if
I could melt away with the exquisite enthusiasm of my sensations. We were called into
the house, and found Mrs. West, a sister of Mrs. Derby's; but more of her by and by.
Friday, Dr. Coffin arrived, and Dr. Lathrop and Hasket Derby dined with us, and set
out for Boston.

Saturday, July 11, 1802.

We rode out, Ellen and myself, with the three boys, in a hack; went to Danvers (Parson Wadsworth's) to see Mrs. Kickman's children; took them in to ride; came down by the mills and went across to Hasket Derby's farm,—all the cherries gone,—rambled about the gardens an hour, and returned home. Charming ride! The country round Salem is delightful, although 'tis situated rather in a plain; 'tis surrounded with beautiful hills, handsome trees, ponds, brooks, etc. We got home at dusk, and found Mr. Coffin just returned from Boston. Mrs. Hasket Derby sent a great basket of cherries and her compliments; she would come over in the morning. I wished very much to see her; she had been gone five weeks to the Springs. I had heard Martha say much of her, and wished much that to-morrow could come.

Next morning, Sunday, went to meeting. Mr. Dana, of Marblehead, preached; very devout, unaffected young man; saw not a soul I had ever seen before, excepting Mr. Gray; thought I should not have known him, as I scarcely saw his face before; found Mrs. Hasket Derby on my return; was disappointed in her personal appearance. Instead of finding the elegant, majestic, beautiful creature my imagination had pictured, I beheld a little, short, plump woman, dressed in black, a coarse complexion, and anxious eyes; yet I had not been in company an hour, without confessing to myself that she was the most agreeable, fascinating woman I ever saw. She continually pleases and delights you; she appears to live for others, nor ever bestows a thought upon herself, yet so perfectly unconscious of it, that it seems inherent in her disposition, and to flow without any effort. She planned parties of amusement, as I was a stranger, and we fixed upon Friday for a fishing party to Nahant; sent to Boston for some to meet us. Monday, a small party at Mrs. Derby's came to tea. I rode in the chaise with Mr. Gray; Mrs. Gray and a Mr. White, an Englishman, in her carriage; Mr. Coffin and Miss Gray, in another chaise; Mr. and Mrs. Hasket Derby. We walked on a hill, near the house, where we had the most extensive prospect I ever saw; the whole world seemed spread before us, covered with the richly variegated carpet of nature. We returned home in the evening, with a fine moon, and all went to Mr. Gray's to spend the evening,—most charming time; treated with great attention by Mrs. Gray, who is, in my opinion, a fine woman, domestic, fond of her children, and never so happy as in contributing to their amusement, and possesses

fine sense, animated, unceremonious, and agreeable. Tuesday, Doct. and Mrs. Coffin and Mrs. Sumner came down from Boston; dined together, and all went to Hasket Derby's farm in the afternoon; Mrs. Gray and Miss Bishop of the party. Glad to see Miss Bishop,—one of my old school-mates. Had a most charming ride; went in the carriage with Mrs. Gray. All returned to Mr. John Derby's and spent the evening. William Gray and his father came in the evening; walked in the garden. Wednesday, large party of gentlemen to dine with Doct. Coffin; in the afternoon, all went to Mrs. Gray's; danced in the evening; Miss Bishop plays and sings charmingly. Thursday, Doct. and Mrs. Coffin went home, and in the afternoon went to Mrs. Hasket Derby's with a party; everything elegant and pleasant. Friday, to Nahant, fishing.—Mr. and Mrs. Hasket Derby, Mr. and Mrs. John Derby, Mr. and Mrs. Kersey Derby, Miss Bishop, Mr. Gray, Mr. Coffin and myself, Miss Heller, Mr. Prince (who looks very much like Horatio), and several others. Met there some smart Boston beaux,—Mr. Amory Parkman, Turner, etc., etc. Spent a most charming day; caught but few fish, and very warm, yet pleasant notwithstanding; set out for home just as the sun was setting. I returned in the chaise with William Gray, Frank with Miss Bishop; rode two miles on the beach, the tide down, sun just setting. 'Twas charming and delightful. Saturday, went out to Kersey Derby's farm to tea; went to the bathing-house, summer-house, and saw the Rumford kitchen!—elegant place, beautiful children; rainy afternoon, we could not enjoy the pleasures of the country so well. Sunday, went to meeting, and to tea with Mrs. Hasket Derby; met company from Boston,—two beaux,—Mr. Lee and Mr. Davis. Monday, a party of young ladies at Mrs. Gray's; danced in the evening, went home at eleven, spent half an hour at Hasket Derby's on my way; Ellen was there. Tuesday, rode out with Mrs. Gray after dining; returned and drank tea with Mrs. Lambert; found company at Ellen's on my return.—Mr. and Mrs. Hasket Derby, Kersey Derby and wife, Mr. Prince and wife. Patty Derby, that was, looks like old Madame Milliken very much. Mr. and Mrs. Hasket Derby wish me to go to the Springs; with them; know not what to do. Ellen says go, by all means; never will have such another opportunity. She thinks my father and mother would not object if I had time to write them, which would be impossible, as they go to-morrow. What shall I do? I must go over after breakfast; I will consult Mrs. John Derby. I would not go for the world if I thought my father or mother would not be pleased. Mr. and Mrs. Derby go alone in their carriage. I must think of it.

ELIZA.

Salem, July 14, 1802.

Dear Mother:

I have just received my trunk, with the letter and key. I perceive you have not received my letter by Mr. Jewell. Fear not, my dear mother; though gay, volatile in my disposition, I feel that I shall return home with the same sentiments with which I left it. True, I am in the midst of gayety and splendor such as I never before witnessed; yet a something within whispers true happiness resides not here. In this family all is calm contentment and peaceful pleasure. Mr. Derby is everything his best friends can wish him, and the whole family consider him as everything good and benevolent. He truly is so, and appears one of the finest men I ever knew. How is Uncle Porter's family? I cannot even now reconcile myself to the idea of leaving them so unexpectedly and so immediately; yet I know not how it could be avoided. I am in the midst of amusement and pleasure,- they drive all melancholy reflection from my mind; but when alone, my feelings warmly pay a tribute to the merit of <u>our departed Moses</u>. Yet I cannot, do not, realize it. Everything contributes to make me think it a delusion, a mere dream. How is it possible I can realize it? Yet sometimes I feel it is, it must be, true. How soon do we reconcile ourselves to the loss of the dearest friends. What would almost distract us in anticipation, we meet with calmness when it approaches; strange, unaccountable. I surely loved Moses with sincerity. I knew of no person so distantly connected whom I felt so interested in. Yet he is dead, he is gone; and I can speak of it without emotion, and — I am called.

Adieu; I will write soon.

ELIZA.

Salem, Wednesday, July, 1802.

What will you say, my dear mother, when you find I am gone with Mr. and Mrs. Hasket Derby to the Saratoga Springs? But I hasten to explain all. Mr. and Mrs. Derby were going in their carriage alone. Mrs. Derby says she never traveled without some lady, and urged my accompanying her. I thought 'twas only a compliment, and treated it as such; but when I found she seriously wished it, and her husband joined his influence, I began to think how it would do. I consulted Ellen and Mr. Derby, and they both thought I ought not to refuse an opportunity of seeing the country which, perhaps, may never again occur,—a better one surely can never offer. To go with Mr. and Mrs. Derby is surely an advantage I can never hope to meet with again. Believe me, nothing would have induced me to think of going with them, unless they had been very urgent. Ellen and Mr. Derby both say they doubt not you would approve the plan if you were here to consult. If I did not think so myself, nothing would induce me to go. Still, I regret not having it in my power to wait an answer from you; but to-morrow afternoon we must set out. Ellen has <u>lent me everything</u> necessary for my journey; indeed, I can never repay her. She is the most generous being I ever saw. She has nothing in the house but is at my service. All her handsome dresses she wishes me to carry; indeed, everything that I can possibly want she has supplied me with. I am glad that I shall not be compelled to purchase anything that would be unnecessary after my return. I think I shall borrow some money of her, as it is impossible I can receive any from home, and if I do not need it, I need not spend it. You may assure yourself I shall remember to economize as much as possible. It seems as if Ellen and Mrs. Derby tried which should most oblige me. As I never determined to go till this morning, Mrs. Derby said 'twas impossible to make any new clothes, nay, unnecessary, and insisted I should take anything of hers I should want; but Ellen would not admit of that. I know not the route we shall take, but Mrs. Derby says we shall probably <u>go</u> or <u>return</u> through Leicester. I shall be gratified very much at an opportunity of seeing our relations there. Ellen promises to write. I never was treated with more attention in my life. Ellen heaps me with favors, and now I have thought of this journey, she thinks she can't do enough. I intend keeping a particular journal while I am gone, which you shall all peruse on my return. We shall probably be gone four or five weeks, as it is two or

three hundred miles from here.   When you write me, direct your letters to Salem, and
Mr. Derby will forward them, as he will know where we are.   Has Octavia returned?
Tell her I shall leave my Salem journal to be sent to her the first opportunity.   If I go
through Newport, I shall endeavor to find Miss Crary and Miss Clarke.   I wish I had
a letter from her.   And now, my dear mother, assure me you approve of my going, and
I shall have nothing to trouble me.   My father, I think, would not object to it, if I
could know his opinion.   Mr. Gray (William Gray) says he is sure he would not
disapprove of it if he knew in what good protection I was.   By the bye, I have received
every attention from Mr. Gray's family, and Mrs. Gray is a remarkably fine woman.
I rode out with her yesterday afternoon, and she sent for me to go to Wexham pond with
her this afternoon.   Called to excuse myself, and tell her of my projected journey.   She
regretted it, as I was to have gone to Medford with her the next week, and she had
planned several parties for me, which would be frustrated.   But she acknowledges I was
perfectly right to go, and that, if 'twas her daughter, she should be much gratified at
the opportunity.   Mr. and Mrs. Derby say I must tell you they will take good <u>care</u> of
me, and they shall take the full protection of me.   Write me soon, or request my father,
or Octavia ; but pray, if you disapprove, do not tell me till I return. 'Twill be too late
to alter or retract, and I should be wretched if I thought you disapproved my going.
Do write, or ask my father.   I shall feel uneasy.   My love to all friends, and believe me,
with great affection,

Your

ELIZA.

Francestown (New Hampshire), July 26, 1802.

My Dear Father:

My letter in which I informed you of my intended journey, my motives for it, etc., you will receive before this. I therefore think it unnecessary to say any more, but rest with full confidence on the indulgent heart of an affectionate father, who, I trust, knows my heart too well to think me capable of acting in opposition to what I know to be his wishes. We left Salem on Thursday evening, and slept at Ten Hills, in Charlestown; breakfasted in Woburn, and dined in Billerica. We had a fine view of the celebrated Middlesex canal, which in future ages must do honor to our country. Such monuments of industry and perseverance raise our opinion of our countrymen. It will be twenty-five miles in length when completed, running from Dracut to Medford River. The river of Concord supplies it with water, boats pass every day, and parties of pleasure are always sailing on it. In my journal I have been more particular; here I say but little, as we are in a miserable tavern and the horses almost ready. I cannot tell you the route we are going.— Mr. Derby's motive is to see the most pleasant part of the country that he has not seen before. From Billerica we came through Chelmsford and Tyngborough, where old Irving lived, and Miss Pitts, now Mrs. Brimby, the heiress of his fortune, has a most elegant, tasty country house on the banks of the Merrimack, which forms a most beauti-ful scene in front of the house and gives full view of the river in each direction. More of this in my journal. We are now on a new turn-pike road from Amherst to Dart-mouth. We shall go up to Dartmouth College, as 'tis wholly a jaunt of pleasure, and Mr. Derby is determined to be in no haste, to inquire about everything worth seeing, and not to mind six or seven miles from a direct road. They are very attentive to me, and have gone a mile from the direct road to show me something they had seen before. Mr. Derby has been such a traveler that he is now one of the most useful traveling companions in the world. His wife is the most engaging, unaffected, fam'ly woman in the world; and instead of feeling myself a burden to them, they make me feel of the utmost consequence. We passed through several pretty villages on coming here, though it is almost a new country,

scarcely cleared up, excepting a small village every six or seven miles; the most hilly, mountainous, woody country I ever was in. Here, as I look around me, I see nothing but enormous high hills, covered with trees, and almost mingling with the clouds. One of them in particular, Francestown, is about twelve miles from Amherst; a number of pleasant houses and a very elegant meeting-house,—how different from our part of the country! Here, if there is but one handsome house in town, there will be a meeting-house. I have passed but one on my journey, in these new back places, but what was painted and had a steeple. From Dartmouth we go down to Northampton, and then to Lebanon Springs, then to Ballston and Saratoga, and return by the way of New Haven, Hartford, etc. I shall have a fine opportunity of seeing the country on Connecticut River. Mr. Derby does not know the route he shall go, but shall depend on what he hears. We shall go through a part of the States of Vermont, Connecticut, and New-York, so that in our tour we shall be in five different States. I shall write very often, and wish you, my dear father, to write me by the return of the mail, and direct to Pittsfield, in Massachusetts, or to Mr. John Derby, in Salem. If we go through Leicester, I shall find out our relations. Tell Octavia and Horatio I shall write them soon; but as I keep a particular journal, which they shall all see, 'tis not so material. I hear the carriage. Love to all.

ELIZA.

Albany, August 8, 1802.

Thus far, my dear Ellen, have we proceeded without anything to mortify or disappoint us. I wrote you the night I arrived at Lebanon. The next morning the bell rang, and we all assembled to breakfast. There were about thirty ladies, much dressed, looking very handsome. It seemed more like a ball-room than a breakfasting-room. We were the last that came in, and all eyes were fixed upon us. Lady Nesbert and the Allston family, from Carolina, were opposite. This daughter of Col. Burr is a little, smart-looking woman, very <u>learned</u>; they say, understands the dead languages: not pedantic, rather reserved. Lady Nesbert, a most interesting woman, full black eyes, with a wild, melancholy expression, and a voice so sweet and plaintive you would think it melancholy music. I never heard her speak a dozen times since I have been here, and rarely ever smile. Old Mrs. Allston, the mother, is a <u>sour-looking woman</u>; nothing affable or condescending. Miss Allston, they say, is a romp; yet her mother restrains her so much, you would never suspect it. Old Mr. Allston is affable and agreeable. We had likewise there a Mr. Constable, of New-York; has lived in great style, very much the gentleman. Miss Ashley, from New-York, whom I mentioned in my last, is a truly fashionable city belle. She has a fortune, but, I believe, not of family. The gentleman she calls her father, and whose name she takes, 'tis said was hired by a British officer, her real father, to marry the mother and adopt the daughter, and a very large sum was given him. The officer's an abandoned old rake, pale and sallow. Oh, he is a horrid-looking object,— in a deep consumption, I imagine. She is very attentive. But, good Heavens! Ellen, I had no idea of a fashionable girl before, one that devotes her whole attention to fashion. I have much to tell you, when I return, about this Miss Ashley's French style of dress. Mr. and Mrs. Rensselaer left Lebanon the day before we did, with Mr. and Miss Westerlo. Mrs. Welch, the Misses Stephenson and Miss Livingston, the Albany belle, all belong to Albany. Mr. and Miss Westerlo, Miss Beekman, and Mr. Rensselaer, who is mayor of the city, called last evening, and we all went to walk. Went into Miss Westerlo's and spent a charming hour. All returned with us, and we engaged to go to meeting with Mr. and Miss Westerlo, and take tea at the mayor's this afternoon. Mr. Westerlo is going to Ballston, in company with us and a Mr. Kane, of New-York, whom we met at this coffee-house,— very genteel man. Another little lawyer from Litchfield, who came in with us from Lebanon, is likewise going on Monday, so we shall have a very pleasant party. Mr. Kane says I shall meet one of their genteelest New-York beaux at

Ballston,— Mr. <u>Bowne</u>. I wonder if it is the same I have heard you mention. I shall find out. About eleven o'clock, or, rather, twelve, I was surprised by some delightful music,—a number of instruments, and most elegantly playing " Rise, Cynthia, rise." I jumped up, and by the light of the moon saw five gentlemen under the window. To Mr. Westerlo, I suppose, we are indebted. "Washington's March," "Bluebells of Scotland," " Taste Life's Glad Moments," " Boston March," and many other charming tunes played most delightfully. I have heard no music since I left Salem till this, and I was really charmed. The bell will ring soon, and I must finish this after meeting.

Sunday Afternoon.

The dinner was brought on the table just as the bell rang for meeting, so that we were obliged to stay at home this afternoon and tell Mr. Westerlo and his sister, who called again for me, as Mrs. Derby did not go out, that I would go to Mrs. Rensselaer's after meeting. In the morning Mr. Derby and I went to the new Dutch church, with Mr. and Miss Westerlo, and sat with them, next pew to the patroon's, whom you saw in Salem with his beautiful wife. After meeting, Mr. Westerlo came with the patroon and his wife to see us. She is really beautiful, dressed very plain,—cotton cambric morning gown, white sarcenet cloak, hair plain, and a black veil thrown carelessly over her head. They urged our dining there to-morrow, but Mr. Derby is determined to set out in the morning for Ballston; the waters, all tell him, will be of great service. When we return we shall go and see them. A great number of elegant gentlemen are here in this house; many from New-York, some going to the Springs. Your Boston Mr. Amory and Mr. Lee would look rusty alongside them. Hush! not a word. Mr. Kane of New-York, whose sister married Robert Morris, is here, and will set out for the Springs in company with us, Mr. Westerlo, and several others. We shall go to Lake George, and probably make a party from Ballston. Mrs. Derby has insisted on my wearing the sarcenet dress to-day, as we shall drink tea at the mayor's, where the patroon and wife will probably be. I am every moment reminded of your affectionate kindness, which I hope never to be insensible to. You wrote Mamma, I suppose. I have not received a line from anybody; shall depend on finding letters at Pittsfield or Lebanon. Do write me everything. I have so much to tell you that I cannot write. Mrs. Derby, I cannot tell you how much I love her. She treats me with so much affection, and says she believes Mr. Derby feels as much interested in me as if I were his daughter; wishes everything I wear should be becoming, and, indeed, they both treat me with all the attention and affection my most sanguine expectation could desire.

I do not wish to be treated with more affection. Think, then, dear Ellen, how sensibly I must feel it; how gratifying to my feelings. I can never forget the obligation I owe to you and them. My best love to your husband, and tell him when I return I shall have a whole world of news for him. I long to hear from you; do write soon. At Ballston I shall write again. Many people will be talking about my going this journey; many will censure me, perhaps. If you, dear Ellen, should hear any of their ill-natured remarks, you could not do me a greater favor than to vindicate my conduct. I have never for one moment since I left Salem regretted I came. The affectionate attention of Mr. and Mrs. Derby delights my heart. It was more than I had a right to expect. I have received much delight in this tour; seen much elegant company, variety of character and manners. I am sensible it will be a source of great improvement as well as pleasure. I shall have seen that style and splendor, which has so many magic charms when viewed at a distance, divested of its false face; find it mingled with as many pains as any other situation in life.—nay, more _poignant_ pains. I feel I shall not be at all injured by this life. Though I enjoy myself highly, and mingle with these people with much delight, I shall return happy and contented. Mr. Derby is quite unwell. He ate nothing but milk since we left Salem; his stomach refuses anything else. I have strong hopes the Ballston waters will have a good effect. Every one tells him so. A gentleman just from Ballston says there is a great deal of company at the Springs.—dance every other night. If the waters agree with Mr. Derby, we shall stay a week or ten days. I have written home a number of times, which, together with my journal, take up all my leisure time, and that is stolen from the hours devoted to sleep. How delighted I shall be when I return. Any news from Martha? If any letter arrives for me, send it to Pittsfield. How charming it would be if we were all together going to the Springs. I have not time to write anything about Albany. Fine society, I believe; full of Dutch houses.

Adieu! Love to all friends.

ELIZA.

TO MRS. JOHN DERBY.

Ballston Springs, August 22, 1802.

My Dearest Mother:

I feel at this moment as if I could fly!—so far from home, received no letters, yet at Albany I expect to find them. Let me at least hope *what 'twill delight me so much to realize. I sometimes almost fear to receive a letter from home, yet my indulgent parents will pardon the liberty I took in coming this journey, as I trust they are convinced by my past life that I would not for the universe act in opposition to what I knew they approved. I am convinced when you know Mr. and Mrs. Derby you will feel that I was both secure and honored in their protection. I cannot tell you half I owe them; never in my life was I treated with more affectionate attention. They appear as much interested in all I do as if I were their daughter. You know my heart, my dearest mother; you know it never was insensible to the smallest favor; what, then, must be its sensation when it is thus overpowered by affectionate kindness. I long to convince them how much I feel, but words are inadequate. My father has seen Mr. D. I wish he would write to him. I think it would be no more than just to thank him for the attention and care he has taken of his daughter. It seems as if he had a right to expect something of the kind. They are the finest couple I know of, so different from what I expected to find them. I thought Mr. Derby a gay, gallant man, like Mr. Davis, but he is a plain, noble-hearted, sincere, generous man; talks very little, and one of the pleasantest dispositions in the world. In Mrs. Derby I thought to find a gay woman of fashion, but not a soul that ever knew her could help loving her. I never saw a person so universally beloved. We have been here at Ballston a fortnight to-morrow; it has been one continued scene of idleness and dissipation. Have a ball every other night, ride, walk, stroll about the piazzas, dress; indeed, we do nothing that seems like improvement. But still I think there is no place where one may study the different characters and dispositions to greater advantage. You meet here the most pleasant, genteel people from every part of our country; ceremony is thrown off, and you are acquainted very soon. You may select those you please for intimates, and among so many you certainly will find some agreeable, amiable companions. For a week we sat down at table every day with sixty or seventy persons; to-day we were all speaking of the table being very thin because we had only forty. There are as many*

more at the other boarding-house, continually going and coming, and now there are scarcely
ten persons here that were here when we came. We went last week to _Lake George_,
about forty miles from here; made up a party and went on Tuesday; breakfasted at
Saratoga—where the Springs formerly most celebrated were—and dined about fourteen
miles this side the lake, at the most beautiful place I ever saw. Perhaps you have heard
of Glens Falls; they are said to exceed in _beauty_ the Falls of Niagara, though in
sublimity must fall far short. I never imagined anything so picturesque, sublime, and
beautiful as the scenery around this enchanting place. The rocks on the shores have
exactly the appearance of elegant, magnificent ruins: they are entirely of _slate_, and seem
piled in regular forms, with shrubs and grass growing in between. I looked around me
for an hour, and I every moment discovered something new to admire: nothing could
exceed the beautiful variety of the scenery. I left this elegant place with painful regret.
About sunset we came in view of the _lake._ It is a most beautiful sheet of water (Morse
says thirty-six miles long and from one to seven broad), full of beautiful islands, 365 in
all, and of every size and shape. It is surrounded by very high hills and mountains,
rising one above the other in majestic grandeur. In the morning we went out to fish,
sailed about four miles on the lake to a little island, where we went on shore. Nothing
could exceed the beautiful grandeur of the prospect we anchored off. I found it very
charming fishing, the water so perfectly transparent that we could see the fish swimming
around the hook. Our first intention was to sail down the lake to Lake Champlain, and
visit the ruins of the fortifications at Ticonderoga, but some of our party dissuaded us
from it. We saw the ruins of Fort George, and the bloody pond where so many poor
wretches were thrown. We stopped on our return at the field where Burgoyne surren-
dered his army; it is now covered with corn, and nothing to distinguish it from the
surrounding fields. We returned by a different route. For ten miles we rode directly on
the banks of the Hudson River. Nothing could be more delightful; our road wound with
the river, which was beautifully overhung with trees. We returned here Thursday
night, found them dining. I joined, and the next night we had a ball at the other house.
There, again, I danced till twelve o'clock, and the next morning got up quite sick.
To-day I am finely again, and have made a resolution not to dance again whilst I stay
here. They all think I can't keep it, but they shall see I can.* Colonel Boyd came here
last week, but went away while we were gone to Lake George,—to Canada, I believe. He
says you had not heard of my coming when he left Portland, so he could tell me nothing new.
We shall probably leave here on Tuesday or Wednesday, stay at Albany a few days, and
go to Lebanon again: perhaps to Williamstown Commencement. We are engaged to spend
one day at Mr. Rensselaer's, the former lieutenant-governor, and one at Mr. Rensselaer's,
his brother, who is mayor of the city. I know not how long 'twill be before we return to

Salem, but I really begin to think of home with a great deal of anxiety. Tell Octavia I never go into the ball-room to dance without wishing for her; how delighted should I be if Horatio and Octavia were here with me. How charming will it be when I get home again. Believe me, my dear mother, I shall love home more than ever. I long to sit me down by the instrument some evening, after the business of the day is over, with you, my father, and all round me, or to hear Octavia sing and play. This scene of dissipation may please for a while by its novelty, but it soon satiates. No regular employment. I have never been in the habit of spending my time in idleness, and they say here that the Southern ladies seem more at home here than the Northern ladies, and do not appear to think industry necessary to happiness. I hope to find many letters at Albany. I have kept a regular journal, which will assist my memory in relating my adventures when I return home. I wrote Horatio last week, and told him to send the letter home for you to read. I look forward to returning with the greatest pleasure. I suppose you are fixed upon a house, and will move by the time I return. Let me know, as I am anxious to hear about it. Give my best love to all my friends, and tell Octavia I have more to say to her than I can gabble in a month. Oh, I long to get home again. I find no time to write, if I lock myself in my chamber, I have so many knocks at the door. " Miss Southgate, go and walk;" " Go down to the spring;" " Somebody wants you below." So many interruptions, 'tis almost impossible. After I retire for the night, I am so tired and sleepy, and my chamber is so hot, I _cannot_ write. 'Tis Sunday to-day (though all days are alike here), and I have determined I would write home. I wonder how it was possible for Martha to write so much. I hear of her from all the Southern people; they all speak in raptures. Give my love to Mrs. Coffin, and kiss all the children, Mamy particularly. What would I not give to have her open my door and run in this moment. Mrs. Derby says I get low-spirited when I write home. The only way is to think as little of it as possible whilst I am so far off. I shall write again from Albany, where I hope to find letters.

Ever your affectionate

ELIZA.

TO THE CARE OF ROBERT SOUTHGATE,
    SCARBOROUGH.
        (District of Maine.)

Salem, September 9, 1802.

My Dearest Mother:

Once more I am safe in Salem, and my first thoughts turn toward home. I arrived last night. The attention I have received from Mr. and Mrs. Derby has been of a kind that I shall look forward with delight to a time when I may be able to return it as I wish. I am in perfect health and spirits, and have enjoyed the journey more than I can express to you. I don't know that I have had an unpleasant hour since I have been gone, and, what is still more pleasing, I look back on every scene without regret or pain. At Leicester, I went to Uncle Southgate's, and Cousin William helped me into the carriage when I left the tavern next morning. We did not return through Northampton, and I consequently missed seeing Aunt Dickenson. I regretted it extremely, but Mr. Derby was in such haste to return, that he left us at Worcester and took the stage. I, therefore, could not say a word of Hadley. I found two letters from Octavia on my return here; felt really grieved at Eliza Wait's death. She must feel it sensibly, as they were such intimate friends; yet time blunts the sharp pangs of affection, and when I return she will feel that happiness has only fled for a while, to make its return more delightful. I have received more attentions at the Springs than in my whole life before; I know not why it was, but I went under every advantage. Mr. Derby is so well known and respected, and they are such charming people, and treated me with so much affection, it could not be otherwise. Among the many gentlemen with whom I have become acquainted, and who have been attentive to me, one, I believe, is serious. I know not, my dear mother, how to introduce this subject, yet as I infer you may hear it from others, and feel anxious for my welfare, I consider it a duty to tell you all. At Albany, on our way to Ballston, we put up at the same house with a Mr. Bowne from New-York; he went on to the Springs the same day we did, and from that time was particularly attentive to me. He was always of our parties to ride; went to Lake George in company with us, and came on to Lebanon when we did. For four weeks I saw him every day, and probably had a better opportunity of knowing him than if I had seen him as a common acquaintance in town for years. I felt cautious of encouraging his attentions, though I did not wish to discourage them. There were so many New-Yorkers at the Springs who knew him perfectly, that I easily learned his character and reputation. He is a man of business, uniform in his conduct, and very much respected; all this we knew from report. Mr. and Mrs. Derby were very much

pleased with him, but conducted toward me peculiar _delicacy_; left me entirely to myself, as on a subject of so much importance they scarcely dared give an opinion. I felt myself in a situation truly embarrassing,—at such a distance from all my friends, my father and mother perfect strangers to the person, and prepossessed in his favor as much as so short an acquaintance would sanction. His conduct was such as I shall ever reflect on with the greatest pleasure,—open, candid, generous, and delicate. He is a man in whom I could place the most unbounded confidence; nothing rash or impetuous in his disposition, but weighs maturely every circumstance. He knew I was not at liberty to encourage his addresses without the approbation of my parents, and appeared as solicitous that I should act with strict propriety as one of my most disinterested friends. He advised me like a friend, and would not have suffered me to do anything improper. He only required I would not discourage his addresses till he had an opportunity of making known to my parents his character and wishes. This I promised, and went so far as to tell him I approved him, as far as I knew him, but the decision must rest with my parents; their wishes were my law. He insisted on coming immediately; that I absolutely refused to consent to. But all my persuasion to wait until winter had no effect; the first of October he _will come_. I could not prevent it without a positive _refusal_; this I felt no disposition to give, and now, my dearest mother, I submit myself wholly to the wishes of my father and you, convinced that my happiness is your warmest wish, and to promote it has ever been your study. That I feel deeply interested in Mr. Bowne, I candidly acknowledge, and from the knowledge I have of his heart and character, I think him better calculated to promote my happiness than any person I have yet seen. He is a firm, steady, serious man, nothing light or trifling in his character, and I have every reason to think he has well weighed his sentiments toward me,—nothing rash or premature. I have referred him wholly to you, and you, my dearest parents, must decide. Octavia mentioned nothing about moving, but I am extremely anxious to know how soon we go into Portland, and what house we shall have. Write me immediately on the subject, and let me know if you approve my conduct. Mr. Bowne wishes me to remain here until he comes on, and then let him carry me home. This I objected to, but will depend on your advice. I shall be obliged to stay a few weeks longer. Harriet Howards expects me a week in Cambridge, Mrs. Sumner a week in Boston, and Mrs. Hasket Derby another week. I am now with Ellen, and shall stay till Mrs. Coffin comes up; then, according to promise, go to Mrs. Lucy Derby's. I feel extremely anxious to hear you have moved into town, and shall most probably be here until then. Write me immediately. If you wish any furniture, Mrs. Sumner will assist me in purchasing whatever you wish. I mentioned in my letter when I set out on this journey I borrowed fifteen dollars of Ellen. I wish you to send it to me immediately after receiving this, if you have not already sent it. I

shall likewise stand in need of a little, as I have unavoidably incurred many expenses in this journey, which I should not otherwise have done. Mr. Derby has loaded me with obligations; all my expenses he defrayed, as if I were his daughter, and in such a manner as endears him more than I can express.

You cannot imagine how interested they both are in the subject I have been writing you upon; my nearest friends cannot feel more; they have witnessed the whole progress, and if you knew them, would be convinced they would not have let me act improperly. They both approve my conduct. I wish my father would write to Mr. Derby, and know what he says of Mr. B.'s character. I don't know but 'tis a subject too delicate to give his opinion, but I can conceive that my father might request it without any impropriety, and do, my dear mother, beg him to say anything in his power to convince him that we all feel sensibly their great attention to me. You know not how anxious I feel for my father to write him something of that kind,—not that they expect it, but, on the contrary, insist that they have been more obliged than I have, and really seem to think so; but this rather strengthens than lessens the obligation. Nothing should have induced me to receive such from people who felt they were conferring favors. I long to hear when we move into Portland,—do write me. My best love to Horatio and Octavia, and tell them I shall write as soon as possible. I found a large packet of five sheets from Martha, dated Paris, June 28th; tells me everything: speaks almost in raptures of Bonaparte; says Uncle Rufus has a little son, about twelve years, at school there, one of the finest boys she ever saw. I find most of the Southern people whom we met at the Springs think Uncle Rufus stands as good a chance of being President as any one spoken of. I have listened for hours to his praises when not one knew how much I was interested; it was known from Mrs. Derby that I was his niece, and it really gave me great consequence. I thought of Mrs. De Witt and laughed. Judge Sedgwick told me he had letters from him as late as June, and that he was determined on returning in the spring. I long to hear from home. My love to all friends, and believe me with every sentiment of _duty_ and affection.

Your daughter,

ELIZA.

Martha sent me a most elegant indispensable, white lute-string, spangled with silver, and a beautiful bracelet for the arm, made of her hair. She is too good to love me, as she says, more than ever.

(Married the next spring.)

Portland, Friday, Nov., 1802.

Mr. Davis is going on to Boston, and will have a letter for you.   I am delighted to hear that Mamma is better.   I send you some of <u>Miss Holmes's wedding-cake</u>; married on Monday.   You say Uncle Rufus Emerson has returned, and tells them a great many stories.   When you write next, tell me what he says, and where he heard them, and all about it, for everything interests me.   Mr. B. has not arrived.   I am out of all patience. Cannot imagine what detains him.   Four weeks to-morrow since he took Mr. Codman's letter.   These Quakers are governed with such a <u>slow spirit.</u>   I wish the deuce had them. I shall be really uneasy if he don't come soon.   I want some <u>money;</u> my last dollar I gave Horatio to buy Mamma's oranges.   I have written to Mrs. Derby to buy me a <u>winter gown.</u>   In her last she says she has bought it, but does not mention the price.   I wish the money to send to her as soon as I hear,—a little, likewise, for occasional expenses; 'tis not pleasant to be without it.   I have been to but one party since Mamma's sickness; shall certainly not go out more than I can possibly avoid.   Mrs. Derby is quite vexed at Mr. B.'s not coming.   I'll not be so ungenerous as to condemn him without giving an opportunity of vindicating himself.   Some circumstances I know not of may detain him.   All our friends are well.   Send me the money as soon as possible, and don't forget to tell particularly what Rufus says, who he saw, what they told him, and where he heard all. In some cases trifles acquire importance, <u>mole-hills become mountains.</u>

Adieu.

ELIZA.

Love to Mamma, and tell her I am out of all patience.

Boston, May 30, 1803.

Here we are, my dear Octavia, at Mrs. Carter's, and though we have endeavored to keep ourselves as much out of the way as possible, a great many people have called to pay their respects to Mr. and Mrs. Bowne. The first person we met, driving through Salem, was Mr. Lee, just coming in town. He bowed very low, and passed. We went to a public-house, and had not been there three minutes before Mr. Lee came in, determined to be the first to call on us. He shook hands very cordially, congratulated us, and went with us up to Ellen's. We promised to drive with Ellen, and went to see Mrs. H. Derby; spent a charming hour, and returned to Ellen's; dined, and all went to Lucy Derby's to tea,—Mr. Lee and a dozen others. Mr. Bowne and myself called on Mrs. Gray, and after a very pleasant day returned to Ellen's, and staid the night, and the next morning, which was Wednesday, came into Boston. 'Twas election day, and all the world was in motion. I could not bear to come to Mrs. Carter's, but Mr. Bowne thought he ought to. Mr. Lee got to Boston as soon as we did, and came immediately to see us, and offer his services. He has been here again this morning, and is going to ride into the country with us, to show us some fine seats. Doctor Boice, Mr. Davis, Mr. Cabot, Charles Bradbury, Tom Coffin, and a dozen other gentlemen, whose names I have forgotten, and who came with the Misses Lowell and the Misses Russell. We have prevented all invitations by constantly saying we were going out of town immediately. Mr. Lee insisted, when I expressed a wish to see Miss Wyre, on letting her know I was in town. He went, and she came immediately back. I was very glad to see her, and she appeared so herself at seeing me. Some ladies and gentlemen came in, and after they were gone, Alicia, Mr. B., and myself went a-shopping. The fashions for bonnets, Octavia, are very ugly. Alicia had a large, white, glazed cambric one, made without pasteboard. But I have not told you how General Knox found us out at Newburyport. We always kept by ourselves, but in passing the entry, General Knox, who had just come in the stage, met Mr. B., and asked where he was from (Mr. Bowne kept here with Mrs. Carter when General Knox was here last winter). He told him from the eastward. "Alone?" "No." "Who is with you,— Mrs. Bowne?" So plump a question he could not evade, so the general insisted on being introduced to the bride. I was walking the room and reading, perfectly unsuspicious, when the opening of the door, and Mr.

Bowne's voice,—"General Knox, my love."—quite roused me. He came up, took my hand very gracefully, pressed it to his lips, and begged leave to congratulate me on the event that had lately taken place. After a few minutes' conversation: "And pray, sir," said he, turning to Mr. Bowne, "when did this happy event take place?" I felt my face glow, but Mr. Bowne, always delicate and collected, said, "'Tis not a fortnight since, sir." The stage drove to the door, and after hoping to see us at Mrs. Carter's, he took his leave, and this morning (he was out all day yesterday) I found him waiting in the breakfast-room to see me. He introduced me to General Pinckney and his family, from Carolina. General Pinckney, they say, is to be our next President. "Mr. Bowne," said General Knox to General P., "has done us the honor to come to the District of Maine for a bud to transplant in New-York." He was very polite, and said he must find us out in New-York. Only think, I never thought of the _wedding-cake_ when I was at Salem. You would laugh to hear _Mrs. Bowne_ and Miss Southgate all in a breath: "How do you do, Miss Southgate?—I beg pardon, _Mrs. Bowne;_" and do it on purpose, I believe. When I hear an old acquaintance call me Mrs. Bowne, it really makes me stare at first, it sounds so very odd. Mr. B. will be in in a moment, and if I don't seal my letter, he will insist on seeing it; so love to all. I depend on finding letters at New Haven. I have a thousand things to say. Some ladies inquire for Mrs. Bowne; so says the servant. I'll tell you who they are when I come up. Mrs. Bartlett and Alicia, they insist on our taking tea and spending the evening. We promised, if we did not leave town after dinner, that we would. Adieu, adieu. Mr. Bowne sends a great deal of love.

Your affectionate sister,

ELIZA BOWNE.

New Haven, June 1, 1803.

Your letter, my dear Octavia, was the first thing to welcome me on my arrival at this city. I cannot describe to you my sensations when it came. I can rarely think of home without more pain than pleasure; and yet, if there is a being on earth perfectly blessed, 'tis your sister Eliza. How infinitely more happy than when I left you. You cannot imagine how delightful has been our journey. We have stopped at every pleasant place, enjoyed all the beauties of the spring in the richest and most luxuriant country I ever saw. I wrote you last from Boston. The afternoon following, Mr. Lee called to accompany us a few miles out of town. He had requested Mr. Lyman to go out to his seat, in Waltham, that Mr. Bowne and myself might have an opportunity to see it, as it is the most beautiful place around Boston. We set out about four o'clock; had a most charming ride. Mr. Lee was remarkably sociable, attentive, and polite, both to Mr. Bowne and myself. He talks just as social, and called me Miss Southgate and Mrs. B. all in a breath, as fast as he could talk. I have no time to tell you of this elegant place; of Mr. Lyman's great taste in laying out the grounds. It surpasses everything of the kind I ever saw; beautiful serpentine river or brook thickly planted with trees, and elegant swans swimming about. You can't imagine,—'twas almost like enchantment. After Mr. Lee had gathered me a bouquet, large enough to supply a ball-room, of the most elegant and rare flowers,—full-blown roses, buds, everything beautiful,—we jumped into the carriage. He shook us cordially by the hand, wished us every happiness, and hoped to see us in New-York ere long. Sunday morning we got to Springfield; staid the day. It recalled so many pleasing sensations. When we parted there, how different were our feelings! our happiness was augmented by the contrast. From Springfield to Hartford was charming. Much pleased with Hartford; staid a day and night there; and from Hartford to New Haven is the most elegant ride you can possibly imagine.—a fine turnpike about thirty miles, and such a picturesque, rich, luxuriant country, such variety and beauty. Oh, 'twas charming! Mr. Bowne is waiting for me this full hour to walk in the mall. What shall I do, he hurries so? Well, I never saw a place so charming as New Haven. We have been all over it, visited the college, everything, and I give it the preference to any place I know of. A particular description I defer. I have no time to say a word of your letter. Write me immediately on receiving this to New-York, where we shall be on Saturday. Mr. Bowne's best love with mine to all the family. Adieu. I have ten thousand things more to say, but can't. Write me immediately.

Ever your affectionate

ELIZA BOWNE

New-York, June 6, 1803.

I sit down to catch a moment to tell you all I have to before another interruption. I have so much to say, where shall I begin? My head is most turned, and yet I am very happy. I am enraptured with New-York; you cannot imagine anything half so beautiful as Broadway, and I am sure you would say I was more romantic than ever if I should attempt to describe the Battery. The elegant water prospect, you can have no idea how refreshing in a warm evening. The gardens we have not yet visited; indeed, we have so many delightful things, 'twill take me forever, and my husband declares he takes as much pleasure in showing them to me as I do in seeing them; you would believe it, if you saw him. Did I tell you anything of Brother John; handsome young man, great literary taste. He is one of the family, nothing of the appearance of a Quaker. Mrs. King, another sister, they all say looks like me. Mrs. Murray, who is very sick now, has a daughter, a charming, lively girl, about nineteen, and the little witch introduced me in a laughing way last night to some of her friends as <u>Aunt Eliza</u>. I protest against that,— her brother Robert seventeen years old, too; I positively must declare off from being aunt to them. Caroline and I went a-shopping yesterday, and 'tis a fact that the little white satin Quaker bonnets, cap-crowns, are the most fashionable that are worn; lined with pink or blue or white. But I'll not have one, for if any of my old acquaintance should meet me in the street, they would laugh. I would, if I were them. I mean to send Sister Boyd a Quaker cap, the first tasty one I see. Caroline's are too plain, but she has promised to get me a more fashionable pattern. 'Tis the fashion. I see nothing new or pretty. Large sheer muslin shawls, put on as Sally Weeks wears hers, are much worn. They show the form through and look pretty. Silk nabobs, plaided, colored, and white, are much worn; very short waists, hair very plain. Maria Deming has been to see me, I was very happy.—several spring acquaintances. Expect Eliza Watts and Jane every moment; they did not know where I was to be found. Last night we were at the play, "The Way to Get Married." Mr. Hodgkinson in <u>Tangent</u> is inimitable. Mrs. Johnson, a sweet, interesting actress, in Julia, and Jefferson, a great comic player, were all that were particularly pleasing; house was very thin, so late in the season. Mr. and Mrs. Codman came to see me. I should have known her in a moment, from her resemblance to Ellen and the family; appeared very happy to see me. Mr. Codman was happy.—Mrs. Codman would now have somebody to call her friend, etc., etc. Maria Deming told me Uncle Rufus was expected every day. We have such contradictory accounts, we hardly know what to believe. As to housekeeping, we don't begin to talk anything of it yet. Mr. Bowne says not till October. However, you shall hear all our plans. I anticipate so much

happiness. I am sure if anybody ought to, I may. My heart is <u>full</u> sometimes, when I think how much more blest I am than most of the world. At this moment there is not a single circumstance presents itself to my mind that I feel unpleasant to reflect on,— the sweet tranquillity of my feelings, so different from anything I ever before felt; such a confidence; my every feeling reciprocated, and every wish anticipated. I write to you what would appear singular to any other. You can easily imagine my feelings. I see Mr. B. now, where he is universally known and respected, and every hour see some new proof how much he is honored and esteemed there,— the most gratifying to the heart you can imagine; cannot but make an impression on mine. We talk of you when we get to housekeeping, how delightful 'twill be. What a sweet domestic circle! I must leave you,— Galys says, "Mrs. Walter" (for so the servants call me, to distinguish), "a gentleman below wishes to see you." Adieu. Who can this said gentleman be?

Mr. Rodman was below, whom I saw at the Springs, and for these two hours there have been so many calling I thought I should never get up to finish my letters. Mrs. Henderson, whom I mentioned to you as one of the most elegant women in New-York, and Maria, came in soon after. Engaged to Mrs. Henderson's for Friday.

Thursday morning.

I have been to two of the gardens. Columbia, near Battery, a most romantic, beautiful place; 'tis inclosed in a circular form, and little rooms and boxes all around, with tables and chairs, these full of company; the trees all interspersed with lamps twinkling through the branches; in the center, a pretty little building with a fountain playing continually. The rays of the lamps on the drops of water gave it a cool, sparkling appearance that was delightful. This little building (which is a kind of canopy), and pillars all round the garden,— and these had festoons of colored lamps that at a distance looked like large brilliant stars, seen through the branches; and placed all round are marble busts, beautiful little figures of Diana, Cupid, Venus, seen by the glimmering of the lamps, which are partly concealed by the foliage, give you an idea of enchantment. Here we strolled among the trees, and every moment met some walking from the thick shade unexpectedly, and come upon us before we heard a sound; 'twas delightful. We passed a box that Miss Watts was in; she called us, and we went in and had a charming, refreshing glass of ice-cream, which has chilled me ever since. They have a fine orchestra and have concerts here sometimes. I can conceive of nothing more charming than this must be.

We went on to the Battery. This is a large promenade by the shore of the North River; very extensive rows and clusters of trees in every part, and a large walk along the

shore, almost over the crowded water, gives you such a fresh, delightful air, that every evening in summer it is crowded with company. Here, too, they have music playing on the water in boats of a moonlight night. Last night we went to a garden a little out of town, Mount Vernon garden; this is surrounded by boxes of the same kind, with a walk on top of them. You can see the gardens all below, but 'tis a summer <u>playhouse</u>,—pit and boxes, stage and all, but open on top. From this there are doors opening into the garden, which is similar to Columbia Garden: lamps among the trees, large mineral fountain, delightful swings, two at a time. I was in raptures, as you may imagine, and if I had not grown sober before I came to this wonderful place, 'twould have turned my head. But I have filled my letter and not told you half,—of the park, the public buildings. I have so much to tell you, and of those that have called on me. I have no room to say half. Yesterday Mrs. Henderson came again to see me, and brought two of my Aunt King's most intimate friends to introduce.— Mrs. Delafield and Miss Bull. Mr. and Mrs. Delafield are Uncle and Aunt's very intimate friends; she is called the most elegant woman in New-York. I was delighted with her, and very much gratified at Mrs. Henderson's attention in coming again on purpose to introduce them; they were so attentive, so polite, and Mrs. Delafield said so many things of Uncle and Aunt King,—how delighted they would be to find me settled near them, how much I should love them, and everything of the kind, that was very gratifying to me. Miss Deming has been to see me three or four times; several invitations to tea, but we declined, as our family friends were visiting us this week. This morning we go to make calls. I have got a list of names that most frightens me. All our brothers and sisters say, "Why, Eliza does not seem at all like a stranger to us." Indeed, I feel as easy and happy among them as possible, which astonishes me, as I have been so unaccustomed to Quakers; but their manners are so affectionate and soft, you cannot help it. Mrs. King (sister) is a beauty. She would be very handsome in a different dress. She looks so like Alicia Wyer you would love her,—just such full sweet blue eyes, charming complexion, and sweet expression; and her little Quaker cap gives her such an innocent, simple appearance. I imagine Alicia with a Quaker dress, and you will see her exactly. Adieu. I am expecting to hear from you every day. Mr. Bowne is out. Would send a great deal of love if he were here. Kiss dear little Mary and all the children. I never go by a toy-shop or confectionery without longing to have them here. Love to all. Our best love to my father and mother, Horatio, Isabella, and all. I mean to write as soon as I am settled a little. Adieu.

New-York, June 18, 1803.

I am just going to set off for Long Island, and therefore promise but a short letter. I have a mantua-maker here making you a gown, which I hope to have finished to send by Mrs. Rodman.   The fashions are <u>remarkably plain</u> *: sleeves much longer than ours, and half handkerchiefs are universally worn.   At Mrs. Henderson's party there was but one lady, except myself, without a handkerchief; dressed as plain as possible,— the most fashionable women the plainest.   I have got you a pretty India spotted-muslin; 'tis fashionable here.   My* <u>husband</u> *sends a great deal of love; says we shall be traveling about all summer, settle down soberly in October, and depend on seeing you as soon as we are at housekeeping.   Sister Caroline has made Sister Boyd a tasty Quaker cap, which I shall send with the gown.   How could you mistake what I said of Caroline so much? Far from being "*<u>stiff and rigid,</u>*" she is most affectionate, attentive, and obliging; nothing was more foreign to my thoughts, and you must have taken your ideas from what I said of her dress, which, you may depend upon it, with Quakers is no criterion to judge by.   I never was more disappointed in my life to find such a stiff, forbidding external cover so much affability and sweetness.*

You must give my love to Miranda.   I wish I had time to write to her, Horatio, my mother, and all, but I expect the carriage every moment.   Tell Horatio he must write to me.   At present my letters to you must answer for all, till I am more settled.   Mrs. Codman has promised to call at our house, and tell you all about me.   Malbone has just finished my picture; I have done sitting!   He was not willing I should see it, as 'tis unfinished.   When you return, 'twill be done; then I'll tell you whether 'tis like.   I have told you in a former letter we shall go to Bethlehem, Philadelphia, and perhaps to the Springs.   My trunk arrived safe.   I shall send a little ring to Cousin Mary Porter; 'tis not the kind I wanted, but I had not time to have one made to send by Mrs. C. Is mine, with Sister Mary's hair, done?   Send it the first opportunity.   Adieu.   Best love to all friends, all the children.   Tell Mamma I mean to write her as soon as I have leisure, that I am very, <u>very</u> *happy, that Uncle Rufus has* <u>not</u> *yet arrived, though every day expected, and that I can look to the time when we shall see her and my father in New York.   Mr. Bowne and myself both will be delighted.   Give my best love to Lucia, Zel*

27

pali, and John, and ask the latter if he has discovered on whom my <u>mantle rested</u>. Tell Zelpali we pass her friend's, Mrs. Bogert's, house every day, and never without thinking of her. The city air has not stolen my <u>country bloom</u> yet, for every one says, "I need not ask you how you do, Mrs. Bowne, you look in such fine health." Dr. Moore would not inoculate me for the small-pox after examining my arm, as he was sure, from what I told him, I had had the kine-pox well, and he would insure me against the small-pox. But Mr. Bowne seems to wish I should be inoculated, though I care nothing about it now. Adieu. My best love to Aunt Porter and Nancy, Mary Porter, and all the other friends. We are going to <u>Flushing</u> to see our cousins before we return. You know how Mary laughed about the name. Yesterday we were at Belvidere, the most beautiful place, the finest view in the world, the greatest variety.—I never shall be done. Kiss dear little Mary; I think of her every time I see a sweet little sight.

Your affectionate sister,

ELIZA S. BOWNE.

P. S.—Remember and put an S. in my name, to distinguish; there are two or three Eliza Bownes in the family.

New-York, June 30, 1803.

Uncle Rufus has just landed! The huzzas have ceased, the populace retired, and I hasten to give you the earliest information. Several thousand people were on the wharf when he landed, my husband among the number. As he stepped from the vessel, they gave three cheers, and escorted him up into Broadway to a Mr. Lowe's (his friend), then three more cheers as he entered the door. He stood at the door, bowed, and they dispersed,— all but a dozen particular friends who accompanied him into the house, and, Mr. Bowne with them, were introduced by Mr. Watson; and immediately after Mr. Henderson said, "A niece of yours, Mr. King, was lately married in New-York to Mr. Bowne." My uncle immediately came up to him, shook hands a second time, and said, "Miss Southgate, I presume?" He staid but a few moments; the acclamations of the people had rather embarrassed Uncle. Aunt King had not landed. This evening we are going to see them. Imagine me entering, presented by Mrs. Henderson, Miss Bull, or Mrs. Delafield,—all her intimate friends; think what a mixture of sensations. I'll tell you all about it. I returned from Long Island this morning; delightful sail, beautiful country, and pleasant visit. Malbone has finished my picture, but is unwilling we should have it, as the likeness is not striking. He says, not handsome enough; so says Mr. Bowne. But I think 'tis in some things much flattered. It looks too serious, pensive, soft; that's not <u>my</u> style at all. But perhaps 'twill look different. 'Twas not quite finished when I saw it. However, he insists on taking it again, as soon as he returns from the southward, and told Mr. Bowne if he <u>must</u> have one, he might keep this till he returned and he would try again. Uncle Rufus brings news that <u>war</u> has actually taken place, hostilities commenced. The king, on the 14th, sent a message to Parliament that he was determined to use every effort to repress the overbearing power of France, and hoped for their united assistance and exertions. So much for <u>Father</u>. The whole city seems alive; nothing else talked of but the arrival of Mr. King and the news of the war. Adieu! I'll write again soon. Best love to all the family. We are in expectation of great entertainment on Fourth of July,—<u>INDEPENDANT</u> Day! as they laugh at us Yankees for calling it,— the gardens, the Battery, and everything to be illuminated; fireworks, music, etc., etc. Col. Boyd called to see me; and Mr. Grelett, whom I was introduced to

in Boston, brought the handsome Miss Pemberton, whom you have heard Col. B. speak of, to call on me. She's from Philadelphia. I was out. I hope none of my acquaintances will come to New-York, pass through, or anything, without finding me out. I just begin to make memorandums of tables and chairs, spoons and beds, and everything else; most turns my brain, so many things to think of; but I am well and happy, and 'tis a pleasant task. Adieu!

Yours affectionately,

ELIZA S. BOWNE.

10 o'clock, evening.

Just returned from Uncle Rufus's. Mr. B. introduced me to Uncle. He took my hand, introduced us to his wife, and they both seemed much pleased to see us. Uncle is so easy and graceful and pleasing, I was delighted with him. Looks very like Mr. Parker instead of Mr. Davis. Inquired particularly after the family, was surprised at hearing of my being here, said everything that was pleasant, hoped we should be very sociable, etc., etc., and after a pleasant half hour we returned home. I broke the seal of my letter to tell you. 'Tis late; I can't be particular.

E. S. B.

MISS SOUTHGATE,
        PORTLAND.

New-York, July 4, 1803.

Dear Mother:

I have written generally to Octavia, but as I meant my letters for the family, 'tis not much matter to whom they were directed. I wrote you of Uncle Rufus's arrival, and our calling on them the evening after. Sunday they called on us, with Mr. and Mrs. Lowe, their friends with whom they are staying till their own house is ready. They both kissed me very affectionately, said everything that pleased me, and were very solicitous that we might get houses near each other in the winter, that we might be sociable neighbors. Uncle Rufus says I remind him of Martha very much. He inquired particularly after all of the family, and asked if I did not expect you would come on to see me, and both appeared much pleased when I assured them I depended on seeing you here. Aunt King told Mr. Bowne he must bring me to see them _very often_, and look upon her as a _mother_.

July 8th.

My letter will be an old date before I finish it. You must have perceived, my dear mother, from my letters, that I am much pleased with New-York. I was never in a place that I should prefer as a situation for life, and nothing but the distance from my friends can render it other than delightful. We have thus far spent the summer delightfully; we have been no very long journeys, but on a number of little excursions of twenty or forty miles to see whatever is pleasant in the neighborhood. Mr. Bowne's friends, though all very plain, are very amiable and affectionate, and I receive every attention from them I wish. I have a great many people call on me, and shall have it in my power to select just such a circle of acquaintance as suits my taste: few people whose prospects of happi

ness exceed mine, which I often think of with grateful sensations. Mr. Bowne's situation in life is equal to my most sanguine expectations, and it is a peculiar gratification to me to find him so much and so universally esteemed and respected. This would be ridiculous from me to any but my mother, but I know it must be pleasing to you to know that I realize all the happiness you can wish me. I have not a wish that is not gratified as soon as 'tis known. We intend going to Bethlehem, Philadelphia, and a watering-place, similar to the Springs, about thirty miles beyond Philadelphia: shall probably set out the latter part of this month. At present we have done nothing toward housekeeping, and Mr. Bowne won't let me do the least thing toward it, lest I get my mind engaged, and not enjoy the pleasure of our journeys. 'Tis very different here from most any place, for there is no article but you can find ready made to your taste, excepting table-linen, bedding, etc., etc. One poor bed-quilt is all I have toward housekeeping, and been married two months almost. I am sadly off, to be sure. We have not yet found a house that suits us. Mr. Bowne don't like any of his own, and wishes to hire one for the present, until he can build, which he intends doing next season, which I am very glad of, as I never liked living in a hired house, and changing about so often. Uncle and Aunt King want we should get near them; they have hired a ready-furnished house about two miles out of the city for the summer, and intend hiring a house in town in the winter. I have been very busy with my mantua-maker, as I am having a dress made to wear to Mrs. Delafield's to dine on Sunday. They have a most superb country-seat on Long Island, opposite Hell Gate. He is Uncle Rufus's most intimate friend, and a very intimate one of Mr. Bowne's. We shall probably meet them there. I have not seen them to ask. My picture is done, but I am disappointed in it. Malbone says he has not done me justice; so says Mr. Bowne; but I think, though the features are striking, he has not caught the expression, particularly of the eyes, which are excessively pensive,—would do for Sterne's Maria. The mouth laughs a little, and they all say is good,—all the lower part of the face: but the eyes not the thing. He wants me to sit again; so does Mr. Bowne. Malbone thinks he could do much better in another position. I get so tired, I am quite reluctant about sitting again. However, we intend showing it to some of our friends before we determine. How do all our friends at Saco and Topsham do? I often think of them; and Mr. Bowne and myself are talking of coming to see you next summer very seriously. How comes on the new house? We are to come as soon as ever that is finished. If you choose to send so far, I will purchase any kind of furniture you may wish, perhaps cheaper and better than you can get elsewhere. Adieu! Remember me to all the children. Dear little Mary! I can't help crying sometimes, with all my pleasures and amusements; 'tis impossible to be at once reconciled to quitting all one's friends. I thought a great deal of the children. I never thought I loved them so much. I never

pass a toy-shop or confectionery without wishing them here. How does Horatio succeed in business,—as well as he expected? How come on Father's turnpike and diking? Tell him I yesterday met a woman full broke out with the small-pox. I was within a yard of her before I perceived it. The first sensation was terror, and I ran several paces before I recollected myself. As soon as I arrived in town, Dr. Moore examined my arm, inquired the particulars, and refused to inoculate me again; that he would venture to insure me from the small-pox; that he had inoculated hundreds, and never had one take the small-pox after the kine-pox. Adieu!

Your affectionate daughter,

ELIZA S. BOWNE.

P. S.—All the family desire to be remembered particularly. Mr. B. is out to dine.

MRS. SOUTHGATE,
   SCARBOROUGH.
     (District of Maine.)

New-York, July 14, 1803.

Friend Greene, from Portland, is here, and will dine with us to-day: a fine opportunity for me to write to my friends. I have quite a packet of newspapers which I shall send by him to amuse you; they contain all the public amusements and shows in celebration of the Fourth of July. The procession passed our house, and was very elegant. In the evening we were at Davis Hall Gardens,—the entertainment there you will see by the papers. 'Twas supposed there were 4000 people there; tickets half a dollar, and 'tis said he made very little money, so you may think what the entertainment was. Indeed, there is every day something new and amusing to me. Whenever we have nothing particular in view, in the cool of the evening we walk down to the Battery, go into the garden, sit half an hour, eat some ice-cream, drink lemonade, hear fine music, see a variety of people, and return home happy and refreshed. Sunday, we dined at Mr. Delafield's, near Hell Gate, Long Island: the most superb, magnificent place I ever saw; situated directly on the East River,—the finest view you can imagine. I was delighted with our visit,—so much ease, elegance, and hospitality. I am very glad you liked your gown: long sleeves are very much worn, made like mitts,—cross-wise,—only one seam, and that in the back of the arm, and a half-drawn sleeve over, and a close, very short one up high, drawn up with a cord. I have just been having one made so. All Mrs. Delafield's daughters, even to little Caroline, no older than our Mary, had their frocks made exactly like the gown I sent you, only cut open in the back, a piece of bone each side, and eyelet-holes laced,—long sleeves, as I mentioned above, short frocks, and open behind. I should admire to be in Portland now; all the Coffin family are there. Give my best love to Mrs. Coffin and Ellen Foster; the others will have returned. I am astonished at what you say about my calling on Mrs. Sumner, and what Mrs. Coffin said. When I got to Boston, I determined to call nowhere but at Mrs. Sumner's, as my intimacy in the family

was such, and I was fearful she might not hear of my being in town, and should not see her. Accordingly, the day I got in town we went out purposely to call there; and to prevent any one calling on us (for I did not wish to see much company), we said we expected to go out of town immediately. However, there were a great many called to see me, notwithstanding. In Cornhill we met Mr. Sumner. I introduced Mr. Bowne, said we were just going to call on Mrs. Sumner, inquired how she did, etc., etc., and Mr. Sumner said they were just going out to ride, but if I would go immediately with him, I could see her. I was fearful of detaining them, and thought I should certainly see her, now she knew I was in town, and had set out to call on her; and Mr. Sumner particularly asked where we were to be found. We told him Mrs. Carter's, and parted. From that time, every time I heard the bell I supposed 'twas Mrs. Sumner.

We staid two days, and neither Mr. nor Mrs. Sumner called. I felt amazingly hurt, as so many ladies I was very little acquainted with called on me immediately. Late in the evening, before we left town, Tom Coffin called in; appeared rather formal; never mentioned Mrs. Sumner, or any reason why they did not call, nor any apology; as I could no way account for such mysterious conduct, it greatly mortified me. This is the true statement, which you may mention to Mrs. Coffin, and then ask her who has a right to feel offended. The great dinner given in honor of Uncle Rufus I have not yet mentioned. 'Twas very superb, and two hundred of the most respectable citizens of New-York attended. Mr. Bowne says, though he has been at many entertainments given in honor of particular persons, yet he never saw one that was so complimentary, and never a person conduct himself on such an occasion with such ease, elegance, and dignity in his life. He returned quite in raptures,—such insinuating manners, such ease in receiving those presented and introduced. He is an amazing favorite here. Democrats and Federalists and all parties attended; French consul on his right, English consul on his left. When Mr. Bowne went up, he held out his hand with all the ease of an old friend; without even bowing, said, "How is it, Bowne; how's your wife?"—so familiar. I went to see the tables,— very novel and elegant. There was one the whole length of the hall, and four branches from it. There was an inclosure about two feet wide filled with earth and railed in with a little white fence, and little gates every yard or two ran through the center of all the tables, and on each side were the plates and dishes. In this inclosure there were lakes, and swans swimming; little mounts covered with goats among little trees; some places flocks of sheep; some, cows lying down; beautiful little arches, and arbors covered with green; figures of Apollo, Ceres, Flora; little white pyramids with earth and sprigs of myrtle, orange, lemon; flowers in imitation of hothouse plants. Nothing could have a more beautiful effect in the hot weather. Those opposite to you were divided; their plates quite hidden. Adieu; some ladies have just called. We are going about twenty

miles to enjoy the sea, a place of fashionable resort. 'Tis intensely hot, exceeded only by Ballston Springs. We don't go to Bethlehem till the last of the month. Mr. Bowne's business detains him in the city only one or two days in a week perhaps, yet prevents a long journey just now. We ride out every day or two, go into the baths whenever we please; they have very fine public ones. Adieu. The ladies will think I am Yankee.

Love to all.

ELIZA S. BOWNE.

Sally Weeks remember me to, and all other friends. Betsey Tappan, tell her Mr. Bowne often speaks of that sweet little Miss Tappan. How comes on Father's house, Octavia? We both depend on its being finished next season. We think very seriously of coming next summer. Mr. Bowne wants to go almost as much as myself.

Love to sister; hope she is well again. Uncle Rufus told me Mr. Boyd had been very sick, but I did not mention it, lest it might alarm sister. Adieu. Love to Zelpat and Lucia. Tell Zelpat Mrs. Bogert came to see me last week, and is in hopes she will come on with her father. Remember me affectionately to all Mrs. Davis's family. I sometimes treat myself with telling my husband all about our charming frolics. Does not Mr. Davis talk anything of coming to New-York? Louise is quite a belle, I suppose.

MISS SOUTHGATE.

Bethlehem, August 9, 1803.

I intended writing before I left New-York, but was so much engaged in preparing for our journey I had no time. My great wish to see this famous Bethlehem is at length gratified. You can scarcely imagine anything more novel and delightful than everything about here, so entirely different from any place in New England. Indeed, in traveling through the State of Pennsylvania, the cultivation, buildings, and everything are entirely different from ours,—highly cultivated country, looks like excellent farmers'. Barns twice as large as the houses, all built of stone; no white-painted houses as in New England. We crossed the famous Delaware at Easton. It separated New Jersey and Pennsylvania. We saw some beautiful little towns in New Jersey likewise; but in Pennsylvania the villages look like so many clusters of jails, and the public buildings like the Bastile, or, to come nearer home, like the New-York State prison, all of stone, so strong, heavy, and gloomy. I could not bear them. The inhabitants mostly all Dutch, and such jargon as you hear in every entry or corner makes you fancy yourself in a foreign country. These Bethlehemites are all Germans, and retain many of the peculiarities of their country, such as their great fondness for music. It is delightful. There is scarcely a house in the place without a pianoforte; the postmaster has an elegant grand piano. The barber plays on almost every kind of music. Sunday afternoon we went to the young men's house, to hear some sacred music. We went into a hall which was hung round with musical instruments, and about twenty musicians of the brethren were playing in concert; an organ, two bass viols, four violins, two flutes, two French horns, two clarionets, bassoon, and an instrument I never heard before made up the band; they all seemed animated and interested. It was delightful to see these men, who are accustomed to laborious employments and all kinds of mechanics, so perfect in so refined an art as music. One man appeared to take the lead, and played on several different instruments, and, to my great astonishment, I saw the famous musician enter the breakfast-room this morning with the razor-box in his hand, to shave some of the gentlemen. Judge of my surprise, and some one mentioned he had just been fixing a watch downstairs. Yester-

day, Daddy Thomas, who is a head one, and who comes to the tavern every few hours to see if there are any strangers wish to visit the buildings, conducted us all around. We went to the schools. First was merely a sewing-school,—little children, and a pretty single sister about thirty, with her white skirt, white, short, tight waistcoat, nice handkerchief pinned outside, a muslin apron, and a close cambric cap, of the most singular form you can imagine. I can't describe it. The hair is all put out of sight, turned back before, and no border to the cap,—very unbecoming, but very singular; tied under the chin with a pink ribbon,— blue for the married, white for the widows. Here was a piano-forte, and another sister teaching a little girl music. We went through all the different school-rooms,—some misses of sixteen; their teachers were very agreeable and easy, and in every room was a piano. I never saw any embroidery so beautiful. Muslin they don't work; make artificial flowers very handsome, paper baskets, etc. At the single sisters' house we were conducted round by a fine lady-like woman, who answered our questions with great intelligence and affability. I think there were one hundred and thirty in this house; their apartments were perfectly neat. The dormitory, or sleeping-room, is a large room in the upper part of the building, with dormant opposite the whole length; a lamp is suspended in the middle of the ceiling, which is kept lighted all night, and there were forty beds, in rows, only one person in each. They were of a singular shape, high and covered, and struck me like people laid out,— dreadful. The lamp,—and altogether it seemed more like a nunnery than anything I had seen. One sister walks these sleeping-rooms once an hour through the night. We went to a room where they keep their work for sale,— pocket-books, pin-balls, toilette cushions, baskets, artificial flowers, etc., etc. We bought a boxful of things, and left them, much pleased with the neatness and order which appeared throughout. The situation of the place is delightful. The walks on the banks of the Lehigh and the mountains surrounding,—'tis really beautiful. The widows' house and young men's are similar to the one described. There were many children at the school from Georgia, Montreal, and many other places as far. There are some genteel people from Georgia at the tavern where we are, and Philadelphia. We intended leaving here for Philadelphia to-day, but it rains. We shall spend a few days there and go to Long Branch. If the alarm of the fever continues in New-York, we shall not return there again, but go in the neighborhood; send in for the trunk which I packed up for the purpose in case I feared going in the city, and set off for the Springs or somewhere else. 'Tis very uncertain when we go to housekeeping. The alarm of the fever hurried us out of town without any arrangement toward it, and may, if it continues, keep us out till middle of autumn; but, at any rate, you must spend the winter with us,—we both depend on it; you can certainly find some opportunity. Give my best love to all friends, and expect to hear from me frequently while I am rambling

about. My husband is so fond of roving I don't know but he'll spoil me. We both enjoy traveling very much, and surely it is never so delightful as in company with those we love. Only think, 'tis just a _year_ to-day since we first saw each other, and here we are, married, happy, and enjoying ourselves in Bethlehem. Memorable day! Horatio's and Frederick's _birthday_ too; mine will soon be here. I long to see you all more than you imagine; hope to next summer, and _depend_ on your spending the winter with us.

Love to Miranda when you write, and tell her I mean to write myself. Mr. B. often talks of her. Is Mr. Boyd _arrived?_ I want much to hear. Love to sister and the children. Adieu.

Affectionately,

ELIZA S. BOWNE.

MRS. SOUTHGATE,
SCARBOROUGH.

Pope and Homer; but I don't believe there can be a greater variety, more sublimity, or more beauty than are to be found on the banks of the Hudson. The Delaware did not strike me at all; I crossed it several times. We were in hopes Uncle and Aunt would come here with us, but Uncle said he must go <u>East</u> if anywhere; but he wanted to be at rest a few months now he was settled. Mrs. Codman told me she saw you all; we called a moment to see her. Mrs. Sumner has a son too. Poor Mrs. Davis, how much sickness she has. On our return from Long Branch, we went to <u>Passaic Falls</u> with a Baltimore family; had a charming little jaunt about twenty miles from New-York. The falls, the rocks, the whole scenery, partake more of the sublime, almost terrific, than Glens Falls, but not so beautiful. I am much delighted to hear of Mr. Boyd's arrival; sister must be very happy. Martha is coming this month. The fever would prevent her coming to New-York; I am sorry. Love to Mrs. Coffin. My mother is quite well, Mrs. Codman tells me. Horatio, Miranda,—there's half-a-dozen wild girls here that would romp to beat her; they are as old as you, but sad romps. We shall stay here about a week, then go to Lebanon, where I wish you to direct a letter to me immediately on the receipt of this. I want to hear much; so does Mr. Bowne. He teases me to death to write home, that we may hear from you. We depend on your coming on this winter. When we shall be to housekeeping, Heaven knows! Not even a napkin made. Just getting a woman to work, fixed the things already, when the fever came, and we all left the city. So here I am, perfectly unprepared as possible. Adieu. Tell Horatio he has more time than I have; he ought to write me immediately to Lebanon. Lebanon has been quite deserted. Poor Hannah Hamilton's mamma died three or four weeks since. The servants at the other house, where I kept last summer, wished me joy; heard Miss Southgate was married to Mr. Bowne. Oh, I have not told you,—saw the tree Major André was taken under, and the house where <u>Arnold</u> fled from, left his wife and family; indeed, 'tis the very house Maria lives in. We staid two nights there, and promised to go and see them on our return,—charming place; such fruit, 'tis delicious. In the Jerseys,—don't laugh at travelers' stories, but we really rode over the peaches in the road; we always kept our case full. William brought us some off the finest trees that hung over the road. Peaches and cream! They laugh and say Boston people cry out, "'Tis <u>so</u> good." Well, what have I written about? A little of everything but sentiment, a dash of that to complete. I am most tired of jaunting. The mind becomes satiated with variety and description, and pants for a little respite of domestic tranquillity. I've done. I have most forgot how to write sentiment. I have not had time to think since I was married. I don't expect to this two or three months; so, good-bye.

ELIZA S. BOWNE.

Lebanon Springs, September 24, 1803.

Your letter, my dear Octavia, has set my head to planning at a great rate. By all means, come on with Mr. Cutts. I am impatient to see you, and I cannot give up the pleasure of having you with me this winter. We shall be at housekeeping as soon as _possible_ after the fever subsides. My husband thinks the plan a very good one. I will write immediately to Aunt King, say that it is uncertain when you arrive; but I have taken the liberty to request Mr. Cutts to leave you with _her_ until I demand you. This settled, I proceed. Tell my good mother not to be afraid. I am as anxious as herself to be settled at home. I am most tired of roving; it begins to grow cold, and I long for a comfortable fireside of my own. What a sweet circle!—Octavia, my dear husband, and myself. When we are alone, we'll read and work like old times. I have spent a most delightful three weeks at Ballston and Lebanon. We had a charming company at Ballston; danced a few nights after I wrote you, and I was complimented as bride again,—manager brought me No. 1; quite time I was out of date. Lebanon is delightful as ever; we have a small party, ride to see the Shakers, walk, and play at billiards, work, read, or anything. Tell Mamma Eunice Loring, that was, is here. She talks a great deal of my mother and Aunt Porter; wants to see them very much, etc., etc. She is married to a Mr. Neufville, of Carolina. She is much out of health; talks of going to England in the spring. She wants to see you, as she says my mother talked of naming you for her; she wishes she had, as she has no children. The box I mentioned was full of sugar things, toys for the children, two little fans, a little frock for a pattern, and another for Isabella's children; "The Children of the Abbey" and "Caroline of Lichfield," for Mamma, —all in a package together; a letter for Mrs. Coffin, and several others. When we left New-York Mr. Bowne sent it to a commission merchant who does business for several Portland people, and requested him to send it by the first vessel. As you haven't received it, I suppose the fever, which broke out immediately after, induced him to shut up his store, or, perhaps, prevented any Portland vessel from coming near the city, and that it now lies in his store. Write me when you set out, and when 'tis probable you will be in New-

York. Direct to New-York; probably I shall be near New-York in a fortnight. I
have but a few moments to write, as the stage passes the village at eleven. You alarm me
about Ellen; pray inquire particularly and tell me all. Go to see yourself, and tell her I
can imagine no reason why I have never received a line from her since I have been in New-
York, nor Lucy Derby neither. Mrs. Coffin I wrote to, but it seems she did not receive
my letter. Love to her, and all Portland friends. I am expecting every day to hear
Martha has arrived. My best love to Sister Boyd and her husband. I wrote a line of
congratulation to her, but that too is in the package. Adieu. I shall soon see you, and
then we will talk what I have not time to write. My husband's best love.

Yours,

ELIZA S. BOWNE.

New-York,   23, 1803.

I have waited till my patience is quite exhausted. What can have kept you so long in Boston? Mr. Bowne has been at the stage office a dozen times, and I have staid at home every forenoon this week to receive your ladyship. I expect to get to housekeeping next week, and am so busy. Mercy on me, what work this housekeeping makes! I am half crazed with seamstresses, waiters, chambermaids, and everything else calling to be hired,— inquiring characters, such a fuss. I cannot possibly imagine why you are not here. I should have written immediately after receiving your letter, but Mr. Bowne was sure you would be here in less than a week. It is possible you may be in Boston to receive this; if not, you will be here or on the way. If you are troubled about a protector, Mr. Bowne says there have been several <u>married</u> gentlemen come on lately, which, if you had known of, would have been proper. Perhaps Mr. Davis may hear of some one. At any rate, come as soon as possible, for I am very impatient to see you. My best love to Louisa; tell her I should be much delighted to see her in New-York this winter. And my husband frequently says he should like to have Mr. Davis's family near us in New-York; I am sure I should, with all my heart. Say everything to Mr. and Mrs. Davis for me that bespeaks esteem. Adieu.

Yours always,

ELIZA S. BOWNE.

New-York, December 24, 1803.

My Dear Mother:

Eliza received a letter yesterday from you, where you say you have not received a letter from either of us for a long time. I am really surprised at it, as I wrote you very frequently from Boston, and am determined to let you have a letter now every fortnight, to let you know what we are doing, and whether I am happy. I begin to feel quite at home, and certainly never was happier in my life. It is true I sometimes sigh for home, but it is generally when in a crowd that I am most there in imagination. But when I am here, and none but our own family, I have not a single wish ungratified. I am much more pleased with New-York on every account than with Boston. As a city it is much superior; the situation is every way as delightful as possible. The inhabitants to me are much more pleasing: more ease, more sociability and elegance, yet not so ostentatious. They dress with remarkable simplicity, and I think I could spend the winter here and not expend half the money that I must unavoidably do in Boston. There every one dresses, and a person would look singular not to conform; but here there is such a variety, and the most genteel people dress so plain, that one never appears singular. To-morrow is Christmas, and we dine at Uncle's. He is a charming man, looks amazingly like you,—so much so that I admire to look at him. She is a very affable, pleasing woman, and they both appear to be fond of Eliza. We were at a concert last evening: the most delightful music I ever heard. We wished for Horatio all the evening. There is not much gayety, they tell me, till after the holidays.—that is, Christmas and New Year. We have been into no parties yet, but have made many sociable visits, which I very much admire. I am very much pleased with all the friends we have visited. Old Mrs. Bowne is a fine, motherly old lady. She treats Eliza with as much affection as an own mother. They all appear to be very glad to see me, and I really feel sometimes as though I were at home. How I long to see you all! How are Arexine and Mary? How I want to see them! How is Papa this winter? Ah, if you were all here! But next spring we shall all be with you. I am afraid you are solitary. If you are, do, my dear mother, tell me: find any opportunity, and I'll be with you as soon as you say. Depend on it, I shall never get so attached either to the inhabitants or the gayeties of New-York as to feel reluctant to return home: even in my happiest hours I think of the time with extreme pleasure. This family is the only thing that would root me to the spot, and there is a charm in that which nothing but home can equal. I have promised Eliza a page for you, so I suppose I must close. Give my best love to Father and the children, and believe me

Your affectionate child,

OCTAVIA SOUTHGATE.

Octavia has reserved me a page in her letter which I hasten to improve. I thank you, my dear mother, for yours, and beg you will often write me now Octavia is with me and cannot tell me about home. I am at length settled at housekeeping very pleasantly, and do not find it such a tremendous undertaking. I have been fortunate about servants, which makes it much less troublesome. The house we have taken does not altogether please us; but, at any time but May, 'tis extremely difficult to get a house. In the spring we shall be able to suit ourselves. Mr. Bowne wishes to build, and is trying to find a lot that suits him; if so, we shall build the next season. Almost everybody in New-York hires houses, but I think it much pleasanter living in one's own. I am more and more pleased with New-York; there is more ease and sociability than I expected. I admire Uncle and Aunt more and more every day, and Mr. Bowne thinks there never was Uncle's equal,— such a character as he had often imagined, though not supposed existed. I believe I sha'n't go to the next assembly; Octavia will go with Aunt King. You say Mr. Bowne must write you, and, as a subject, mention the dividends from the insurance office. In the summer there was no dividend, no profits; the next dividends will be soon. Mr. Codman thinks there will be a tolerable one. You shall hear as soon as it takes place; we have received nothing as yet. Uncle and Aunt always inquire particularly about you, and desire to be mentioned. Make my best love to all friends; kiss the children, and tell them not to forget Sister Eliza. I live in the hope of seeing you next autumn,— Heaven grant I may not be disappointed. Remember me, with my best love, to my father and all the family. Adieu. Write me soon, and believe me your affectionate

ELIZA S. BOWNE.

MRS. ROBERT SOUTHGATE

New-York, March 1, 1804.

Dear Miranda:

I have been talking of writing to you so long, that I think it is quite time I should talk no longer, but _act_; but you should not have waited for me to write. You knew both Mr. Bowne and myself would have been very glad to have heard from you,—all about your school, your acquaintance, amusements, or anything; and I have a thousand things to take up my attention that you have not. Do you return home this spring? We shall find you at home when we come. I have got one or two trifles I want to send you, but can't find an opportunity; there are so few people from our way come to New-York, that 'tis very difficult to send anything. I hear a strange story about Isabella Porter; she is a silly little girl, and, when she is older, will think she acted very foolishly. One ought to know more of the world before she decides on a thing of so much importance; she is a mere baby, and has seen nothing of life. Do you often hear of Caroline, Miranda? I feel anxious lest she should not conduct herself with as much discretion as she ought, as she never knew the blessing of having a kind, indulgent mother to watch over and guard her from harm.

When I was in Bethlehem last summer, I got some little caps such as the girls at school wear, and such as the sisters or members of the society wear. I want to find an opportunity to send them to you. Did you ever read a description of Bethlehem? If you never did, you may find one in some of the Boston magazines. We had a little book called "A Tour to Bethlehem," which, if I can find, I will send you; it will give you a very correct idea of the place, society, and customs. When I was there, there were eighty-three girls, from four to sixteen, at the school, from almost every part of the United States. They all wear these little caps, tied with a pink ribbon, which look very pretty where you see so many of them together; they learn music, embroidery, and all the useful branches of education; likewise to make artificial flowers, and many other little things of that kind. Do you ever attempt painting? 'Tis a charming accomplishment, and if you have any taste for it, I would certainly cultivate it. Write me soon and tell me when you are going home, and of anything else that interests you. Mr. Bowne often talks of you, and now desires to be particularly remembered. Adieu. Remember me to any of my friends who inquire, and believe me

Your affectionate sister,

ELIZA S. BOWNE.

MIRANDA SOUTHGATE.

32

New-York, July 23, 1804.

Octavia :

I have sent a few sugar toys to the children, which you must divide : the cradle for Mary, the basket for Arexene, etc., etc.; pair shoes apiece; two little dogs I put up in the music,—one looks like Sancho ; a little frock I send as a pattern for Miranda, Arexene, and Mary,—long or short sleeves, as you please, whalebone in the back, laced. I have sent another box of things to Isabella's children; the paper box I mean for them ; two little fans for Arexene and Mary, with their names on them, you'll find in the bottom of the box ; the two songs I send you are all I could find that struck me, for the "Death of Allen" I never heard, and bought it because it was a composition of Floyd's ; "The Wounded Hussar" I admired, and knew you could not get it set for the piano. I don't know but 'tis different from Miss Sandford's. I write in great haste. We are going to dine at Uncle Rufus's, out of town,—'tis past eleven. They have a delightful place on the North River ; took tea there last week. Mr. Bowne joins me in love to Father and Mother and all. How comes on the house, Octavia ? We want to come very much next summer. Adieu.

Yours,

E. S. B.

P. S.—I have some fine peaches and apricots on the table before me. Mr. Bowne brings me a pocketful of fruit every time he comes home. I have eaten as many as I want to, and have been thinking how much I would give to get them to you ; but this early fruit won't keep at all. I was at the theater night before last, at Mount Vernon Garden. Hodghison is a fine fellow. We commence our Southern journey in about ten days. Oh, I'm sorry ! Mr. Bowne just came to tell me the vessel has sailed. Well, I must wait for another. Love to Mary Porter, and give her the ring I enclose of my hair ; tell her I long to see her, and ask if she means to be Mary Porter when I next come to the eastward.

Love to all friends.

ELIZA S. BOWNE.

New-York, July 30, 1804.

I received your letter, my dearest mother, three days since, and every moment of my time and attention since has been taken up with our dear Eliza. I am grieved that you are so low-spirited about her, though, as you predicted, her trouble has again ended. I yet feel confident, if we can once get her home, that she will gain strength and do well. Her physician has been in great hopes that she would get through this time without any difficulty. Indeed, the first week we were in the country she was so finely that we all felt encouraged about her. She had been as prudent as possible, and she can't with any reason reflect upon herself. The last week we were there, she began to droop again, and Mr. Bowne brought her into town with an intention of carrying her to Flushing. But this accident has frustrated all his plans; but I assure you we are making more pleasant ones, for now we shall set off for home as soon as she is strong enough to travel. I am astonished at her spirits, they are as good as mine; and yet to-day she is so much better I feel finely myself. I hope with us you will rejoice that, as it <u>was</u> to take place, it did so early.

She has had no pain through the whole, but only suffers from weakness. We shall go in three or four days to Flushing, which has a fine, bracing air, and stay there a few days, till Eliza is smart enough to travel ten miles a day. I place full confidence in this journey. I am sure that the change of air and scene, and, more than all, the prospect of home, will render it truly beneficial. We are at Mr. Bowne's mother's, for we have shut our house up. She is a fine old lady, and Caroline is perfectly amiable and as attentive as possible. I am glad we are here and in the neighborhood of Mrs. Bogert, for she is all goodness. I grow more and more anxious every hour to get home. The city is quite deserted, though it never was more healthy. There are as few deaths as there were in the winter. There have been two weeks of <u>very cool</u> weather. I go wandering about and see scarcely a face I know. I used to complain last winter of our large acquaintance, and having the house full of company; but now I exclaim out half a dozen times a day, "I wish I could see some one I knew." There are gentlemen enough, but no ladies. Uncle and Aunt, I suppose, have nearly set out for Scarborough. I wish we were to be there whilst they are with you. You can have no idea how very anxious I am to return. Were

I not so much occupied, I should be positively _homesick_, but I have no time to _think_ but upon one subject. Kiss the dear children for us all, for we are equally anxious to see you. Remember me very affectionately to Sister Boyd and to the children. Before I leave here, I shall be in need of a little money. I won't seal my letter to-night, but will write you how she is to-morrow.

July 31st.

I did not finish my letter this morning, because Eliza did not feel as well as usual, but this afternoon she has taken a good dose of physic, which has had a most excellent effect. She is in charming spirits, and so very well that we are delighted. She gives her best love to you, says _she_ don't feel _at all_ obliged to you for your wishes, and is determined not to join with you. The old lady desires to be remembered, and says: "If thee was here, thee could do no more for thy child than we have." Indeed, she is the most tender, affectionate of women. My best love to my father. We are full of seeing you soon. I shall not make it long before I write again.

Yours affectionately,

O. SOUTHGATE.

Rockaway, August 24, 1804.

Dear Girls:

I enclose you a piece of Mr. Blowell's poetry on the Misses Broome's country-seat at Bloomingdale, as you both know him. I think it will amuse you. I expect Eliza and Jane Watts down here in a few days, and should be delighted if you could be here at the same time. I wrote to you, Octavia, on Monday last, a long letter; answer it soon, and tell me how far you mean to comply with my proposals. I spent several days at Flushing last week. They all inquired very affectionately for you; but I don't know but Miranda is your rival; she is a monstrous favorite among some of them. I believe Mary is engaged, and all matters settled. I met the Murrays and Mrs. Ogden at Miss Curtis's; they came up from New-York the same day we did from Rockaway. Very fortunate meeting them, for it rendered my visit doubly pleasant. 'Twas the season for peaches; we feasted finely. I shall attend to your memorandums as soon as possible. Give my best love to Horatio and Nabby, if I may be allowed to connect the names, and tell him my plan. Mr. Bowne says I must write another letter to urge it more strongly. It must be so.

Yours ever,

E. S. BOWNE.

Bloomingdale, November 2, 1804.

Mr. Bowne has just brought me a letter from you, in which you mention coming on with Mr. Wood. I am fearful my answer will arrive too late, as your letter has been written nearly a fortnight. At any rate, come on with Mr. Wood, if he has not set out. You should not wait for an answer from me. I shall be ready to receive you at any time, at housekeeping or not. We go in town next Monday,—everybody is moving in. For the last three days there has been no death, and for five, no new cases. If, unfortunately, Mr. Wood should have gone, and you not accepted of his protection, come the very next opportunity, without consulting me or waiting a moment. I hope to get to housekeeping very soon. We have just returned from Uncle's, where we had been to meet Mr. and Mrs. Paine (Mrs. Doble) from Boston. She is less beautiful than I expected,—charming little daughter. I am more and more delighted with Aunt King, she is so unaffected, easy, and ladylike. Margaret and Mr. Duncan married. I expect to hear still stranger things from Portland, now Ellen Foster is married. I _suppose_ she is, though I have not heard. I am hourly and impatiently expecting to hear from Martha. How unfortunate,—what would I give to be nearer! Adieu, 'tis late ; come as soon as possible. Give my love to all friends.

Yours affectionately,

ELIZA S. BOWNE.

Husband scolds at your waiting so. I heard of Isabella in Boston. I wrote my mother not long since how unfortunate I was in missing Martha. But I am fully determined to see Boston and Portland next summer : that in part consoles me. Ask Mary Porter to write by you, and if she wishes anything purchased, and can think of any way for it to be sent her, she may command my services at all times ; so to Sally Weeks, and all my other friends. My love to Miranda. I want to write her, but I seem to have no time. Horatio is very lazy ; he won't give me an opportunity to write home.

Again adieu.

E. S. B.

New-York, November 9, 1804.

I have been in daily expectation of a letter from you ever since my return, and none has yet come. I have not heard a word from Isabella, though I have been very anxious. The trunks arrived yesterday, with an old letter for me enclosed by Horatio in a <u>blank</u> cover; not a word to say how all the family did, particularly Isabella. We are still at our mother's, and shall probably remain a fortnight longer; the house would be ready in a few days, but we think it is too damp at present. Everybody expected you back, for the Murrays had told most of our acquaintance you were to return with me. John and Hannah Murray came to see me the day after I arrived. John rattles as usual, talks much of getting married,—his old tune, you know. He has completed his thirtieth year now since we have been gone. He says: "I begin to feel the approach of old age." Mr. Newbold called to inquire particularly after your ladyship, and Mr. Rhinelander spent last evening with us. I think he improves fast; he told me a deal of news. Miss Farquar and Mr. Jepson were married last night, Miss Blackwell and Mr. Forbes, and one or two others. Rhinelander says half the girls in town are to be married before spring,— Maria Deming for one; and the world says Amelia and James Gillispie will certainly make a match; that I was surprised at. Miss Burmmer and John Duer are married. Sally Duer is soon to be, and Fanny is positively engaged to Mr. Smith—whom you saw several times last winter—of Princetown. So you see all the girls are silly enough to give up their fine dancing days and become old matrons like myself. Mrs. Kane is in town; looks older, paler, and thinner. Oh, this having children, how it spoils every-thing! She has got a charming little girl, fat and good-natured as possible. Mrs. Ogden stays out of town all winter. We are engaged at Mrs. Bogert's this afternoon, but it storms so violently I believe I sha'n't go. She regrets very much your not coming, and Lucia she would be delighted to have. Our things arrived yesterday, but are not out of the vessel yet. At present there is no gayety, quite dull; there will be a reviving soon, I suppose. Mr. Poinsett has been to see me several mornings; he goes on Monday to Caro-

lina. Miss de Neufville spends the winter in New-York with her Aunt Stonton. I meant to call on her this morning, but it was stormy. The few days I was in Boston I was constantly engaged. We dined at Sheriff Allen's with a very large party.—Lady Temple, Mrs. Winthrop and daughters, Mrs. Bowdoin, Mrs. G. Green, Mrs. Stowton and daughter, and many others (about thirty),—and we were at Mrs. G. Blake's at a tea-party. She inquired particularly after you. She is a very fine woman, I think. Our journey on was tolerably pleasant. We arrived before Uncle and Aunt. Eliza Watts told me she had a letter from you after I left home. Adieu. Write me soon, and tell me all the news. Give my best love to Father, Mother, and all the family. I am very well, and grow fat. Everybody says I am wonderfully improved. Write me soon.

Yours ever,

ELIZA S. BOWNE.

June 3, 1805.

Dear Octavia:

Mamma arrived safe and well on Wednesday morning, to our great joy, after having a pleasant passage from Newport, staying two days in Boston, two in Newport, and one in Providence. We are going to Uncle's to dine to-day, and I can't persuade Miranda to write a line to let you know Mamma had come. Company coming in every minute, and can but just steal a moment to write. Louise is with you. I am more than half vexed that I am to be disappointed of the charming winter I had promised myself, with you and Louise to spend it with me; so you need not be surprised if I am rather ill-natured at times. The secret is out, and all your friends (beaux, I mean) walk the other side of the street when I meet them. Mary Murray called this morning; seemed rather disappointed at not having a letter. Eliza Watts thanks you for the wedding-cake, as well as myself. Give my best love to Louise, as well as all my other friends. We go over into Jersey to-morrow; E. Watts and Susan go with us,—John Wadsworth. I wish you could have been here while Mamma was. Adieu. Write me soon, and expect a longer letter as soon as I can command a little more time.

Your affectionate

E. S. BOWNE.

P. S.—Remember, I don't call this a <u>letter</u>, so no lectures on that head.

Jamaica, October 6, 1805.

I am delighted, my dear Octavia, to hear you are so finely, and the more so as I hear it from <u>yourself</u>. I did not so soon expect such fine effects from the new system of living; I am sure all will be well now. A wedding, I suppose, next; for I conclude, from the melancholy pathos with which you say you shall " neither have the independence of a married woman nor of a single," that you don't mean to try the half-way being. However, let the man tease if he will, do not think of being married until your health is perfectly confirmed.— I would not, for the world. 'Tis so late in the season 'tis not possible I can come to see you this fall, even though there should be two weddings in November. And so you talk of spending the winter with me. How you love to tantalize, and wish me to give you the pleasure of refusing me. You know I should be delighted to have you, but you know you never mean to visit New-York as Miss Southgate again. Somebody would put on a graver face than he did last fall on a like occasion, and, as he had as <u>much influence</u> then as to counteract my wishes, I won't subject myself to the mortification of another defeat now I know his power to be much greater. However, I won't ask, though I shall be very happy to have you with me. As for news, you give me more than I can you. We have left Rockaway more than a week ago, still exiled from our home by this dreadful calamity. We are at lodgings in Jamaica, where we shall probably remain until 'tis safe removing to the city. Uncle and Aunt, Mr. and Mrs. Bogert, have gone about thirty miles down the island sporting for <u>grouse</u>, and return to Jamaica until we can all go in town. Mr. and Mrs. Rogers (Cruger that was) have taken a house in Jamaica during the fever, the next door to this I lodge in. Mr. and Mrs. Hayward are with them, but leave here for Charleston this week. I am in there half of my time. We make a snug little party at <u>brag</u> in the evening frequently, and work together mornings. Mr. Bowne goes to Greenwich, where all the business is transacted, on Mondays and Thursdays, but returns the same night, so I am but little alone. As to news, Miss Charlotte Manden Heard was married last week to a <u>gentleman</u> from <u>Demarara</u>, whom nobody knew she was engaged to until he came a few weeks since and they were married. John Murray, I believe, is at last really in love, though 'tis not yet

determined whether the lady smiles or not,—a Miss Rogers, from Baltimore, whom he met at the Springs; a sweet, interesting girl, 'tis said. Wolsey Rogers and Harriet Clarke were talked of as a match at the Springs. Mrs. Kane staid at the Springs till she was so near her confinement she could not venture to ride to Providence with her mother, and the fever kept her from New-York, so she was obliged to stop at Mrs. Livingston's, Mr. Kane's sister, at Red Hook, until able to resume her journey home, which will probably be in November. Mrs. Fish has a daughter,—great joy on the occasion. Give my love to Paulina, and tell her I congratulate her on the birth of her son. What do Mary and Paulina call their boys,— Nathaniel and Enoch? I hope not; never keep up such ugly names. Mr. B. says you must spend the winter with us. He will come under bonds to somebody to return you safe. Give my best love to Sister Boyd, Horatio, and all the family at home. Has any progress been made on the new house? I am sorry to say I fear not; 'tis pity,—I had almost said 'tis wrong. I am half mortified when I hear of my acquaintance visiting Portland,—'tis true, I declare, though husband would scold me for saying so. Papa is an affectionate father, yet therein he acts not up to his character. I must check my pen; I am too much interested in this subject. Adieu. Make my compliments to all acquaintances and write me again soon. Love to Miranda; tell her Mrs. Bogert talks much of her, and remind her from me of Aunt's sleeves. Are they finished? If they are, I hope she will send them by Mrs. McKersen. I am working me a beautiful dress: it will be when 'tis done. By the bye, any purchases for the coming occasion will be executed with pleasure. Give my best love to (sister, I had almost said) Nabby, and tell her I shall feel myself flattered by any commission she will give, either in clothes or furniture. Do away with modesty in this thing, if you think I can be of any service in that way, for I assure you 'twill gratify me. Tell Horatio I am impatient to thank him for giving so pleasant an acquisition to our family, but I could do it more heartily in person in New-York, if so I might be indulged. Since you won't be honest and tell the truth, I won't tell you what I'll say to you. Do ask Papa if he could send us six or eight barrels of potatoes; there is like to be a great scarcity in New-York. Put them in the hold of the vessel or anywhere. Col. Barclay has sent to Nova Scotia for a vessel-load.

Yours, a housekeeper.

E. B.

What a romantic conclusion.

New-York, November 10, 1805.

Horatio is really married then, and we married, and I suppose the next account your ladyship will be added to the list. How swimmingly you all go on! What a tremendous marrying-place Portland is! New-Yorkers don't marry,— sad set of them. I am half angry to think you are marrying in such an out-of the-way season, that 'tis impossible any one can come to see you. However, I hope to come early in the summer, if nothing happens to prevent, and spend three or four months. I shall have so many new relations, that 'twill be necessary to come often to keep an account. Robert Murray came home quite delighted with his eastern visit, but disappointed at seeing so little of Miranda. What has been the matter with her,— anything more than a heavy cold? I wish she were here with all my heart. I am quite alone, and require a companion more than ever; but I suppose Mamma could not hear of that. I wish Arexine and Mary could have found a good opportunity to come this fall, and we could take them home in the summer; but I suppose I must be content. We have been in town since the 31st of October, the day your letter was dated. It has been a long time in coming; I got it only last evening. Mr. Bowne had found out Captain Libby, and we were preparing to send the sheeting and diaper by him; he sails the last of the week. The other things you wish we will send, as many as can be procured before the vessel sails; but 'twill be impossible to get any plate made to send for several weeks. We will order it immediately, and as it will not be bulky, there will probably be no difficulty in finding a conveyance. We made a sketch of the articles you wished and of the prices, which cannot be very incorrect, as I took them all from our own furniture book, and we calculated that the whole of Mamma's plate, and another suit of curtains for Nabby included, would come at about four hundred dollars. Mr. B. has three hundred and forty in his hands of Papa's, about the sum that would buy all the things but Mamma's plate and Nabby's curtains. However, that makes not the least difference to Mr. Bowne, as he desires me to say he shall execute the commissions with great pleasure, and 'twill be no inconvenience to him to purchase the other articles; and I merely mentioned it as I did not know that you knew the real sum in Mr. Bowne's hands. 'Tis very lucky there is so direct an opportunity to Scarborough; we shall endeavor to send as many things as possible. Shopping at present is a prohibited pleasure to me; but as all

the things can be better procured at wholesale stores, and my husband has both a great deal of taste and judgment in those things, and makes better bargains than I do, you will be no sufferer by the loss of my services in that; and I can have anything sent to me to look at, and therefore 'tis quite as well as if I went for them. I don't mean you shall understand because I don't go shopping I am confined to the house; on the contrary, I am much better than could be expected, and hope with care to do very well. I shall go out very little until the middle or the last of the winter, when I hope, if I continue well, to be most as smart as other people. My husband does not allow me to go into a shop. I laugh at him, and tell him I don't believe but the health of his _purse_ is _one-half_ his concern,— a fine excuse! Mrs. Bogert is in expectation of seeing Lucia Wadsworth when the general comes on. You never told me what became of Zilpah's expectations. Mrs. Kane has another daughter,— in eight days after she left the Springs. Only think, she was a tremendous figure to sit down at table with an hundred people. She got in town on Tuesday. I have not seen her, as I have been confined to the house with a severe cold since Thursday. Friday and Saturday was quite sick, and to-day feel unfit for anything almost but my bed. Adieu. My best love to all the family. You mentioned nothing of the cipher on the plate: O. S., or B., or your crest, or William's crest,— if you can find them out: I suppose we could here,— or what? Mamma's, I suppose, will be S. only. I have great mind to tell you what a saucy thing my husband said on your anxiety that the bowls and edges of the spoons should not be sharp.— but I leave you to guess; or, if you can't, perhaps William may help you to an explanation.

Adieu. Yours ever,

E. S. BOWNE.

MISS OCTAVIA SOUTHGATE.

November 14, 1805.

Capt. Libby sails to-morrow. We have got as many things as possible. There is not a piece of embossed buff in New-York, nor of plain either. There is not more than two pairs alike; therefore I have done nothing about the trimmings. I fancy Boston is a better place for those things than New-York. The most fashionable beds have draperies the same as my dimity window-curtains. However, if you think best, I will look farther, and perhaps there will be something new open in a week or two. There is but one barrel urn in the city. Mr. B. was two days in pursuit of one; he purchased this and sent it back,—'twas brown, and no plate on it except the nose. I can get you one like mine for twenty-five dollars. Let me know immediately respecting these things. Yesterday the silversmith came for instructions respecting the plate, and brought patterns for me to look at. I ordered a set of tea-things for Mamma, the same as mine. I think them handsomer than any I see. The man is to send me some patterns to look at, which he thinks are similar to your description. On the next page I will make a list of the goods and prices copied from the bills.

1 piece Irish sheeting, 48 yards at	5	.	$30.00
1 piece " " 55 "	"	6,6.	44.69
6 yards fine linen	"	7 6.	5.62
12 Damask napkins	"	8/.	12.00
1 piece fine diaper, 27 yards	"	5 6.	18.56
2 breakfast cloths	"	14. .	3.50
1 plated castor, best kind. . . .			12.00
1 plated cake-basket, silver rims			18.00
2 pearl tea-pots, $2.25: 1 trunk, $2.50.			4.75
			$149.12

The sheeting is quite as cheap as mine; the fine I like very much, and think it quite a bargain. The diaper is not quite so cheap as mine, but it has risen; the table-cloths

are cheap; the linen is high, I think.   The cake-basket is very cheap,— two dollars; cheaper than mine and rather handsomer, I think.   I could get no crimson marking, but send you a few skeins of cotton which I procured with great difficulty.   The napkins are not the kind I wished, but there were none of those excepting at two places, and they were eighteen to twenty-two shillings apiece.   I thought these pretty, and would answer your purpose.   I enclose the marking-cotton and the key of the trunk.

Adieu.   Yours ever,

E. S. BOWNE.

P. S.— The bills are in Miranda's book in the trunk.

New-York, March 30, 1806.

My Dear Mother:

I am most impatiently looking for Miranda, and hoping, though I dare not place too much dependence on seeing my father. I am better than when I wrote you before, though still subject to these faint turns. I have become more used to them, and they don't alarm me. I ride frequently and take the air every fine day in some way or other. I have been free from a return of the nervous headache for a fortnight till the night before last I had a return of the numbness and pain, though not so severe as the last. The physician says I have got on safe ground now, though I may frequently be very uncomfortable. I look forward with impatience to have it all happily over. I have a very good appetite, and look very fat and rosy, but really am very weak and languid. I don't know why I look so much better than I feel. Mary Murray is to be married a week from next Wednesday; she is very desirous that Miranda should get here. I really hope she may. Perhaps I may get courage enough to go myself if she come in time; otherwise, I don't believe I shall venture. However, 'twill depend upon my feelings at the time. I shall look out the last of the week for Papa and Miranda very seriously. I hope they are on their way now. Uncle's oldest son, John Alsop, arrived here about a week since; he seems a very fine young man, rather taller than his father. He will be a second Uncle William, for he does not appear to have got his height. Charles has gone to Holland.

E. S. B.

MRS. MARY SOUTHGATE.

New-York, April 27, 1806.

My Dear Mother:

Before you receive this, my father will be with you. He says I need not fear anything, that I am in a very fair way of doing well. He will tell you all the particulars better than I could write. He got quite home-sick; we could not prevail on him to lengthen his visit, or go to the Springs and return here. I promised to let you hear from me once a week how I got along. For the last three days I have been finely for me. The fore part of the day I am often very faint,—all the forenoon, but generally better toward evening. 'Tis a great comfort to me to have Miranda with me, as I am a great part of the time unfit for anything. My head has been much more clear and comfortable for the last few days than for some time past. I am so glad to get along so far, that it prevents me from being impatient for the time. You shall hear immediately when there is any change, and some of us will write once a week at any rate. Tell Father there was a meeting called last evening of the Federalists in the city, to make some further remonstrances on the defenseless state of the port of New-York, occasioned by an accident that has set the whole city in an uproar. There are three British frigates at the Hook, a few miles from the city, that fire upon all the vessels that come in or go out, and search them. They have sent several on to Halifax, and yesterday they fired in a most wanton manner upon a little coaster that was entering the harbor with only three men on board, and before they had time to come to, as they were preparing to do, they fired again, and killed one of the men dead upon the spot. He was brought up, and the body exposed to view on one of the wharves, where several thousand people were collected to see it. It put the city in great confusion, and this meeting was called in consequence, where Uncle made a very eloquent speech. I am very sorry Father had not been here; it would have gratified him. 'Tis the first time he has spoken in public since his return to this country. The British consul had sent several boats of provisions down to the frigates, which, as soon as 'twas known, the pilot-boats went after and brought them all back. They were loaded upon carts, and carried in procession through the streets to the poor-house, attended by a prodigious mob huzzaing, and the English and American colors fixed on the carts. They demanded the commander of the frigate to be given up as a murderer by the British consul. He replied he had no power over him. It has made a prodigious noise in the city, as you may imagine. So much for Father. I shall expect to hear to-morrow when he got to Providence. Adieu, my dear mother.

Ever your affectionate

E. S. BOWNE.

To Miss Miranda Southgate.

New-York, May 18, 1806.

By way of punishment, if it is any, I have denied myself the pleasure of answering your letter till I thought you would begin really to wish for a letter. However, I quite want to hear again, and as there is little hope of that until I answer yours, I'll e'en set about it at once. William Weeks told me he saw you in Portland the day before he left there. I wonder he did not tell you he was coming to New-York. Mr. Isaac McLellan is here too from Portland. You did not write to me half particulars; you said nothing about Arexine.

Sunday, May 25.

After a week has elapsed I resume my pen to finish my letter. I was expecting Mr. Isaac McLellan to call and let me know when he should return, as I intended writing by him; but he has left town without my knowing it. Now for news, which I suppose you are very anxious to hear. In the first place, Miss Laurelia Dashway is married to Mr. Hawkes. On Saturday morning, eight o'clock, Trinity Church was opened on purpose for the occasion; something singular, or it would not be like Miss Laurelia. But what do you think? Mr. Grellet has taken French leave of New-York; sailed for France about a fortnight ago, without anybody's knowing their intention until they were gone. There are many conjectures upon the occasion not very favorable to the state of their finances. 'Tis said his friends were very averse to her going with him. If she had not, I suspect she must have sympathized with Madame Jerome Buonaparte and many other poor madames that have founded their hopes on the fidelity of a Frenchman. Poor Mrs. Ogden has another little petticoated little John Murray,—four daughters! I am sorry it was not a boy. What should you think to see me come home without Mr. Bowne? I strongly fear he won't have it in his power to leave the office more than once in the season; if so,

I would much prefer him to come for me in the autumn. However, we have made no arrangements yet. Walter grows such a playful little rogue, he is always in mischief. I am just leaving off his caps. I want his hair to grow before his grandmamma sees him; he won't look so pretty without his caps. He creeps so much, I find it impossible to keep him so nice as I used to. Poor Harriet Brain, I think, is going rapidly in a decline; she has been confined to her room five or six weeks. I have not seen the Wattses this some time. They are gone to Passaic Falls with a little party.—Maria Laight, Mr. Delort, Robert Harney, etc. My love to all; write me soon particularly. I hope soon to be with you. How is Sister Boyd's infant?

Yours ever,

E. S. BOWNE.

New-York, Spring, 1806.

My Dear Mother:

I find it quite in vain to wait for a letter from Miranda, and she has left me to chance and uncertainty to know whether she has ever arrived at Providence; but luckily, from constant inquiries, I have learnt she did arrive safe, and, from some other accidental information, that she was to leave Boston last Thursday for home with Judge Thatcher. I presume by this she is with you. As the spring opens, I begin to look forward to my eastern visit. I can't make up my mind to wean my child; but they tell me 'twill never do to wean him in warm weather. If I don't do it now, I must nurse him till October: that is too long. I would not hesitate to nurse him through the summer if I thought I was hearty enough. Octavia's boy is as beautiful as a cherub, I hear,—Miranda, Saturday, 18th. Mrs. Derby has returned from Philadelphia, and intends leaving here for Boston on Tuesday. She spent a long, sociable day with me yesterday, and I found it quite a treat. I have seen so little of her but in mixed parties that it hardly seems like a visit. She is almost worn out with dissipation, and I greatly fear her constitution has suffered an injury from this kind of life it will never recover. She has absolutely refused all invitations since her return, and means to rest for a few days while she remains here. She takes one of our belles on to Boston with her,—Miss Fairlie. Miranda knows her. Martha had a letter from Mrs. Sumner yesterday, where she mentions Miranda leaving there for home the Sunday before with Mr. and Mrs. Kinsman. I am really hurt at her unaccountable silence. I promised to tell her all the news and account of all the parties after she left me, but I was quite provoked at her not writing. Tell her, however, that there seems no end to the gayety this spring: it does not abate as yet at all. The day after she left me, I paid the bride's visit to young Mrs. Murray; there was a prodigious crowd, a hundred and fifty at least, and many never sat down at all. Madame Moreau wore a long black velvet dress with pearl ornaments, looking elegantly. The next day I dined at Uncle's with company; on Tuesday following went to a ball at Mrs.

Stevens's, next day a ball at Miss Murray's; very pleasant. They regretted her not being here very much; she was intended to be one of the brides-maids, and the day after the last assembly, as you may suppose, was completely tired dancing three nights in succession. Last Friday I was at a ball at the Watts's, and the week before at Miss Lyde's to a ball, and Mrs. Turnbell's to a monstrous tea-party. Yesterday at Mrs. Morris's. On Monday next Aunt King has a very large party. On Tuesday I go to Mrs. Stoughton's, on Thursday to Mrs. Hopkins's, and on Friday dine at Mrs. Bogert's; and this evening to Mrs. Henderson's to a _ball._ I think it will be one of the most elegant we have had this winter. I wish Miranda were here,—so much for Miranda. Adieu! I have promised to go shopping with Mrs. Derby this morning, and 'tis growing late. I look forward with delight to the approaching summer spent amidst all my family. Give my affectionate regards to all.

Ever yours,

E. S. BOWNE.

New-York, November 8, 1806.

My Dear Octavia,

 I am quite anxious to hear good news from you ; keep up a good heart, 'tis soon over. I wish I could send you my darling boy to look at. I am sure he would make you think no price was too much for such a little cherub, and I am so proud of making such a fine nurse. He is a hardy little creature, and so lively and playful : cries after his father, and has so many winning ways that I am amused all day with him. He is as quiet as a lamb ; sleeps in his crib all night, and never cries in the night. As for myself, I am so hearty, feel so active and light,— indeed, I never was better in my life. Have milk enough for my child, and am happier than ever I was in my life : so much for encouragement. Miranda has been in Jamaica this fortnight. She has taken a frock and cap along with her to work for you. I hope she will have it finished when she returns. Mary Perkins will be confined in January ; she says you did not suspect her at all. Mary Parsons is not going to have any. I believe she has been married as long as you have. A sad disappointment, for her husband is the only one of the name ; it dies with him. Maria Deming is married, and William has returned to New Orleans : left her with her friends for the winter. Amelia was married to Mr. Gillespie in the spring,— lives at home yet. Miss Pell was married last week to Robert MacComb ; they are making a prodigious dash. I went to pay the bride's visit on Friday. They had an elegant ball and supper in the evening, as it was the last day of seeing company. Seven brides-maids and seven bridemen ; most superb dresses ; the bride's pearls cost fifteen hundred dollars. They spend the winter in Charleston. Adieu. Love to all friends, and tell your husband to write me immediately after this great event. I am looking forward to a happy summer spent among you. Best love to Isabella and family, Horatio and family. How is Robert Southgate, Jr. ? That is as it ought to be. Papa is pleased, I dare say.

Yours ever,

ELIZA S. BOWNE.

New-York, January 24, 1807.

My Dear Miranda :

Mr. Abbot is here from Brunswick, and will take letters for me to any of my friends. I should not have been surprised any more to have seen the cupola of the college itself walk into the room than I was to see Mr. Abbot. I could hardly believe my eyes, but I could not but know him, as I know nobody like him ; he always seems like a frightened bird,— so hurried in his manner and conversation. How much he looked like some of Timothy Dexter's wooden men at Commencement last year,— it came across my mind while he was sitting by me yesterday; 'twas well I was alone, or I should have certainly laughed. Frederic, I suppose, is at home ? though Mr. A. could not tell me. John and Charles King have some thought of going to Portland. I have told them they had better go some other time, as they will find Portland so dull, and none of you in quite so good spirits. James is here, and they return with him. You ask about Jane Watts,— sees nobody : she is entirely confined to her room. Doctor Burchea attends her now. Her cough they think a little better, but she is not able to sleep at all without laudanum. I have no expectation she will recover; the family seem to have.

As to news, New-York is not so gay as last winter; few balls, but a great many tea-parties. I believe I told you Mrs. Gillespie has a daughter ; and still more news. Mary Parsons expects an heir in May. Sammy looks as smiling as a basket of chips. 'Tis a prodigious fine thing; they are all mightily pleased with it. You never wrote me anything about the muslin for Arexine to work her a frock ; 'tis so good an opportunity to send it, that I have a great mind to get it not withstanding. If youcan, send the things I left to Louisa Davis, in Boston : John and Charles would bring them on to me. Walter will want the shirts as soon as the weather becomes warm. You say I have said nothing of Walter in any of my letters. He is so hearty and well I hardly thought of him when I wrote : he has not had a day's sickness since I returned. I send him out walking frequently when 'tis so cold it quite makes the tears come ; he trudges along with leading very well in the street : he never takes cold, though he walks in our damp streets

without a diaper, for he has not worn one since I returned. He goes to bed at six o'clock, away in the room in the third story you used to sleep in, without fire or candle, and there he sleeps till Phœbe goes to bed to him. You know I am a great enemy to letting children sleep with a fire in the room. 'Tis the universal practice here, and as long as I can avoid it, I never mean to practice it : it subjects them to constant colds. They think I am very severe to suffer such a child to be put in the third story to sleep without a fire. Mary Parsons still nurses her boy : he is a fat, hearty fellow, and I think improves. Nabby is not yet confined. I presume Aunt King and family are all well ; they are going to have a fine waffle party on Tuesday. I wish you were here to go, for the boys want to have a fine frolic. Kitty Bayard is to be married in April to Duncan Campbell. All engaged since Wolsy and Susan were married. Mary is engaged to the big Doctor Romaine,— that is quite a surprise to every one. This is rumor. And now I have written all the trifling, I come to what is nearer my heart. You are not half particular enough about Octavia. Does Isabella live in the same house she did when we were there ? Has Octavia nobody with her to take care of her child ? I am very glad to hear they are so cheerful. Papa, you say, has been sick, but is quite recovered. How is Mamma this winter,—quite recovered her health ?

Adieu.

E. S. B.

To Miss Miranda Southgate.

New-York, December 1, 1807.

You won't write a line, I find, without a punctual answer, letter for letter. Could you not make any allowance for domestic engagements, etc., etc., and write me at present two for one, or were you afraid of the precedent I might claim as a right hereafter what I owed merely to your indulgence? I have anxiously wished to hear again from little William, for notwithstanding your flattering accounts of his returning health, I felt so fully persuaded he would never recover that I could not but think he would relapse again. How happy I shall be to hear that my fears are groundless. If you have not written again before this reaches you, lose no time, but write at once. I do not write to Octavia till I know whether she is in Boston or Portland. You must make it a rule, Miranda, to write me once a fortnight, whether I answer or not. Charles will tell you all the news of the fashionable world. I have been in no parties yet. The theater is quite the rage. I have been several times. You have no idea how much it is improved; entirely altered.— looks light and gay,—a perfect contrast to its former appearance. Cooper draws crowded houses every night. I have been much delighted. Mr. Wolsey Rogers's approaching nuptials seem anticipated as the opening of the winter campaign. Of course the event is much talked of; not a mantua-maker in the city but will tell you some particulars of the bride's wardrobe, length of her train, etc., etc. A fine lady here, as Mustapha says, is estimated by the length of her tail. If it were not for using a most homely proverb, I would say, "Every dog has his day." Here was our friend John Murray and his bride last winter, making all ring; this winter quietly settled in Nassau street, just what I call comfortable. (You have not seen this new play about comfortable.) Poor Sterlitz, who has no way to discover his taste or judgment but by finding fault with everything, seems quite in a <u>fuze</u> (is there such a word?) that Mr. Murray prefers his own comfort to dashing in high style, and, in his own language, wonders that a man that has seen so much of the world should so soon get into a <u>humdrum family way</u>. By the bye, you must know this is <u>not</u> the case in more than <u>one</u> sense; quite a trouble I suppose. Mrs. Bogert begins to feel all the palpitations and trepidations of a doting anxious mother in introducing her favorite daughter to the world. The next winter is

the all-important era for the exhibition. Miss Arma, in my opinion, will make a little coquette; the bud seems expanding even now,— that extreme simplicity, which her mother encouraged by always talking of it before her, as if she were too young to understand, is now changing for an affectation of simplicity. I hope she will correct it; time will convince her that simplicity is only charming in inexperienced youth,— or rather the kind of simplicity which she possesses. There is a simplicity which gives a softness, a tone, as a painter would say, to the whole character, but it springs uncontaminated from the guileless purity of the mind. All affectation of this serves but as a tattered veil through which you constantly penetrate to the original deformity. Where have I rambled? Poor Mrs. Greene is dangerously ill; her friends have little hope of her recovery. On Saturday she was not expected to live the day; bled several quarts at the lungs. She is a favorite with all who know her; a most valuable woman. On business: Mamma told me something about getting muslin for Arexine,— a frock to work,— but I have forgotten whether she afterward told me to get it or not. I can get very pretty for two dollars or two and a half. Let me know. Tell Octavia I received the little hat which Mr. Brown bought for me in Boston, and shall send the little tub and the rest of the money as soon as I know she is in Boston. Fashions: Ladies wear fawn-colored cloth coats and bonnets of the same, trimmed with velvet trimming, same color, with lappels, cape, and inner waistcoat. If I could find an opportunity, I should send you a bonnet and Mamma a cap. Adieu. Tell Arexine to write to me. James writes to Charles he liked Arexine best of all the cousins.

ELIZA.

New-York, December 13. 1807.

I have been waiting some time to hear you were in Boston, but as I have not heard from any of the family for some weeks. I shall write you and direct to Portland. I am rejoiced to hear that little William continues to recover fast, for Mrs. Derby writes me, still later than Miranda, that he is almost recovered. How happy you must feel! None but those who have suffered the anxiety can conceive the happiness of such a change. I don't hear half often enough from you : Miranda writes but seldom. Charles told me last evening, in his last letter from her she says she is going to spend part of the winter in Boston with you. From that I conclude you intend going to house-keeping before spring. I have been making a plan for you to make me a visit next spring. I think there can be no objection to it ; your husband can make arrangements to leave Boston for a month or a few weeks, I am sure. The accommodations in the stage to Providence are so good you can go in half a day, take passage in a packet, and be in New-York in three days with ease. You can either bring William with you, which I should wish you to, or leave him, if you prefer it. Indeed, I can see no objection to the plan. To be sure, <u>married</u> ladies are liable to so many interruptions to their plans that one can hardly calculate five or six months forward ; but no particular circumstance to prevent, I shall certainly look for you. Your friends in New-York have made particular inquiries respecting you. Mary Murray says you have quite given her up ; that she has not received a line from you for some time, I don't remember how long. I believe I told you Mrs. Ogden had lost her youngest child, about five months old. Harriet Beam, whom I believe you knew, died last week ; melancholy, so young. Mrs. Derby writes me her father is still far from strong and firm, though much better ; very probably his constitution will never entirely recover this shock. I was quite surprised to find Mrs. Codman expects an addition to her family :- her youngest child must be seven years old. I am much obliged to Mr. Brown for pur-chasing the little hat for Walter. It was not the kind I meant, however ; those here are worn only by girls,— square crowns altogether for boys. Give my best love to Horatio and Nabby, Isabella and husband, Arexine. I want to send her a pattern to work a frock in. I have a very pretty one, with but little work on. Adieu. Write me very particularly about William.

E. S. BOWNE.

New-York. January 13. 1808.

I have been in daily expectation of hearing further from you, my dear Miranda. I received a letter from Octavia by the same mail that brought me yours, informing me of the melancholy change in their prospects, which I answered immediately, and used every argument I thought could console her at such a time. Her firmness and resolution in relating the particulars, her reasoning on the subject, displayed the real superiority of her mind. She has had severe trials,— the danger of her child, and now this stroke. I tremble when I think with how much less firmness I should probably have acted in the same trials. I am extremely anxious to hear all the particulars of their failure; how Mr. Brown bears it; where they will spend their winter. I wish with all my heart Octavia and her child would come and stay with me until Mr. Brown could arrange his affairs a little, but I suppose 'twould be in vain to urge her to leave her husband at this time. You mention that you were in hopes Papa would secure Octavia's furniture for her. I wish you would write me particularly if he did. Octavia writes me he attached all the personal property he knew of at the time; Papa, too, I fear, will be quite a sufferer by their failure. I hear Webster is gone ; he, I think, had money of my father's. Mr. Bowne has always thought he played rather a hazardous game in letting out money in that way. I hope he is not materially injured; he will, at any rate, have the consolation to know that the education of his children is principally accomplished. He will always have enough to live with comfort and ease, and as to leaving a great deal, I think 'tis immaterial. I am glad to find his stock here has produced a very good dividend this month. I hope this won't depress his spirits any; old people feel the loss of property much more than younger ones. However, Papa's is nothing to mention at these times, as he is not in debt, has a good farm, and will always have all the comforts of life,— indeed, I think 'twill have a good effect. He has always been determined on leaving such a sum untouched, and because of that darling object has deprived himself of the comfort of a comfortable house for many years past. Accident has interfered with the fulfillment of his plan ; he will now enjoy

what he has left without thinking of leaving just so much.   His children are, or
soon will be, grown up, and he ought to have no other care, but to enjoy now, in
his old age, what he has dearly earned.   I am sure all his children most heartily
wish it, if he should not leave a farthing for them.   Old Mr. Codwise has failed;
a dreadful thing for so old a man.   Mr. Macomb (Ann and Robert's father) is
gone too; all the Franklins too, and a great many others I do not recollect.   Adieu.
Write me immediately, and tell me every particular.   My love to Arexine.   Is she
at Miss Martin's, for I have never heard *

E. S. BOWNE.

MISS MIRANDA SOUTHGATE.

February 15, 1808.

Octavia:

    I must hear all the important events of the family from anybody who casually may have it in their power to communicate them. Horatio has a fine son, I hear, of which I am very glad; congratulate them for me. Do they mean to call him the same name as their other little boy? I suppose you have heard from John and Charles since they have been in Boston. If you would send the little bundle for them to bring on, I should be very glad, and I wish you to get me three pairs of Mr. Smith's little white worsted socks, such as I bought for Walter, only two or three sizes larger, big enough for him next winter. Don't neglect it, for I wish for them very much. Let them be full large for a child three years old. How are all the family? Octavia, I don't hear from anybody: you ought to write once a fortnight certainly. Poor Jane Watts is very low, confined to her bed. I fear she will never go out again. Love to all. This is my second letter since I heard from you. I write more particularly that you may send those things by the boys.

Yours ever,

E. S. B.

Boston, December 21, 1808.

My Best Friends:

In consequence of a letter from Mr. Bowne, received this day, I have to inform you that instead of proceeding to Scarborough, my next journey is to New-York. He writes me that by the advice of Mr. King, they have concluded it will be best for Eliza to go to Charleston, South Carolina, in order to avoid the severity of our winter; that he is under the necessity of remaining in New-York till February himself, and that he wishes me to return and go on with Eliza and Octavia as soon as I can. As I have nothing of consequence to prevent me, I shall leave here in a day or two for New-York, and shall be fully satisfied if I can render them the least service by my attentions. With sentiments of the brightest esteem and regard,

I am, your obedient servant,

W. BROWN.

TO MR. AND MRS. ROBERT SOUTHGATE.

New-York, December 27, 1808.

You are anxious, my dear mother, to hear from my own hand how I am. Octavia has told you all my complaints: my cough is extremely obstinate, I have occasionally a little fever, though quite irregular, and sometimes a week without any. I have a new physician to attend me; he is a Frenchman of great celebrity, particularly in pulmonary complaints, and has been wonderfully successful in the cure of coughs. He keeps me on a milk diet, but allows me to eat eggs and oysters; he does not give any opiates,—paregoric and laudanum he entirely disapproves of; he gives no medicine but a decoction of roots and flowers,—the <u>Iceland moss</u> or <u>lichen</u> made in a tea he gives a great deal of, and for cough I take a white pectoral lotion, he calls it, made principally of white almonds, gum arabic, gum tragacanth (or something like it), the syrup of muskmelon seeds. He thinks I am much better already. I have no pain at all, and have not had any. My cough seems to be all my disorder. He thinks he can cure that; indeed, he speaks with perfect confidence, and says he has no doubt as soon as I get to warmer weather my cough will soon leave me. Mr. Brown got here last night, and we shall probably sail by Sunday at farthest. Octavia will write particularly. You will hear from me, my dear mother, often. At present my mind seems so occupied leaving my children, preparing to go, and making arrangements to shut up my house. 'Tis quite a trial to leave my little ones; I leave them at their grandmother's. My little Mary has a wet nurse: she is a fine, likely child and thrives fast. Adieu, my dear mother. I did not think I could have written half as much. Love to all my friends.

ELIZA S. BOWNE.

Charleston (South Carolina), January 1, 1809.

Our Most Esteemed Friends:

We have now been in the city a week. We find that Eliza has gained a little strength since she arrived, and that her cough is not quite so distressing as before we left New-York. She complains of no pain, but her fever and night-sweats continue to trouble her every other day and night, as was the case before. She can walk about her room with ease, and she rides when the weather is fine, which she is much pleased with, and no doubt it is of great service to her. The streets are entirely of sand, as smooth as possible, no pavements, not a stone to be seen, which renders it very easy riding for her. It is as warm as our first of May (if not the middle), and when the weather is fair, the air is clear, very mild, and refreshing. The change is so great between here and New-York, that I cannot help thinking it must have a great and good effect on Eliza. I find, as to myself, that my cough is done away with entirely, and I had a little of it most all the time at home in winter. Octavia has certainly grown fat, and our little Frederic is very well indeed. Eliza eats hominy, rice and milk, eggs and oysters cooked in various ways, vegetables too, which we find in great perfection here; fruit is plenty, of almost every description. The oranges raised here are not sweet, but are very large. Their olives, grapes, and figs are excellent. Their meats and fish are not so good as ours. Their poultry is fine; a great plenty of venison, wild ducks, and small sea fowl. Green peas we shall have in about a month, so that beside the change of climate, we have many of the luxuries of a Northern summer. Uncle King gave us letters to Gen. C. C. Pinckney and his brother, Major Thomas Pinckney. Both of them being out of town, at their plantation, their sister, Mrs. Hovey, received the letters, and has been very attentive and kind to us all. She is a widow, about fifty-five, I judge, of the first respectability, and appears a very pleasant, amiable, and cheerful old lady. She sends some nice thing to Eliza almost every day. Her daughters, Mrs. Rutledge, two Misses Pinckney (daughters of the general), Mrs. Gilchrist and daughter, Mr. and Mrs. Manigaults, Mrs. Middleton, Mr. and Mrs. Izard, Mr. and Mrs. Dessasue, and Mr. Heyward make an extensive acquaintance for us. They all seem very kind and hospitable to us; plain and open in their manners, and yet the most genteel and easy. Eliza has seen only Mrs. Hovey

Mrs. Rutledge, and the two Misses Pinckney yet, but she thinks in a few days to be able to receive short visits from a few of her friends, and even thinks it may be of consequence to enliven her. She rides whenever the weather is fine, and is very much pleased with the appearance of everything growing in the gardens here so like our June. We have had one visit from a physician only; he thinks taking a little blood from her would be of service, but she has not yet consented. He approved of her diet and of the Iceland moss tea which was recommended at New-York, and which is said here to have had a great effect in removing complaints of the cough. Mrs. Manigaults told us yesterday she found immediate relief from it after she had been sick a long time. We expect Mr. Bowne in the course of a fortnight, and then I expect to return toward Scarborough immediately. We hope to hear from you in a few days; not a word have we yet from New-York since we arrived. Our darling boy we think we see every day playing about us, without thinking who admires him at the distance of eleven hundred miles.

Our best wishes attend you always.

Affectionately,

W. BROWN.

ROBERT SOUTHGATE, ESQ.

Charleston, January 22, 1809.

Monday Night.

Eliza has had a poor day: she thinks it is owing to some little cold. She had a hard chill in the morning, succeeded by considerable fever, headache, and sick stomach: poor appetite.

Tuesday.

Last night Doctor Irvine gave her a powder to take on going to bed, which, apparently, had a good effect: she coughed less on going to bed, and instead of having a violent burning in her feet and hands as usual, it put her into a gentle perspiration, which was not, as usual, succeeded by a more profuse one. She ate her breakfast with a better relish than common. She raised more than usual in the course of the forenoon, a thick yellow matter, but very easy. She had a slight chill, but very little fever: ate her dinner with more appetite, but was extremely sick at her stomach all the afternoon and evening. She has had a bad spell of coughing since she has been in bed this evening.

Wednesday.

Another poor night: coughed a great deal, but I think less fever and sweating than usual. She has, almost regularly, a chill about eleven o'clock, which lasts two hours: nails as purple as possible. At this time her stomach is much distressed, and she complains of the headache. As the chill goes off she is sick at her stomach, and very faint: and yet her stomach, she thinks, is not foul. Her circulation is extremely languid. I rub her feet and legs once or twice in the course of a day. They are very cold, seem a little swelled on the instep. 'Tis not a good day for her,— raw and chilly.

Mrs. Rutledge has been here, and says if to-morrow is pleasant, she will come for us to ride. Mr. Brown is sick to-day. He is afraid 'tis the fever and ague, but hope 'tis only a common cold. I have been first in one room then the other all day. Frederic was never more fretful, poor fellow. I am afraid he, too, will get sick. My spirits almost gave out to-day,—all sick among strangers; but I am wrong. Never was there such a friendly set of beings as these Charleston people. Every day they are sending some nice thing for Eliza. Our dear, good friend Mrs. Hovey has gone to the country. Much indeed do we miss her; but she has left behind her her excellent daughter, Mrs. Rutledge. We find her, though not as sensible and dignified as her mother, quite as amiable and kind.

Thursday.

Eliza had a better night last night; coughed a good deal, but slept more, and had less fever and sweating. She had her fever, however, at eleven o'clock, but has had but little fever. She was extremely faint and sick about one. The afternoon and evening she has passed pretty comfortably. Moved into a more pleasant room; exchanged a north for a south room. She is much pleased with it. She has taken another powder to-night. I hope it will have as good an effect as the other had.

Friday.

Eliza had a tolerable night; her cough easier, her fever and night-sweats less than they were last week, but her stomach out of order, sick and sour; chill and fever as usual. I am convinced 'tis this fever and ague which keeps her down so; it is regular every day.

Saturday.

Her cough is easier, she raises rather more, cough don't distress her, less burning in her hands, but more on her face. Dr. Irvine sent her some quassia to take in the morning before her chill comes on. She took it to-day without effect, but he says she ought to have taken three wine-glasses instead of one. This evening she has taken an emetic ipecac, divided in four parts, taken every ten minutes. She was not sick at all till she took the last one, which she threw directly up. It operated three times, brought up a good deal of bile. After it had done so, it distressed beyond everything I ever saw. We had to get her to bed, and I really was frightened, she looked so distressed. I gave some Hoffman's drops, which in the course of an hour composed her to sleep. I

wish her doctor had seen the operation of this emetic; it certainly operated very hard upon her, and relieved her but little. She has now a little gruel, and sleeps quietly. I hope it will give her a good night.

Sunday.

'Tis a cold, rainy, comfortless day, and Eliza never feels smart such weather. Dr. Irvine has not been here. One thing they say is favorable, — her chill comes on three or four hours earlier than usual; 'tis said it grows irregular as it goes off. Dr. Irvine says she certainly is better of her other complaints, and if he can knock this intermittent on the head (to use his own phrase), she will do very well. The next month they invariably have fine weather: 'tis the most pleasant month in the year; the blossoms and flowers all come out. The sweet-scented shrub is delightful; it grows wild, and a small bunch of it perfumes a room. You would be delighted with the appearance of vegetation you see here. Ride out, and you will see the gardens full of vegetables, orange-trees frequently full of fruit, — hardly could you believe it was the depth of winter. We have every day fine cabbage, cauliflower, carrots, and salad, greens, spinach, etc., all fresh from our landlady's garden. It is not a good place for our Northern fruit. They have no winter apples that grow here, peaches but few, no plums or pears, but all imported fruits they get in great perfection, — indeed, I tell them they seem to have nothing but what they get from the Northward. They have no manufactories, no mechanics; the shop-keepers import almost all their goods from Boston, New-York, and Philadelphia. You may conclude, of course, that everything is extravagantly dear. We pay ten dollars a week for board. Our landlady pays half a dollar a pound for butter, quarter of a dollar for mutton, two dollars for a turkey, and in English goods there is generally one-third difference in the price between them and New-York, so you may conclude I make but few purchases in Charleston; indeed, I have not been into a shop, and can tell you but little about the city. It certainly does not strike a stranger agreeably, particularly one from New-York, which is, perhaps, one of the cleanest, freshest-looking cities in the world. Owing to their painting and white-washing, they make their old homes look like new. This seems never done in Charleston; they put a great deal of sand into their bricks and burn them a great deal, — they are a kind of chocolate color; this gives the town a very gloomy appearance. Many of the buildings are plastered outside, and owing to the saltness and humidity of the air, they turn very black. They are mostly ancient-looking buildings, nothing of that lightness in their style of building which of late has been so fashionable; a great deal of wood-work and heavy carved wood in the finishing. Mr. Russell (an old gentleman of Rhode Island) has a most

superb modern house. I was introduced to him at Mrs. Hovey's.—a good, plain New England man. I felt as though he were an old friend, he was so cordial and kind. He called to see me next day with his wife and two charming daughters. Mrs. Russell is an extremely plain woman, but seems very motherly and kind: she said Eliza was away from her mother and she should be glad to supply her place as far as lay in her power. I could tell of many others who are equally kind had I room. Judge and Mrs. Dessasue are extremely attentive to us, and Mrs. Manigaults is the most charming woman I ever saw: she is a relation of Eliza Watts. And now what a little place have I got to say what my heart is full of. Why do we have no letters? Miranda, you ought to have directed here sooner; I am so impatient to hear, I know not what to do. Do let me hear from you once in a fortnight at least.

January 29.

How is my precious William? Dear little fellow, how much I think of him. Poor Frederic has been quite unwell the last week: he cries almost all night constantly: he seems to have something of a dysentery: he took two grains of calomel yesterday, and has since been taking salts, and will you believe, with all the fatigue and anxiety I undergo, I grow fat. You will all rejoice with me to know that I am fat, rosy, and in finer health than I have been in many years. What a favor! I hope I am grateful for it. I won't close my letter till I can tell you what kind of a night Eliza has. She lies down but once in the day; her hands and face burn this evening, her feet cold. She wishes me to be very particular that Father may judge of her situation, but much do I fear I shall make you very anxious; but comfort yourselves, my dear parents, with the assurance that I will do everything in my power, and whatever may be the event, you will not charge me with keeping you ignorant.

OCTAVIA.

TO MRS. KING.

P. S.—I am rejoiced to have something good to close my letter with. Eliza had a poor day yesterday, but, contrary to my expectations, she was up before me this morning; the time for her chill has gone over and she seems comfortable.

Charleston, January 28, 1809.

Dear Caroline:

I send by Capt. Crouch a little pair of shoes for Mary, a little cuckoo toy for Walter, and a tumbler of orange marmalade for Mother. I have had only one letter from New-York since I have been here, and that from Mary Perkins; not one line from my husband. I can tell you nothing flattering of my health. I am very miserable at present; I have a kind of intermittent fever; this afternoon I shall take an emetic, and hope a good effect. How are my dear little ones? I hope not too troublesome. Octavia is in fine health and grows fat for her. Freddie has been unusually troublesome. My dear little Walter. I hardly trust myself to think of them. Precious children! How they bind me to ——. Adieu. I have a bad headache and low-spirited to-day.

ELIZA.

TO CAROLINE BOWNE,

    No. 288 PEARL STREET, NEW-YORK.
       (With two small parcels.)

(BLAZING STAR.)

[*This appears to be the last letter she wrote.*]

Charleston, February 2, 1809.

I have been waiting day after day, my dear aunt, in the hope of having something pleasant to communicate to you; but I do very much fear I shall now have nothing, if ever, to say about our dear Eliza but will give you pain. I sat down to write you without knowing what to say. I have been so in the habit of dissembling lately that I can hardly throw it off, for when I write my father and mother, everything is so glossed over 'tis impossible to come at the truth. You know not how I am affected, my dear aunt. I fear I am doing wrong in deceiving them, for it is my firm opinion she never will be well. Do advise me, tell me what I ought to do. I think to you I may say the truth,— I think she has been growing sicker every hour since she left New-York. Her voyage had a singular effect upon her: she suffered but little from sea-sickness, but every bad symptom she had before seemed increased; she coughed a great deal and very hard, her fever and night-sweats were excessive. You may imagine she was much weakened, but I hoped this was a temporary thing, and a few days of quiet and of rest would restore her; but instead of that, directly after our arrival a sort of intermittent fever took place: she had a regular chill and fever every day, she lost her strength very much, no appetite at all. This last four or five days her disorder wears another appearance. 'Tis now Thursday. On Saturday last she took an emetic; it distressed her exceedingly and yet did not operate well. On Sunday Dr. Irvine ordered her to take quassia, in order to prevent a chill; she took it according to his direction. It brought on her fever at one o'clock in the morning and it never left her till twelve o'clock at night; it absolutely raged all day. Since then she has had no night-sweats, no chill, but her cough and fever very much increased. Her nerves are extremely disordered,— such a tremor that, to-day, she cannot feed herself at all. She is so weak and exhausted that she cannot walk alone. 'Tis now eleven o'clock; I am sitting by her side and she is still coughing, and in such a hot fever she can bear nothing to touch her. I have not asked her physician's opinion concerning her; 'tis unnecessary; I feel I know what it must be. Yet is it not strange she keeps up her spirits? She is looking forward with the greatest anxiety to warm weather. God grant it may not be too late. Dr. Irvine was the physician Mrs. Hoxey recommended; he is indisposed, and has left his patients in the care of Dr. Barron. The exchange has

pleased us very much, for Dr. Barrow is considered quite as skillful, and is extremely kind and fatherly in his manners; indeed, he reminds us so strongly of our dear father that we already love him very much.

February 3.

Poor Eliza had a most distressing night last night. She coughed so long that she was entirely exhausted; her fever was very high, and she has scarcely spoken a loud word to-day. Her nerves are in a dreadful state. I inquired of Dr. Barrow what he thought of her situation. He says he can say nothing encouraging. He said the disorder had taken great hold upon her, and had shattered her nerves in a terrible manner,—he very much fears a nervous fever; that her pulse was very bad: as nearly as he could count, up to 150. Is it not very evident from his being so candid, my dear aunt, that he has but little or no hope of her recovery? And yet so strongly do I sympathize in every feeling of hers, that seeing her easier and more comfortable this evening has renewed my hopes and put me quite in spirits. She has been much better this afternoon and evening, less fever, less tremor upon her nerves, and since she has been in bed has had no bad coughing-spell. The mail went to the Northward to-day. I have so little time to write that I have missed it. I will let you know to-morrow how she is, and the next day is post day again. I know what a kind interest you and my uncle take in our dear Eliza, and I know I cannot be too minute. Our friends here are kinder than I can express to you. It seems sometimes as though we were among our own relations. They think of every little thing for Eliza's comfort and convenience that I could myself.

Monday, February 6.

This morning Eliza was better, my dear aunt, than she has been for a week past. Her voice has returned, and she appears stronger in every respect. Yesterday and last night she had a little fever; this morning is delightful and she is going to ride. You shall hear again from us before long. I know Mrs. Rogert will need no apology, I am sure, for my not writing. The repetition of such symptoms are distressing to me beyond expression.

Your affectionate niece,

O. S. BROWN.

TO MRS. RUFUS KING,
    NEW-YORK.

12

New-York, February 4, 1809.

Your letter, my love, of the 13th and 14th has comforted me.   You must keep up your spirits; you will do well.   Dr. Bergere says attacks similar to yours are not of the dangerous kind that some think.   He approves of your taking the lichen again.   I have sent a bundle from Mr. King by Capt. Slocum, who sails to-morrow.   I am distressed I cannot go with him, but so it is: it is next to impossible I should leave here till about the 25th of this month.   Mr. Jenkins, my assistant, is absent, and I cannot leave the office until he returns without relinquishing it altogether, and I have most of my houses to let this month, those I have lately built included, and which are not finished; but I am determined to leave all in this month.   I hope you have a comfortable place now.   What abominable lodgings the first were.   Don't mind the expense; get everything and do everything you like.   We can afford it.   I wish my presence in this place could as well be dispensed with, but so it is.   I think it right you should have a physician. I will bring the things you mention.   Our children are well.

The ship General Eaton has not yet arrived.   I will write to Mr. Brown by this vessel if I have time; if not, by mail on Monday or Tuesday.

W. BOWNE.

With a bundle of lichen for E. S. B.

It is a fortnight since I sent my last and third letter to my dear aunt, without having received a single line from either herself or Octavia, which, I must acknowledge, has been no small disappointment. However, I feel disposed to put the most favorable construction on their silence, and still hope there is one on its journey. All the information we can learn of thee is through Uncle Walter, who says thou thought thyself rather better, but we want something more particular. We feel interested, and are anxious to know just how thou art situated in every respect. Do gratify my curiosity. What sort of a family do you board with? Is it a pleasant situation, and have you been regaled with green peas yet? Our deep snows and cold, whistling winds, which almost occasion chill from the very sound, even when a rousing fire is before us, seem to put all prospect of returning vegetation at a great distance, and bid defiance to the very idea. Walter and Mary were pretty well last evening. It storms so violently to-day, I have not heard from them. They look finely, and Mary grows very fast. Their father treated them with a sleigh-ride a few days since. We have had as delightful a season for this amusement as I recollect, and our citizens have really taken advantage of it. The streets are quite alive with the swift passing steed, and our ears are assailed on almost every side by the noise of the bells which attend them. But the walking is and has been so extremely bad, I have scarcely ventured from the threshold of our door for this long while. Grandmother and Aunt Caroline are both unwell, with colds of which very many are complaining, and my father has had a severe turn of pain in his breast and side, occasioned, we suppose, by cold; so that he was not out of his bed yesterday, but seems now very much relieved. Dr. Seaman attends him, and inquired particularly after thee.

8th (fourth day).

Not having heard of an opportunity before to-day to forward this, I deferred the conclusion, that my aunt might have the latest information from her dear children, who are perfectly in health this morning, and in good spirits. I wish I knew as much of their

beloved mother, but Uncle Walter does keep his letters so close, that we cannot hear anything particular; so I do entreat thee, write to some of the rest of us, or beg dear Octavia. Grandmother and Aunt Caroline have nearly recovered from their colds, and my father is rather better.

How is Octavia, her husband, and dear little Frederic, and above all, how is my aunt's health? I have not time to add more, than as much love as this paper can possibly carry, from my dear parents, grandmother, Aunts Townsend, King, and Caroline, and be sure a large portion from thy Douglas and Mary, to all your party.

FROM MARY MURRAY PERKINS.
*(Wife of B. Douglas Perkins, who was nearly
the same age as her Uncle Walter's wife.)*

TO ADAM GILCHRIST,
      FOR ELIZA S. BOWNE.

Second Month, 7th, 1809.

I have just received my dear Eliza's letter, and the information thou gives of thy health was affecting. We shall anxiously wish to hear again in hopes of a more favorable account. I have received Mary's shoes, and they fit her very well. The other articles we have not received yet, but hope to have them from the vessel to-morrow. The little children are pretty well; have slight colds, but are lively, quite amusing to us, this stormy weather. We have had it very cold, snowing or raining most continually since thou left us. Sister King desires her love, and would write if her time was not so much engrossed with her children having the whooping-cough, though not very unfavorably. Thy Aunt King sends frequently to inquire after dear little Mary and Walter, and intends visiting them soon. Neighbor Bogert was here a few days since and desired her love to thee. As Mary Perkins writes frequently to my sister, I hope she will get every information she wishes. Mother unites with me in much love to thyself and Octavia.

CAROLINE BOWNE.
(Her husband's sister.)

Charleston, February 12, 1809.

The day has come for me to give an account of our dear Eliza for the last week, and yet nothing has occurred that can give them the least satisfaction. How painful is the task. But my duty commands it, and I will be faithful to it. I will not flatter with hopes which never visit my heart. You have your own feelings to bear, my dear parents; you shall not be distressed with mine. I will compose myself to give as distinct an account as possible. Her chief affliction the last week has been sore mouth,— it has, indeed, been dreadful, and still continues nearly as bad; she has constant fevers, hardly ever off her; she generally has a chill every morning. She takes nothing but jellies and a little chocolate for breakfast, but no meat or bread. Her strength goes very fast; 'tis with great difficulty she can walk from the bed to the easy-chair with two to assist her; her countenance and voice have altered very much.— indeed, she seldom speaks loud.

She rode a little on Thursday, but it was too much for her strength. We have given it up for the present. Different from most persons in her condition, she seems well convinced she will never get well. She says very little about it; never frets at being away from her children or friends,— never mentions it. She asked me yesterday if she would be able to get back to New-York. I told her 'twas impossible to say what changes might take place; that I wished to see her mind in such a state that she would be perfectly resigned whichever way it turn. And just so she seems. Thank God, I am spared the pain of seeing her sink away insensible of her danger. I told her to-day was the day for me to write home. She said I could say nothing encouraging, that her lungs had only one more state to go through, but that she was resigned to the will of God. This, my dear parents, is a comfort to me beyond description, and I am sure it will be so to you. The doctor has been fearing that the sore mouth would produce a diarrhea; she had a touch of it Friday night, but it has disappeared again. Poor Mr. Bowne! I don't know what we shall do when he comes. He has no fortitude, and is not prepared to find her so greatly changed. He will be here in the course of another fortnight, I hope.

She has had a comfortless day to-day, that distress which I have mentioned before has troubled her very much. She is hardly ever free from it an hour. I will not close this comfortless letter until morning.

Monday, February 13.

Eliza is much the same this morning.—as usual, very feeble; her mouth and throat excessively sore. This morning she had a most profuse perspiration, particularly about her head and face. She wakes quite wandering; asks strange questions, owing to extreme weakness, I suppose. The diarrhea still threatening; of course, her strength diminishes daily. I dare not think what another month may produce; she certainly, it appears to me, cannot survive another like the last. She has no pain, and Dr. Barrow says she raises matter from the lungs. Mr. Brown and myself are in very good health; our darling little Freddie has one tooth. I very much fear he is going to have a sore mouth. I think a great deal of my darling William, but my anxieties are so centered here that I feel none on his account. No letters yet from Scarborough; I am quite sick to hear. Do, my dear Miranda, write every week, and be the means of affording me the only comfort I am capable of receiving. Tell me that my dear father and mother are well, and not too much distressed, my dear boy in health. Yourself, Arexine, dear Isabella; how much I think of you all, and how much dearer you all seem to me than ever.

Your child,

OCTAVIA S. BROWN.

Charleston, February 21, 1809.

I will permit no one but myself to transmit to you the dreadful intelligence this letter
will convey to you, my dear parents.   A good and merciful God will not forsake you in
this awful moment.   Our dear Eliza is freed from her earthly sufferings, and I humbly
trust is now a blessed spirit in heaven.   I offer you no consolation ; I commit you into
the hands of a good God, who has supported me when my strength failed me.   She had
her senses at intervals for the few last days of her illness.   She spoke of her approaching change with great composure ; said she had thought much of it ; that she trusted in
God for further happiness with great satisfaction and confidence ; wished her time
might come speedily, that she might be relieved of the pain of seeing her distressed friends.
She suffered with wonderful patience ; never murmured. At the very last she looked the
satisfaction she had not the power to speak.   At two o'clock yesterday afternoon was the
most afflicting scene. Octavia had great fortitude to sit by her when she could speak only
with her eyes.   She knew us, and listened with apparent satisfaction to a prayer I read
only an hour before the sad moment.   It was a day of trial with us most severe.

With much affection and regard to all.

W. BROWN

Poor Mr. Bowne has not arrived.

Mrs. Rutledge:

Nondescript rose.
Sweet-scented shrub,
Yellow jessamine,
English honeysuckle.
) In two boxes.

Daily rose.
} In one box.

Mrs. Russell:

Yellow jessamine,
Nondescript rose.
} In one box.

Mr. Jose Winthrop,
Jno. Simon, Bre.,
Wm. Dawson,
Lewis Morris, Esq.,
James Gregorie,
Lieut. R. Izard.
Invited as pall-bearers.

Adam Gilchrist, Esq., Mr. and Mrs. Manigault, Mr. and Miss Middleton, Mr. and Mrs. Cogdell, Mr. and Mrs. Gregorie, Mrs. Hovey, Mrs. Rutledge, and Mr. and Mrs. and the two Misses Pinckney, Mr. A. Middleton and Lieut. Izard, Mr. Crocker, Mr. J. Stoney, Mr. and Mrs. Dessasau, Doctor and Mrs. Irvine and Miss Bee, Mr. and Mrs. J. Manigault, Mr. and Mrs. Russell and Miss Russell, Mr. and Mrs. Hasket and Miss Hasket, Mr. Crafts, Mr. Bee, Mr. and Mrs. Loundes, Mr. Winthrop, Mr. McKinzey and McNiel, Mr. Wm. Heyward, Jr., Mrs. Heyward and Miss Hamilton and Miss Heyward, Mrs. Morris and Mr. Morris, Dr. Barrow and two daughters, Mr. John Rutledge, Mrs. Brown, Major Thomas Pinckney and son, Rev. Mr. Hollenshead, two Misses Winthrop, Miss Craft, Mr. and Mrs. Kerr, Major and Mrs. Thompson, Mrs. and Miss Roxana Theus.

Died at Charleston, S. C., on the 19th ult., Mrs. Walter Bowne, consort of Walter Bowne, Esq., of New-York, and daughter of the Hon. Robert Southgate, of Scarborough, Maine, aged twenty-five years. The bereaved husband and infant children, the afflicted parents, brethren, and sisters, and the numerous respectable friends and acquaintances by whom she was so justly respected and beloved for her talents and virtues, will deeply mourn this early signal triumph of the King of Terrors. But they will not "sorrow as those without hope." Her immortal spirit, liberated from the body, is, we trust, already admitted to a clear and perfect, an immediate and positive, a soul-transforming and eternal vision of God and the Redeemer. Why the most endearing ties of nature should be dissolved almost as soon as formed, why the dreadful law of mortality should be executed on the most worthy and dearest objects of conjugal, parental, and social love, in the moment of sanguine expectation of reciprocal enjoyment, is among the dark and mysterious questions in the book of Providence. The ways of God are inscrutable to man, "clouds and darkness are round about him, yet righteousness and judgment are the habitation of his throne." All afflictive events are readily resolved into the wisdom of God. To his sovereign will reason and religion, duty and interest, require us to bow with reverence. What a dark and gloomy veil is spread by the early death of our friends over our earthly enjoyments! How tenderly are we hereby admonished not to expect satisfaction in this empty, fluctuating and transitory state! How strongly urged to place our affections on things above to secure an immediate interest in those sublime and durable pleasures which flow from the service and favor of God, and the prospect of complete and endless felicity in his presence.

SACRED

TO THE MEMORY OF

ELIZA S. BOWNE,

WIFE OF WALTER BOWNE, OF NEW-YORK,
DAUGHTER OF ROBERT SOUTHGATE, ESQ., OF SCARBOROUGH,
DISTRICT OF MAINE.

WHO DEPARTED THIS LIFE
ON THE 19TH DAY OF FEBRUARY, 1809,

AGED 25 YEARS.

Take, holy earth, all that my soul holds dear;
    Take that best gift which Heaven so lately gave.
To Bristol's mount I bore with trembling care,
    Her faded form she bowed to taste the wave
And died!   Does youth, does beauty read the line?
    Does sympathetic fear their breast alarm?
Speak! dead Eliza, breathe a strain divine;
    E'en from the grave thou shalt have power to charm.
Bid them be chaste, be innocent like thee,
    Bid them in beauty's sphere as meekly move;
And, if so fair, from vanity as free,
    As firm in friendship and as fond in love.
Tell them, though 'tis an awful thing to die
    ('Twas e'en so to thee), yet the dread path once trod,
Heaven lifts its everlasting portals high
    And bids the pure in heaven behold their God.

Charleston, March 12, 1809.

I hope, my dear Miranda, this will be the last letter you will receive from me at Charleston. Poor Mr. Bowne arrived here on Thursday. Not a word had he heard, and owing to his having left New-York, he had not received a single very alarming letter. He was entirely unprepared for that which awaited him. Never did I pity any one so. He is indeed borne down with the weight of his grief, but the violence I dreaded I see nothing of. There is no judging from the effect little troubles have upon people how they will bear great ones. I know it by myself. I see it in him. He is more composed to-day, and we are making arrangements to get away. He is much gratified that we waited here for him, which we had some doubt about, on account of the great expense of these houses. The Minerva, a very fine packet, arrived from New-York yesterday. We shall return in her. She will go in the course of a week or ten days. What a melancholy voyage! But yet I will not think so. I am going to my dear father and mother, my kind sisters: indeed, 'tis a delightful thought.

Your sister,

O. BROWN.

New-York, Sunday, April 23, 1809.

Your afflicted brother, my dear sister, again finds himself in the place which so lately contained everything his heart could wish; but oh, the sad reverse! all is changed. Accustomed to approach the city with so much pleasure, now it seems to have lost all its delights. All is gloom. Business, which after a short relaxation I used to resume with so much satisfaction, has lost its charm, and more than all, how shall I describe my feelings on again beholding my dear children? Can it be possible, my bleeding heart seems to say, they have no mother: how shall I support myself? The loss of your society, dear sister, I feel very much. Your presence gave support. What would I not give were yours and Father's families near to me. Perhaps I do wrong to assail others with my distress. I have not at any time since our return from Charleston felt resolution to enter that residence that so lately contained my beloved. I dread it; my heart is ready to burst at the thought. Do, my dearest sister, write me and console me.

Adieu.

W. B.

New-York, April 29, 1809.

I am much gratified, my dear sister, in receiving your letter. I was anxious to hear from little Frederic. I hope you will write me often and particularly; you must not think any incident too trifling to relate: everything you can say will interest me. Father's family are very near and dear to me. I feel great solicitude for our sister Isabella; frequent riding might be of service to her.

I had a most gloomy journey home, my dear Miranda. I felt the loss of Brother and Sister Brown's company very much. I remained in Boston only a part of a day, and did not see Mrs. Derby (I called, but she had company) nor Louisa; she was out. I sat an hour with Mr. and Mrs. Gray. William was part of the time with us: he is a young man that stands higher in my estimation than any other I know.

After leaving Boston, and riding two days and nearly two nights, a most distressing accident happened to one of the passengers: the stage upset and broke his leg in a most shocking manner. Four of us escaped unhurt, or very little. We carried him about a quarter of a mile on a board; he suffered dreadfully. We left him in good quarters, and procured a doctor. I have not heard from him, but expect to: how thankful ought we that escaped to feel. My dear little children are quite well. O my sister, were Father's family only near me! With much love to our friends.

Your very affectionate brother,

W. BOWNE.

My love to Arexine. I wish she, too, would write to me. I wrote to Octavia a few lines the day I arrived.

MISS MIRANDA SOUTHGATE.

New-York, May 13, 1809.

I have, my dear sister, been at that mansion,—but enough! I am unhappy. Two trunks are sent by the brig Scarborough. I have kept a number of things for Mary. I thought of selecting a few things for Sister Isabella, but could not. I leave it to Mother and yourself, if you think well of it. The keys are sent by Mr. Wood, and two letters for you that came enclosed to me by Mr. Gilchrist. My dear little Mary is quite well. Walter has a cold. Mary has taken possession of her afflicted father's heart. She will come to me from any one, and seems so pleased when with me that I frequently don't know how to leave her. I have not had a line from you, my dear sister, and I want to hear from you very often. Your good husband's letter I received. One box of roots Caroline has sent; the other roots are not alive. Let me know if the trunks arrive in good order; and if you have the new velvet coat, it is yours. Present my love to Father and Mother.

Your affectionate brother,

W. BOWNE.

MRS. OCTAVIA BROWN,
  SCARBOROUGH.
   (District of Maine.)

New-York, June 23, 1809.

I have your kind letters, my dear sister, and if you could know the comfort they afford me, and how anxious I am to hear very often from you, I think you will, when a leisure moment does occur, gratify me. My solicitude for your husband and yourself is unchangeable. He is young. How different would be the prospect if he were advanced in years, with a large family,—and we see many in this situation. I very much doubt the expediency of Mr. Brown seeking a clerkship. To spend his best days with so little prospect of permanent independence does not appear to me to be right,—his knowledge and extensive capacity for business will certainly enable him to do better. I see no insurmountable difficulty to his commencing the dry-goods or other business in Portland or some other place, except that he is not clear of the old concerns. If unavoidable, he loses two or three years to effect this: it is certainly a misfortune, but he has youth on his side. I talked with Mr. Gray: he appears justly to appreciate Mr. Brown's mercantile knowledge, and I think is very ready to aid him in commencing business, or, if his old affairs prevent that at present, to employ him.

My dear little children are very hearty. Walter's head, I hope, is nearly well.

Our good friend Mary Murray has copied the miniature, and only waits a private opportunity to forward it to dear mother. O my dear sister, how many things occur to rend my heart, and how few to soothe the sufferer's tortured mind.

I have let my house, sold the greatest part of the furniture. Mother and Caroline, with my dear little ones and nurse, are going to Flushing for the summer, and I shall stay at Mrs. Loring's.

Your ticket, I fear, has only drawn a prize of ten dollars. I am not certain of the number: send it in your next. I have purchased another ticket in the same lottery, No. 4,481, for you: it will finish drawing in about three weeks. Miranda and Arexine must write to me.

W. BOWNE.

MRS. OCTAVIA BROWN.
    SCARBOROUGH.
       (District of Maine.)

New-York, August 2, 1809.

Mrs. Octavia Brown:

Your good husband, my dear sister, passed a week with me on his way to Baltimore, and a great comfort it was. I hope he will stay longer on his return. The reflection which is constantly with me, that I am so distant from my ever dear friends of Scarborough, is painful in the extreme,—could I conveniently leave insurance office and make you a visit this autumn, how fondly should I anticipate it. I feel I must defer the agreeable prospect to another season. My dear little ones are quite well; I pass every Sunday with them. May can walk very well,—hold of the hands,—but she has not cut any teeth; it is not quite time. Mr. Brown and myself dined at Jamaica with Mr. King, and in the afternoon went to see my darlings; the night following, at Cousin Ann Bowne's. Your husband has probably informed you of our visit. Mr. and Mrs. Davis are now in this city; I see them frequently. They lodge near Mrs. Loring's; they met their son here from Baltimore. Mary Murray has finished the miniature; I have it, with a letter for you. I intend to forward them by Mrs. Davis.

I feel great comfort that my children are in the country; the city is not a proper place,—great mortality prevails among very young children. We have some alarm of fever, though it does not appear to gain ground at Brooklyn. The fever prevails, and our Board of Health have interdicted the intercourse. At Philadelphia they have also had some cases. Believe me, my dear sister.

Ever your affectionate brother,

W. BOWNE.

Thursday Morning: Mr. Brown arrived last evening.

To convince you, my dear sister, how much I value your letters,—to leave no excuse, if possible, for such long silence on your part, I will not delay making you my debtor. I acknowledge this is selfish. To hear from my dear friends at Scarborough is so great a comfort to me, when I receive a letter my wish is that I may soon receive another; and the more to entitle me to the favor, I will not delay to write, though I confess to you, I am liable to feel reluctance at commencing a letter. I think you, my sister, have expressed feelings of the same kind; we must not give way to them.

Mr. Brown and myself dined at Mr. King's on Sunday; the family are well. John intends to make a visit to Ballston Springs. Mr. Brown can tell you how finely my little darlings look. Little Mary is so sprightly and so good, you would all be charmed with her. O my dear sister, if I could frequently make you a visit with my little ones, what relief it would be to me. I think you and Arexine might have come on with Mr. Brown; it would have been a great comfort to me. I shall fondly anticipate the pleasure another season. My mother, sisters, and all would be highly pleased. I will return with you at any time. Our friends, I believe, are generally well. Mary Parsons has a fine son. Mrs. Bogert is happy in imitating Aunt King. Mary and Hannah Murray, their mother and grandmother, with John, with Mrs. M., seem gloomy at their summer house. Mrs. J. R. is much altered in her appearance for the worse. The Misses Watts, lovely, unhappy girls! their father has taken them up the North River. It was with great difficulty he prevailed on them to leave Broadway; they will not visit their country house.

My love to Father and Mother. I do think Father does very wrong to work so hard. I wish he would pay more attention to his health; he ought to, certainly. Accept my best wishes for your happiness, my dear sister.

Your affectionate brother,

W. BOWNE.

P. S.—Mr. Brown left here yesterday.

New-York, September 15, 1809.

You have grand times, I suppose, with Governor Gore, and Commencement too. Write to me all about these grand doings. Did the governor stop to see you? Has James King made you a visit? Frederic is at home. You are, no doubt, all very busy moving or preparing to move to the new house. Let me know everything. I am distressed about Sister Isabella: perhaps a journey to this place might be of great service to her. My mother and sisters would make her as comfortable as possible. My dear children are quite well, and continue in the country. Mary has five teeth, and runs alone, without fear. It is proposed to wean her. Ask Mother and Octavia what they think of it. I am anxious for her. Mother and Caroline intend returning to the city in about two weeks with the children.

Mr. King's family are well. John has been at the Springs some time. Charles, I believe, is content without going further than Hell Gate, the seat of Mr. Gracie.

What a cool summer we have had; scarcely any hot weather. It is now like late fall weather, and excessively dry. The farmers near this are alarmed, fearing they will not have any pasture.

Present my love to Father, Mother, and sisters, and remember me affectionately to other friends. How are our relatives at Topsham, Bath, Saco, etc.? Sister Octavia is indebted to me a letter, but I will excuse her, and write to her shortly; dear woman, she has much to do.

Your lonely brother,

W. BOWNE.

MISS MIRANDA SOUTHGATE,
   Care ROBERT SOUTHGATE,
      SCARBOROUGH.
        (District of Maine.)

New-York, November 25, 1809.

It is now my turn to apologize, my dear sister, for the delay in writing. I am ashamed of myself, for really it is more owing to laziness or a want of attachment to writing, which I have a thousand times wished to overcome, than anything else. This, you will say, is a pretty apology. I admit you have a right to say, No more apologies unless better can be made. I plead guilty. I must correct one idea in my sister's letter. You think you cannot say much to interest me. Very different indeed is the reality,—everything, the most trifling, no matter what, if it interests one of your family, doubly interests me. I am in need of comfort. My dear little Mary is now finely, but, poor thing, she has been far otherwise. She has had a most dreadful sore mouth, which nearly deprived her of taking all refreshment; during the time weaned herself entirely; slept with nurse the whole time, about two weeks, and would not be nursed once. If the nurse offered to nurse her, she would push her away and be quite displeased. She is now quite well, and a most interesting little thing: mild, sprightly, and everything I could wish; playful,— says, "Pa." I wish you could see her. I must not venture my all on the little darling. Caroline is devoted to her. The nurse has another place. I am very sorry to hear your dear little Fred is still an invalid. I hope, before this, he is restored to health. Miranda is a bad girl; she did not write a line to me from Boston. Do scold her very hard for me. I wish she had extended her journey to this place; we should all have been very glad to have seen her. We are all frightened here on account of the early setting in of winter: the cold is very severe, and there is now a great deal of snow on the ground,— not less than twelve inches. I have been much concerned for Sister Boyd; I am consoled at your intelligence that she is much better.

I sympathize, my dear sister, with you in your very many trials. The family who are likely to meet with the greatest of losses, I suppose, is Major McLellan's. 'Tis hard indeed. I am very glad your friend Miss Davis is to be connected so agreeably; all your friends have a conspicuous place in my consideration. Present my love to your husband, and all my other dear friends. I want very much to see you all.

Ever your affectionate brother,

W. BOWNE.

To Miranda.

New-York, January 18, 1810.

I was very glad, my sister, to receive your letter. It was so long since I had heard
from my dear friends, and such a long letter too, you will please accept my thanks, and
forgiveness of neglect to write to me from Boston, provided, nevertheless, you write more
frequently. My dear children are very well, and have grown a great deal. Walter is
quite tall, and Mary has fine red cheeks, and could not be in finer health. You do not
mention how dear little Frederic was; I hope he has recovered. In your letters you
must mention everybody by name. Aunt King is troubled again with a bad cold. The
rest of the family are well. James is here; John was married last night, and report
says Charles and Miss Gracie are to be before a great while. Miss Champlin was
married, Tuesday, to a son of Mr. Richard Harrison. Our city, I am told, is very gay.
Mr. Jackson, British minister, is here, and report says great attention is paid to him
and Mrs. J.,— every day invited to dine out, and every evening at a party. You know we
are very Anglo. The Misses Watts are well. You don't know how much I feel obliged
to Eliza and Susan for calling to see my little darlings. Octavia must thank them very
particularly when she writes. Anna Bartlett has made her appearance at the assemblies, is much pleased; says you don't write to her. If you want to hear all about
fashions, and a great deal about the young folks' marriages, and such things, you had
better write to her. Your Aunt King, too, complains that you had not written to any
of her boys. Isaac Bell is to be married soon to Miss Ellis, a very handsome young
lady about eighteen. I am told he capers about at a great rate. Write to me soon; give
my kindest love to Father, Mother, and Octavia.

Affectionately,

W. BOWNE.

June 8, 1810.

My Dear Sister:

Again at housekeeping. I am rejoiced. Oh, how I want to see you all. You must write to me soon all about yourself. I like your husband's plans. Be supported, my dear sister, by the hope that things will be better for you. The enclosed is yours; it may be convenient at this moment. You know your brother.

Most affectionately,

W. BOWNE.

To Miranda.

New-York, May 4, 1811.

To begin a letter by apologizing is what I dislike, but it is due to my sister. I am in fault. Soon after receipt of your favor I went to Philadelphia, and since my return I have been very busy. Mr. Tilton's information of your intended visit is, my dear sister, very pleasing to all your friends, and to myself most grateful. I shall be much grieved if you do not fulfill this promised gratification. On your arrival you must repair immediately to my mother's. There any arrangement can take place you like. I am indeed happy to hear you all have such good health. I suspect you should have excepted yourself. The visit this way, I trust, will establish that also. Truly, my dear sister, does everything interest me that is interesting to your family, and you should much oftener let me hear very minutely from you. I have no intelligence whatever of Uncle Richard since he left this city. How dreadful to his family. What can be his views? I yesterday sent on board the schooner Relief, Captain Obed Baxter, for Boston and Portland, a box, directed to Brother Boyd, containing a silver tea-pot, sugar-dish, and cream-pitcher. I have long wished to present something to Sister Isabella, and this tea-set must be it. Mother will permit me to have this gratification. Present my love to all our friends, and do not defer your journey, but set out the first opportunity. My dear children are quite well.

Your affectionate brother,

W. BOWNE.

New-York, October 12, 1811.

I hope, my dear Arexine and Mary, this is the last time I shall write to you from New-York; for I am now in a state of preparation for a removal of my quarters. There is a Mr. and Mrs. Winthrop from Boston, who intend shortly to return to that place, and if they will take charge of me, I intend to go with them. I look forward with a great deal of pleasure to the time of my arrival at home, where I shall again be returned to the bosom of my dear family. I have received every attention and kindness from my dear friends in New-York, and hope ever to retain a grateful sense of un-merited favors; but my heart lingers about its home. I hope Father and Mother are well, and I shall find them in as good health as I trust they will find me; for the last time I was weighed, which was a few weeks ago, I weighed one hundred and twenty-five pounds. Tell Mother I have, with the kind assistance of Caroline, made her a fine pot of peach, which, together with some other things, I shall leave to be sent by Walter. And tell Mr. Smith, I must answer his repeated favors of pen and ink, paper and ideas, by word of mouth; he will not think I do not love him because I do not write to him. Remember me affectionately to him, and to Father and Mother. Do not expect me with any anxiety, for whenever I am safely on my journey, I will, if nothing prevents, let you hear from me. Little Mary and Walter are very well, and Mary desires her love to her grandma Southgate, and her grandpa also, and her aunts and uncles. Give my love, she says, to Dranma Southgate,—she talks very crooked.

FROM MIRANDA.

TO MISS AREXINE SOUTHGATE.

New-York, November 30, 1811.

My sister reached home, but not a line from her to her brother. I did not expect to be so long deprived of that pleasure. My dear little Mary frequently talks of Aunt Miranda,—says she must not stay at Miranda's house only a little while, for she can't leave Grandmother and Aunt Caroline, and often asks why Aunt Miranda don't come to see her. This little darling of mine has certainly more discriminating powers than children usually have,—don't laugh, for I think my sister discovered an unusual smartness in her niece. Walter, too, is a fine boy. They are quite well. My mother has been very ill. I hope she will be restored to health in a few days. You must write me a long letter,—give me an account of everybody. I like very much to receive long letters, though I write short ones myself. Nancy Watts is much indisposed, though I do not know that the family are much alarmed, nor do I know that she is dangerously ill, but I fear, for she has been confined to her bed or room ever since you left us. The rest of our friends, I believe, are well. Now I will tell you a piece of news, but you must not talk about it or write about it: Robert Murray is engaged to the young lady at Coldenham. It is not known when they will be married, and they wish it kept a secret. Give my love to my dear friends, Father's family. I have not heard from Octavia for a long time. I have sent the things you left per schooner Dolly, Captain Greely, to sail for Portland ; has probably gone two or three days since. It will be well to inquire about them on receipt of this letter.

Affectionately, your brother,

W. BOWNE.

One Jar of Peaches,
Small Thread-Trunk,
One Bandbox, Two Brushes,
One Rolling-Pin and Water-Pail.

(SENT BY SCHOONER DOLLY.)

New-York, January 18, 1812.

I cannot but think my dear sister might write to me oftener, when I assure her it would gratify me much to hear very frequently from my valued friends. Dear Octavia has entirely neglected to give me the pleasure of a line. Always mention her particularly in your letters, Sister Isabella and all. How does Cousin Mary Coffin do, and Uncle Porter's family? Sister Arexine and my cousins have my best wishes for their happiness in their proposed change of situation. Robert Murray is not married, but will probably be soon, and I have no doubt his family will be very much pleased with his wife. She is a charming girl, I am told. My mother has recovered from a very ill turn and is in good spirits. My dear children are well. Walter goes to school, Mary prattles all day and plays with Sally and Sonny, two miserable dolls. Mother and Caroline desire their love to you all. Nancy Watts is very ill. I have the greatest apprehension for her; indeed, I believe her friends have scarcely any hope left. Betsey, dear girl, looks worried out. You can, my dear sister, in some measure realize her situation. Oh, how much sympathy is due her; her lot would seem to be hard; I trust she will be supported. What would become of that family without her! I seldom see John or Charles King; indeed, I do not go anywhere,—my children and the office take my time. Present my affectionate love to Father and Mother. My regards to Mr. Tilton. Accept my best wishes.

W. BOWNE.

TO MISS MIRANDA SOUTHGATE.

1811 — Account with W. B.:

June.	Paid B. Willis for Miranda	$14.00
July 12.	Paid to herself	20.00
August 16.	Paid to herself	30.00
October 9.	Paid to herself	10.00
October 12.	Paid to herself	50.00
November 15.	Paid for fourteen chairs for Sarah Leland	29.75
		$153.75
	Due Robert Southgate	96.25
		$250.00

1812 —

January 17. Received from Wm. Codman, Two hundred and fifty dollars dividend, on New-York Insurance Co's Stock.

I can send Father a check on one of the banks in Boston for the money.

New-York, March 20, 1812.

I am determined not to remain in debt. My sister shall not have that excuse for depriving me of the pleasure of receiving letters from her. I have received a letter from dear Octavia. Give my love to her. She is very often the subject of my thoughts. How does Mr. Brown make out? The eye-water for Sister Boyd shall be procured and sent on the first good opportunity. My dear children are well. Mother and Caroline are also well. You may imagine the solicitude and affection my mother has for the children. When she was very sick lately, it gave her great trouble their being removed into another room to sleep, and the second night she would have them back. She said she felt more easy and contented when they were near her. Then and not otherwise could she be certain they were safe. Brother Murray is laid up with a strain from a fall on the ice at Albany. His wife and Lindley have gone there to remain with him till the ice breaks up and the steamboats run. Robert has returned with his wife; they are at his father's; she will be quite a favorite with them all. Robert has done well. You have, no doubt, heard of William Gracie's duel with Hamilton, from South Carolina. The story is this: Hamilton was in love with a Miss Hayward, of Charleston. She remained in this city to pass the winter. Hamilton heard Gracie was very frequent in his visits, and came on from Charleston to inquire into the business; immediately on his arrival, wrote to Mr. Gracie and informed him of his attachment for Miss Hayward, and what he had heard (all this without consulting the lady, as is said). Mr. Gracie sent him a verbal answer that he had no intention of interfering with him. Hamilton was, at the time, satisfied. In the evening he called on Miss H., and Gracie was there. The next day Miss H. and her mother were engaged to dine at Mr. Gracie's father's, and did dine there. The morning following H. wrote G. a very harsh letter, and in such terms that Gracie thought proper to challenge him. They went out, and Gracie is now laid up with a wound, though no way dangerous,—the ball passed through his thigh. What shocking, horrid mode this is of obtaining satisfaction. Present my affectionate love to our friends, not forgetting the valued Mr. Tilton.

With great truth, your affectionate brother and sincere well-wisher,

W. BOWNE.

New-York, June 18, 1812.

I have for ten days had the pleasure of Mr. Brown's company. He can inform my valued friends all that writing to my dear sister would convey; nevertheless, I cannot let him depart without a line. My dear children are quite well. Little Mary has commenced school, and is highly delighted with this new employment of her time. Our friends are all pretty well, except Brother Murray, who is in a very unpleasant situation, from a fall at Albany. He is almost helpless, can scarcely walk with the aid of crutches. Mother and Caroline, with the children, intend shortly to make their annual visit to Flushing. Our friend Eliza Watts is well, and proposes, if not prevented by war, to visit Niagara Falls in company with Mr. and Mrs. Kearnet. And I do almost promise myself the pleasure of seeing you all this season. If, however, war should be declared, it will disarrange all plans of this kind. This most dreadful calamity, I do fear, will be our lot.

Present my love to Father and Mother, and do not omit to remember me affectionately to Sister Boyd. Mr. Tilton has my regards at all times. I enclose a check on the Boston bank for ninety-six dollars and twenty-five cents, the balance due Father of the money received from Mr. Codman. Truly, my dear sister.

Your affectionate brother,

W. BOWNE.

MISS MIRANDA SOUTHGATE.

To Miss Miranda Southgate.

Spring, 1813.

My Dear Sister:

I have been on a visit to Washington City, which prevented my receiving your kind letter until my return last week. Say to Arexine and Brother Smith, they have my most ardent wishes for their happiness. I should be glad of the opportunity of rendering a visit here pleasant to them. My children are well, except Mary a cold. They have had the measles, but so favorably that they were very sick but a single day. They grow very fast; you would be surprised to see them so tall. My dear mother does not seem quite so well this spring as usual. Caroline is well. They desire much love to you all. Brother John is married; my new sister, I believe, is a most amiable woman. John has surprised most of his acquaintance in this affair, yourself, I think, of that number. Make my love to Father and Mother, and dear Frederic. If he would make a jaunt this way his health might be improved. I will take good care of him. You say nothing of your own health; I hope it is good. Present my regards to Mr. and Mrs. Tilton.

Your affectionate brother,

W. BOWNE.

New-York, October 19, 1814.

My ever dear Sister:

I have received your kind letter. I am indeed among the number of your friends made happy by your recovery so far, and pray a complete restoration of health may take place. Do, my dear sister, take every possible care of yourself; your dear children, husband, friends, all have so high an interest.

The constant alarm for the safety of our sea-ports is very distressing. Many of our citizens at this time are very apprehensive. Lord Hill intends to make New-York his head-quarters this winter if he can. My visit to my dear friends is necessarily deferred for the present; I want to see you all very much. My dear children are quite well; they have just returned to the city, and their school. As usual, they have passed the summer at Flushing. Father has, I believe, a pretty good idea of my property and manner of conducting my affairs. I have not been in trade for a long time. The war has caused my property to be comparatively unproductive. Failures have been very numerous and very distressing: Robert Bowne and one of his sons, Minturn & Champlin, Post & Minturn,—these are all closely connected, and have large families, accustomed to live in affluence, and two of them, M. & C. (of late) in great luxury. It would gratify me to hear often from those I so much value.

Affectionately,

W BOWNE.

Scarborough, September 23, 1815.

I hope my dear brother does not attribute my long silence to a decreased affection for him or his precious children, but to causes which have been of a nature to unfit me for this or any other exertion. Since our Octavia's death my health has been very poor. I do not think my complaints are consumption, although I am quite subject to a cough, but I believe it arises from debility. I am now, however, recruiting quite fast, and expect soon to enjoy my former state of health. Father and Mother are in very good health, as is Mary, who is now at home. She is quite fleshy and very blooming. Arexine is pretty well, and Mr. Smith is in fine health. Sister B. has not been well this summer, but is now getting better. She, I suppose you have heard, is the mother of twelve children, the youngest of whom is not very healthy. Horatio is in fine health; they have four children; his wife is in very poor health. She has bled at the lungs a number of times, but latterly in much larger quanties,—Arexine says a half of a pint at a time. Her constitution is much shattered, and we have but little hope of her recovery from those repeated shocks. Uncle Porter's family are in pretty good health, but in poor circumstances. Isabella Porter is very well married, and King likewise. Harriet and Lucy are still single. Mrs. Coffin lives at Wiscassett; her husband has the office of clerk in one of our Eastern courts. He owns a small farm, and lives very comfortably. Mrs. Coffin has lately become the mother of twins, a little boy and girl. They have lost their two youngest children before these,—a little Sarah and John, for whom they are named. Mr. Brown is very well, and is very much supported. His heavenly Father regards the sorrows and petitions of his heart, and comforts him by the rich influence of his Spirit. He is still at housekeeping with his little Frederic, who is of the same age as your Mary. William is at an academy at Saco, and is doing very well. Little Octavia is with Arexine; she is a nice little girl, but she is unhappily affected by a scrofula in her neck which injures her looks more than her health. Little Harriet and Elizabeth are with us; they are fine, healthy children.

I give you a particular account of the family, my dear Mr. Bowne, because I feel assured that everything which belongs to the source from whence Providence once permitted you to derive the richest treasure you ever possessed is, and will ever be, interest-

50

ing to you; and, although the stream which diffused joy and tranquillity through your heart is now shut up, yet is not the fountain precious? You are bound to us by ties which nothing but death can dissolve, and I feel as if in your heart there is almost something which reciprocates this feeling. How are your precious children? You cannot fully realize our desire to see you and them; consider how long a time it is since you have been to see us. My mother is sometimes hurt, and always grieved, when she thinks or speaks of your long absence from us. Do, my dear brother, come and bring our dear Walter and Mary; if you will bring them here next year, unless something in Providence occurs to prevent, I will return with you to New-York. Let not tenderness or sympathy in our afflictions prevent you. I know you dread to meet us, but do not let this prevent you from coming. We have been and are deeply afflicted, but, my dear brother, we are not unhappy; you will not find us so. We heard you were going to the Springs,—did you go? I wish I could have been in New-York and accompanied you. Does Mary remember her Aunt Miranda? If so, remember me most tenderly to her and Walter, and tell them that Aunt Miranda and Aunt Mary, and Grandmamma Southgate wish to see them very much. How is your mother and Caroline? Do give my love to them; it would afford me a great deal of pleasure to see my dear New-York friends again. Remember me affectionately to your brother Murray's family, Mrs. Townsend, and Mrs. King, if she is in New-York. Mr. Tilton is very well, and if he knew I was writing, would send particular remembrance. Father and Mother desire an affectionate remembrance to you, and join me cordially in wishing you to come to S. Write soon, my dear brother, and believe me.

Yours very affectionately,

MIRANDA SOUTHGATE.

TO WALTER BOWNE,
    NEW-YORK.

Albany, March 14, 1820.

My Dear Mary:

The packet with Aunt Mary's and brother's letters came safe to hand, and since I have had the pleasure to receive my dear daughter's letter. Walter has written to me lately, and before this, mine in reply has most likely reached him. Brother seems to express a willingness to leave Burlington for rather a longer time than vacation. I want to see him very much, and all of you ; it is too bad to be so long from those we love.

I do not feel as if I should object to thy going to drawing-school ; drawing is in my mind a pretty and seasonable accomplishment, and why may not delineating objects upon paper be useful? I shall want thee to make maps for me ; I do not recollect from whence those lines were taken,—most likely from some work on education. In thy next thou can give me a kind of diary, suppose suited to the previous day, something like this : "Dear father, I got up at six o'clock sunrise, washed, studied my lessons one hour—sewed half hour—breakfasted—went to school—up head in rhetoric and French, next to head in philosophy, grammar, and spelling, down foot in ciphering—came home at three o'clock, dined, looked over my lessons, wrote ten lines to father, knit half hour, sewed half hour, jumped rope and played one hour—drank tea, talked, put questions to Cousin Mary in geography and grammar—Cousin Mary put questions to me in geometry, trigonometry, and mathematics—studied lessons one hour, knit and sewed half hour, jumped rope and played half hour—warmed, went to bed at half-past eight o'clock." The weather is most unpleasant, walking wretched, sleighing pretty good. The Hudson remains frozen ; horses and sleighs cross on the ice. The hour has nearly arrived for me to go to the house to my daily avocation, as thine is to school.

Entirely affectionate, etc.

W. BOWNE.

TO MARY KING BOWNE,
    No. 288 PEARL STREET,
        NEW-YORK.